FIRE
ON THE FENS

A gripping crime thriller with a huge twist

JOY ELLIS

Detective Nikki Galena Book 9

Revised edition 2024
Joffe Books, London
www.joffebooks.com

First published in Great Britain in 2018

This paperback edition was first published
in Great Britain in 2024

Cover art by Nick Castle

ISBN: 978-1-83526-610-6

This book is dedicated to my friend Peggy Fujimura, and all the people who have lost their homes and suffered as a consequence of the Kilauea eruptions. Our hearts go out to you. Aloha, Joy.

There is something both exciting and exquisitely dangerous about a glowing ember, whether it be a spark of inspiration that leads to a great idea, the gently smouldering ashes of an old memory, or the first lick of flame that ignites a roaring fire.

However, if you combine all three, you have the makings of a treacherous and unstoppable inferno.

CHAPTER ONE

'Not much left of that lot, is there?' Denny said. The young firefighter stood with one of the big hoses draped over his shoulder to clear the water remaining inside it.

Josh, one of his crewmates, nodded at the massive piles of smouldering charred wood. 'Farmer reckons that's a couple of thousand pounds worth of pallets there, nothing but ash now.' He looked at a car standing just beyond the fire appliances. 'He's here again. Third time this week.'

Denny glanced across to the tall man staring at the scene of the fire. 'Is this what happens when you retire from the fire service? You spend your days chasing blue lights?'

'He's one of the best fire investigators you'll ever meet, I'll have you know. In his day, John Carson solved some of the country's most complex arson cases. Why he's trailing us around these bored yobs' attempts at arson beats me.'

Denny pulled a face. 'Mmm. I heard he was the top banana. So what's his interest here, I wonder?'

Josh grinned. 'Ask him. Go on, I dare you.'

'No way,' Denny said. 'If the old guy's some kind of legend, he's hardly going to talk to me, is he?'

Josh shrugged. 'Too late now, he's back in his car. You lost your chance.'

'Come on, you two!' yelled the crew commander. 'Get those hoses away and stop gossiping!'

Denny and Josh completed their task and scrambled back into the fire engine. Josh watched the investigator's car until it drove out of sight. John Carson was onto something.

* * *

A few hours later, John Carson was back at the site of the fire, now deserted.

His boots squelched in the muddy black residue, all that was left after the hoses had quelled the flames. The stench of burning hung heavy in the air.

'Bloody vandals!'

John had been so deep in thought that he hadn't heard the farmer walk up behind him.

'At least the stack was some way from your farmhouse — and the main outbuildings.' John tried to sound reassuring. 'You've lost a bit of money here, but it's nothing compared with what a serious fire could have done.'

'Scared me though.' The farmer ran a beefy hand through his thatch of greying hair.

John nodded at the blackened mess. 'You have every right to be scared, sir. Only a fool underestimates fire.'

'You with the fire service?' the farmer asked.

In response, John stuck out his hand. 'John Carson. I've spent my whole working life involved with fire, first fighting them and then investigating them.'

The farmer shook hands with him vigorously. 'Lewis Rhodes, and I've spent my whole life, every minute of it, here at Birch Farm. Born here, Mr Carson, and we've never had a single fire.' He sighed. 'The kids in these parts are getting more and more bored and out of hand. No boundaries any more. Threaten them with the police and they laugh at you. Little hooligans.'

John's nod was perfunctory. 'Did you see anyone around here before the fire?'

'We were all tucked up in bed, fast asleep,' Lewis said. 'Busy time this, up and out long before dawn.'

'Well, let's just be thankful no more harm was done. Nice to meet you, Mr Rhodes. Take care.'

He left the farmer shaking his head over his lost pallets. John knew just how lucky this particular farmer had been. If the stack had been next to a barn, as they often were, and the barn close to the farmhouse, he might be mourning the loss of his family.

He opened the boot of his Land Rover and replaced his wellingtons with a pair of shoes. With one final look back, he put the car into gear and pulled out into the Greenborough Road. It was time to talk to an old acquaintance of his.

* * *

DI Nikki Galena had started work early, hoping to slope off mid-afternoon and spend some time with her mother. Eve Anderson had been working all spring and summer to get a new fern garden laid out, and now that it was almost finished, she wanted Nikki to see it before the evenings got too dark.

Her mother's new home, a converted chapel in the village of Beech Lacey, was a real showplace. Prior to inheriting the beautiful old chapel, Eve had known nothing about gardening, but now she was a born-again Gertrude Jekyll. Nikki smiled to herself. At least it kept her out of trouble, and boy, did her mother need it! She shivered when she considered the danger Eve had been in last year. Her new role as head gardener was much safer than that of private investigator.

Nikki went back to the reports that she needed to get ready for the new superintendent. This was to be his first day, and she and the whole team were on tenterhooks, wondering what he would be like. Rumour had it that he was a fast-track university swot from the direct entry programme, who didn't look old enough to drive, let alone take on the responsibility for all the operations in their division. Though the grapevine

3

was often wrong. Only time would tell. Nikki glanced at her watch. A couple of hours, to be precise.

After the sudden death of Superintendent Greg Woodhall, they had muddled through, with everyone temporarily stepping up a post. Today they would be back to full strength, whatever that might mean. Nikki grimaced. A new super, especially one who needed to prove something, or maybe just make his presence felt, could be a big problem for her and Joseph. Ranking officers were not allowed to work together if they were married or in a personal relationship, and she and DS Joseph Easter were now in a relationship. For a very long while, for the sake of the team and their working partnership, they had remained just friends. Then, following a traumatic case that affected both of them badly, they had decided that life was just too short. They had never actually moved in together. Joseph retained his quaint Knot Cottage, and she still lived in her family home, Cloud Cottage Farm, but they spent most of their time together. They hadn't made a thing of it. In fact they never spoke about it at all. Canny Superintendent Greg Woodhall had chosen to ignore the rumours, well aware that half the station believed they'd been a couple for years, while the other half didn't give a damn. But a new super? Nikki wasn't sure how things were going to pan out.

She loved her job and had no intention of losing it. But equally she loved Joseph, and didn't want to lose him either. If her new commanding officer asked her outright, she wouldn't be able to lie. Maybe he wouldn't find out how close she and Joseph were. It was all she could hang onto. They always drove to work in separate vehicles, and they always appeared slightly distant when in company, so it was now in the lap of the gods.

There was a soft tap at her door. She looked up expecting to see Joseph, but it was Sergeant Niall Farrow, Joseph's son-in-law.

Whenever she saw Niall, Nikki always had to look twice. She still thought of him as the young, gung-ho constable who had joined them years before, all fired up and full of an enthusiasm that sometimes clouded his common sense. But now he was a responsible man. He had a wife, a home, and three stripes on his shoulder, and it made Nikki's heart sing. She had a very good reason for being especially fond of him. She owed him her life, although he still hotly denied it. He could have played the hero, but instead he played it down.

'Superintendent would like to see you in his office, ma'am,' Niall said

'Good heavens! It's barely eight! He's not due till ten. What's this all about?'

'New broom and all that.' Niall grinned at her, and then his smile faded. 'When you're through, if you have a minute, I wondered if I could have a word?'

'Of course. Something wrong, Niall?'

'No, not exactly, we've just got a few odd things going on in Greenborough that I'd like to run past you.'

'I'll come and find you after my meeting with, er, Superintendent Lucien Crawford.' She pulled a face. *Lucien*? What kind of name was that for a copper? The mess room would love that. She'd have put money on "Juicy Lucy" for his nickname.

'I'll be downstairs, ma'am. Just give me a bell and I'll come up.' Niall paused in the doorway. 'And good luck.'

Nikki gathered up her paperwork, thankful that she'd started work so early.

Outside the superintendent's door, she stopped and took a deep breath. It didn't seem right somehow. It should be Greg sitting behind that desk, not some fast-track egghead. She sighed, knocked and went in.

'Cam? What are you doing here?' Her voice shot up an octave. Rising from his seat behind the desk was her old friend, DCI Cameron Walker from Beech Lacey, not "Lucien."

'Not exactly who you expected, am I?' The big man's smile was warm. 'How are you, Nikki?'

'I'm fine, but what on . . . ?'

They both sat down.

'Your new super had a skiing accident, and it seems he won't be fit for action for a good long while, so,' he spread his hands, 'guess who's your acting superintendent?'

'But that's brilliant!' Relief flooded through Nikki.

'I'll tell you if I agree after the first month, shall I?'

Nikki frowned. 'Hang on. You always said that no matter what, you'd never step further up the ladder than DCI. You hate all the management stuff!'

Cam's face became serious. 'I had no choice, Nik. They're closing Beech Lacey and we're being integrated into the surrounding districts. My job'll be gone in a couple of months' time and I need a few more years under my belt for a full pension.'

'You said "acting?"'

'With a view to a permanent position. They can't wait for Lucien Crawford to recover — this station needs stability." Cam leaned towards her across the desk. 'And I had an ulterior motive for taking this. It concerns you.'

Nikki stared blankly. 'Me?'

'I heard something on the jungle drums about the only other candidate for this position. Do you know a Superintendent Cresswell?'

Nikki groaned. 'Do I! Everything by the book, and no deviations. No grey areas and no sense of humour at all. He makes anal retention look positively hedonistic! Lord! Did he apply?'

'Yes, and those drums I was talking about said he was very interested in you, Nikki, and your private life.'

'What?' Nikki gaped. 'Oh, shit!'

Cam smiled angelically. 'I, on the other hand, want to know nothing at all about such things, and would be most grateful if your private life was never spoken of again.'

Nikki could have hugged him. 'We owe you big time, Cam.'

'So how is Joseph?'

Nikki beamed. 'Good, really good.'

'You look happier than I've ever seen you, Nikki Galena.'

'That's because I am.'

'And you can hack having me as your new super?'

Nikki had known Cameron and his wife, Kaye, for many years. He was an honest man and a damned good detective. It was nothing short of a miracle that he had stepped in. 'Cam, you'll be a great super, and I promise not to give you too much of a hard time.'

'Mmm. Greenborough does have a reputation for its stroppy DIs, doesn't it?'

'All lies! Don't believe a word of it!' Nikki said, and smiled. 'Welcome aboard, Superintendent Walker. It's good to have you here.'

'Only acting superintendent, don't forget. But I don't think the job's going to be as quiet and gentle as I'd hoped.' Cam's brows furrowed.

'Why? We've got nothing major on at present. In fact, it's all pretty mundane stuff.' She looked at his worried expression. 'You know something I don't?'

'I've had a call from an old friend of mine, Nikki. John Carson, ex fire-service investigator.'

'I know him. He came out when a psycho torched my garage a few years back. He really knew his subject. I was dead impressed that he managed to discern *anything* from the mess that remained, but he told us how and where the fire started almost immediately.'

'He's the best there is, or he was. Shame he retired. But anyway, he told me he's been monitoring a lot of small fires in the last few weeks.'

Nikki nodded. 'Yes. Uniform have reported a whole spate of them. Wheelie bins, skips, a shed, a chicken feed store. Nothing big though. They reckon we have a group of idiot kids with a bulk buy of matches and lighter fuel.'

'John thinks otherwise. He's recorded each fire — time, date and location. Last night a farmer had a twenty-foot high pallet stack torched. Hundreds of wooden pallets burned to a crisp.'

'Oh. They're expanding their repertoire, are they? That means they're becoming dangerous — to property, the public and to themselves. Little shites!'

'Not quite that straightforward, Nikki. John is certain these fires are carefully planned practice pieces. The last one was cleverly prepared to do the maximum amount of damage to that stack. He's seen it before. He believes that someone is doing an apprenticeship, learning their new trade. He thinks we have an embryonic arsonist in Greenborough, Nikki, and he's certain they're escalating.'

'An arsonist?' Fear trickled down Nikki's spine like melting ice. A deep, primeval fear. 'He's certain of this?'

'I trust John's judgement. But on the plus side, he's prepared to help us. He's lived a whole life dealing with fires of one sort or another, and there's nothing he doesn't know about them. With him on board, we have a massive advantage.'

She was silent for a moment, contemplating the type of person who would deliberately start fires. They made her blood run cold. These crimes were usually committed under the cover of darkness, and the victims never saw their attacker. It was an insidious, callous and cowardly crime, and she didn't want it on her patch. 'If he's right, we'll gratefully accept his help. I don't want a single building, or more to the point, a single human being, to come to harm in this lovely old town.'

'He's coming in later to talk to us,' Cameron said. 'Great start to the day, huh?'

'So far nothing's gone as I expected, but having you here is a real bonus.' Nikki stood up. 'Will you take daily orders this morning?'

'I'll be there, but you take it, Nikki. I'll just introduce myself. I've had a brief glance at what's going on here, but I need to get up to speed on everything and put names to faces.'

'They are a good bunch, for the most part. There's a few wild cards, but not many. And you know my team from the investigation involving my mother.'

Cameron gave an exaggerated shiver. 'Don't remind me of that case! Anyway, I'm pleased to report that Eve has settled in to become a pillar of the community in Beech Lacey. She's the go-to woman for horticultural advice.'

'A far cry from sleuthing, thank goodness! Long may it last.'

As she left, Nikki heard him mutter, 'You can say that again!'

CHAPTER TWO

After the meeting, Nikki and Joseph sat in her office discussing the unexpected news.

'If Cameron Walker takes the job permanently, we couldn't ask for better,' Joseph said. 'He's straight as a die, and the station would certainly benefit from having him at the helm.'

'*If* he can put up with the red tape, and the deluge of new initiatives, policies and strategies. He's a proper copper, and he's always hated the managerial crap.'

'Doesn't sound like he had much choice. Though if I know Cam, he'll give it his very best shot. He's that kind of guy.' Joseph lowered his voice to a whisper. 'And you and I have a stay of execution for a while longer.'

Nikki looked rather sadly at him. 'Thanks to Cam. Still, I guess one day . . .'

'Let's not get ahead of ourselves.' Joseph returned her look. 'This is a blessing. Let's just accept it.'

He was right. Joseph usually was. But having to make decisions that involved a change in their future together was one bridge she never wanted to cross.

'Plus,' Joseph said, 'if Cam's friend is right, we have something nasty brewing in our area, and we need to nip it in the bud.'

'Absolutely. And your son-in-law wants to talk to us about something that's bothering him.' She grinned at him across the desk. 'Right. Brain back into work mode, Galena!'

'I'll go and nab Niall, shall I?'

They returned quickly.

'It's probably nothing, ma'am, but Vonnie mentioned this to me the other day, and since then I've heard a few other rumours.' For a moment Niall seemed hesitant to go on.

'Spit it out, Niall, for heaven's sake,' Nikki said.

'There've been one or two disturbances in the town recently, involving a group that call themselves the New Order Luciferians.'

'Oh, Jesus!' Nikki exclaimed.

'Just the opposite,' Joseph quipped.

'But you're joking, aren't you, Niall? These people aren't serious?'

Niall looked apologetic. 'Now you can see why I didn't mention it before. But, yes, they're quite serious. I think it's some quasi-religious sect. The thing is, on each occasion they weren't the ones causing the trouble. It was a gang of hard-nut local yobs, and they seem to be targeting the group.'

Nikki groaned. 'Where do they meet? Do they have a church or something?'

'They meet in a place called the Black House. It's a property in Ferry Street.'

'Ferry Street? But that's an upmarket residential area.' Nikki frowned. 'Aren't the neighbours complaining?'

'That's the odd thing, ma'am. The Black House is owned and maintained by a businessman with a lot of connections. The group is very orderly and according to local residents, polite, quiet and no trouble at all.'

'So no slaughtering chickens at midnight?' asked Nikki. 'No raising the Goat of Mendes for their diabolical purposes?'

'Ah,' said Joseph. 'Someone else who used to smuggle Dennis Wheatley books out of the library when they were a kid.'

'*The Devil Rides Out* is about the extent of my satanic knowledge, I'm afraid,' admitted Nikki. 'But seriously, who are these people? Do we know them?'

Niall shrugged. 'I get the feeling we'd know them all if we looked closer, but they've done nothing wrong. I can't start poking my nose in. It's the local yobs that need tracking down and given a talking to.' He grimaced. 'Local, as in the Carborough Estate.'

Although nowhere near as bad as it used to be, the Carborough was the roughest area in Greenborough. You didn't venture into the Carborough alone at night — or in the daylight for that matter.

'Whatever, it doesn't sound like a CID matter. We might just have ourselves a new problem to sort out. Niall, get your lads and lasses to keep their eyes peeled for anyone starting fires and report to me directly, okay?'

Niall nodded. 'Of course, ma'am. I just thought you should know about the presence of a group of that nature in our area. It could attract trouble.'

'Thanks, Niall. Let us know if anything else happens regarding our band of devil worshippers. I prefer to be fore-warned, just in case we need to pay them a visit.'

After Niall had left, Nikki smiled. 'Is that the same lad we used to say needed a pair of reins to keep him in check?'

'He's a married man now, Nikki, and he knows the seriousness of marrying a detective sergeant's daughter.' Joseph laughed. 'Poor kid. It's a heavy responsibility.'

'Rubbish. He loves you to bits.'

'I'm pretty fond of him too.' Joseph's expression changed. 'But I wouldn't mind keeping my ear to the ground regarding our not-so-secret society. I have a theory that they're not followers of the Dark Lord at all, that's just a cover.'

'So what are they?' asked Nikki.

'Let me do a bit of ferreting, and I'll tell you.'

'Don't go all mysterious on me, Joseph Easter!'

'I'm not! It's just that I read something recently about such groups. And if their HQ is in Ferry Street, they certainly aren't squatters or down and outs. They must be very well off.'

'Okay, ferret away, but the fires come first,' Nikki said.

Joseph offered her a smart salute, and she stuck her tongue out at him.

'What time is Cam's fire investigator arriving?' Joseph asked.

Before she could answer, her phone rang. 'DI Galena. How can I help?'

She recognised the desk sergeant's voice. 'Ma'am, there's been an incident in a small caravan park, out beyond the Fairweather brothers' farm estate. One fatality. We think you need to see it. Can you attend?'

'Certainly. What was the incident?'

'One of the caravans was set on fire, ma'am, with the occupant still inside. *Locked* inside.'

She frowned. 'As in, by someone else?'

'Key was still in the outside of the lock, so yes, definitely.'

'We're on our way. Thank you, Sergeant.'

She told Joseph and added, 'I'm going to tell Cam to get his investigator John Carson to meet us there. You get a car, okay? I'm pretty sure Mr Carson's theory about the arsonist escalating is about to be proved correct.'

* * *

Rory Wilkinson met them in the car park of the small campsite. Known as Mud Town, it was a collection of low-cost caravans that the migrant fieldworkers used.

'I don't think it'll ever rival Butlins, do you?' Rory asked. 'Not a Redcoat in sight.'

Before they began to trudge across the uneven ground, he produced a large white envelope from his bag and handed it to Nikki. 'In case I forget — your invites. Well, invite singular, actually. Don't read anything into that. I've lumped you and Joseph together simply to save expense on the gold-leaf, deckle-edged, wildly extravagant wedding invitation cards.' He winked at Nikki. 'And if you believe that, you'll believe anything.'

'Wedding?' Joseph looked at him quizzically.

'David and I have decided that as we've put up with each other for the past twenty years, neither of us is probably going anywhere else, so . . .'

'Oh, Rory, that's wonderful!' Nikki slipped her arm through his and hung on tightly. 'When? Where?'

'Next month. We're having the service at Greenborough Registry Office and reception at the old Second World War airbase at East Enderby.'

Joseph grinned. 'What a great venue! Complete with a Lancaster bomber and spitfires!'

'As long as the meal isn't NAAFI style, we should all have fun.' Rory looked across to the burnt-out caravan, and the one remaining fire appliance nearby. 'Unlike this poor soul.'

Little was left but a skeletal framework. The kitchen end was reduced to ash and scrap metal, but the bedroom was still vaguely recognisable.

'What do we know?' Nikki asked the fire crew.

One of the men pointed to the charred and partially destroyed door, where a metal key still hung from the lock. 'Locked. From outside. One occupant, still in situ.'

Nikki didn't want to look, but knew she had to.

Thankfully, Rory moved forward and peered inside, blocking her view. 'I hate them when they're all crispy! I like the residents of my morgue to look relaxed and finally at peace, not like something from a Blitzkrieg newsreel. Oh dear. What a state!' He gave Nikki a dark look. 'Usually I can say they would have known nothing because the smoke got to them first. But not in this case. Looks like he'd been drinking, but he knew exactly what was happening and tried desperately, and unsuccessfully, to get the door open.'

Nikki gathered herself and looked at the body, and then at the smoky remains of a bottle lying beside his blackened bed. 'Whisky,' she muttered.

'Expensive whisky,' added Rory. 'Not what you'd expect to find in a crappy little caravan in Mud Town.'

The body was curled up on the floor, just inside the door, twisted and inhuman. One arm reached up, as if in supplication.

Nikki closed her eyes and stepped away, trying not to breathe too deeply. All around her was the acrid stench of burning. Of all the deaths they saw in their job, to her this was the worst. It must be so painful. She knew that deep, full thickness burns destroyed the nerve endings, but the pain felt at the initial touch of the flames must be indescribable.

'Time for us to take over, I think.' Rory was watching her.

'I'm okay, it's just . . .'

'Yes, it's one of the cruellest ways to kill. And this was undoubtedly murder.' Rory looked up. 'Ah, good. My trusty SOCOs are here.'

Two women were pulling on protective suits and shoe-covers, and bringing out equipment from their car. Nikki realised that the tall one, pushing long white-blonde hair into her hood, was Ella Jarvis. Ella had a reputation for being the best there was when it came to forensic photography.

Nikki went to find Joseph. He was talking to the fire crew that had attended.

'Anything interesting?'

Joseph shrugged. 'It looks as if the person who did this was male. One of the other migrant workers caught sight of a man leaving just a few minutes before the caravan went up.'

'I shouldn't think there are too many women arsonists, would you?' said Nikki.

'Doubt it, although these days, nothing would surprise me.'

'This caravan seems to have been specifically targeted, so do we know who the deceased man was?'

Joseph looked at his notebook. 'Ronnie Tyrrell. A bit of a loner, but he seems to have got on well with the other workers here. Most are foreign. They did their best to try and save him. One man ripped out the gas canister from the back before the fire could get to it and take half the park up with it. Another couple of lads tried to break the windows, but the heat drove them back.'

A small group of men were silently watching the emergency services. They all wore expressions of shocked disbelief. 'Is this Ronnie Tyrrell known to us?' she asked.

'I'll check.' Joseph pulled out his phone and made the call. 'Nothing. Clean as a whistle. I've asked Cat to do a full background check on him. We'll need to trace his relatives.'

'And find out who employs these workers, Joseph. Whoever it is should have details on file, assuming he was kosher and not moonlighting.'

'These men tell me Tyrrell was employed by the Fairweathers. He worked for them on a permanent basis. Bit of a jack of all trades, apparently, did whatever was needed, not just land work.'

'Okay. When we've finished here, we'll go see these Fairweathers.' Nikki looked up. The crunch of tyres on gravel announced a car pulling into the site. 'John Carson, I believe.'

John strode over to them and held out his hand to Nikki. 'No more garage fires out on Cloud Fen, I hope?'

She smiled. 'You remembered. I'm impressed.'

'I remember every fire I've ever dealt with. And each one is different.'

'I suppose they must be,' said Joseph. 'Different locations, different weather conditions, different material burning.'

'Our new superintendent, Cameron Walker, brought us up to date with your rather alarming thoughts, John,' Nikki indicated the murder site, 'and this seems to prove you right.'

'I'm afraid so. Though I would have expected more smaller fires first, and none involving loss of life. This is a major step — assuming of course that it's the work of the same person.'

'Fire isn't exactly a popular method of killing someone, not compared with a knife or a blunt object,' Nikki said. 'And considering your theory that we have an apprentice fire-setter on our hands, I'm thinking it's the same man.'

'Probably.' Carson's eyes gleamed darkly. 'But in fire investigation, the first thing we learn is to assume nothing, and never make snap judgements. Can I see the site, please?'

Nikki really didn't want to see Ronnie Tyrrell's twisted remains again, but she nodded and led the way.

Rory almost fell over himself in his enthusiastic greeting. 'John! Good to see you! How's retirement treating you? Though I see you are staring longingly at my grimy crime scene. Are you back in the saddle?'

'No, Rory. Just keeping my mind active. Though it's probably rather overactive at present.'

'Well, as soon as I've got what I need, the shots are snapped and anything useful collected, feel free to tiptoe through the debris — metaphorically speaking.'

John grinned. 'You're too kind.'

'My pleasure, old bean. Now, if you'll forgive me, I need to fathom out a way of transporting this man back to the morgue intact. Can't afford to lose bits, can we?'

Nikki looked pained. 'I wonder about you sometimes, Wilkinson! I'll leave you to it.' She turned to John. 'Joseph and I are going to visit the victim's employer. Shall we meet back here?'

John nodded. 'Yes, I'll be here for quite a while. And don't worry, I know it's a crime scene. I won't do what Rory suggested and tiptoe through the ashes.'

CHAPTER THREE

Brodie Fairweather sat in silence. He looked stunned. His brother Clay did all the talking. In fact he didn't seem able to stop. 'Ronnie? I just can't believe it! What on earth happened? He didn't smoke. He never smoked, so it couldn't have been that. Some sort of electrical fire, maybe? I mean, I know the caravan was old, but he kept it nice, didn't he, Brodie? Really nice. We always said that about Ronnie.'

'How long had he worked for you?' asked Joseph.

'Oh, well, a good while now. Must be seven or eight years. Yes, I remember, he joined us the year Greenborough Town Football Club got into the National League, and that's seven years ago.'

'He's lived in Mud Town for seven years?' Nikki wondered at this. It was hardly what you would call a desirable location.

Clay nodded. 'And not a bit of bother in all that time. If any of the transients played up, Ronnie was the one to calm things down. Thoroughly nice bloke, Ronnie. Salt of the earth. I can't believe he's dead!'

Brodie raised his eyes. '*Two* detectives? For an accident?'

Bright man, thought Nikki. 'Sorry, sir, but can either of you think why Ronnie's caravan would be locked from the outside?'

The silence seemed to last an age. 'You mean this was foul play?' Brodie said. 'Ronnie's caravan was deliberately set on fire?'

'We won't know until forensic tests have been carried out, and we have a fire-investigation officer with us.' Nikki decided to leave out the retired bit. 'Did he have any enemies that you know of?'

'Ronnie? No. He kept himself to himself. Mud Town was his home. He was a good man, a quiet man.'

'And his family? Are they local?'

Clay looked at his brother. 'He never mentioned family to me. Did he say anything to you about them?'

Brodie shook his head. 'No one ever visited him, and he hardly ever went out. He had no mail to speak of, and never once did he mention family.'

Oh great, Nikki thought. 'How did he come to work for you, and what did he do exactly?'

'Because he needed money, like everyone else,' Brodie said flatly. 'And he didn't care what he did. He'd have a go at anything. We're vegetable farmers, you know. Between here and our Cornwall farms, we have over five thousand acres of brassicas. Ronnie understood the land. He knew farming from before he came to us, but he never talked about his past, and we never asked him.'

'Why? What about references?' asked Joseph.

'I could tell he was a grafter the minute I set eyes on him. I trusts my own judgement, Officer. No doubt like you does.' Brodie looked hard at Joseph. 'I reckoned if I pumped him about where he'd been and what he'd done, he'd have given me a load of lies anyhow, so we decided to just try him out, and we came up with a winner.'

Joseph shrugged. 'I just wondered if his reluctance to talk was because he was hiding something. Is there anyone here that he was particularly friendly with? A close mate?'

'He was a private man,' Brodie said. 'He'd help anyone if they needed it, but as for going down the pub for a few jars, no. That wasn't his way.'

'Did he drink much?' asked Nikki, thinking of the whisky bottle in Ronnie's caravan.

'Don't think so. You smell it on some of the migrants.' Brodie wrinkled his nose in distaste. 'I swear some of them have vodka for breakfast. But not Ronnie. I think he liked the odd beer, but in all the time he was here, I never saw him drunk, or even tipsy.'

Another mystery, thought Nikki. 'Well, thank you for your help, gentlemen. We may be back if we think of anything else, but now we need to return to Mud Town.'

'Uh, Inspector? What happens now? To Ronnie, I mean,' Clay asked.

'He'll be taken to the morgue in Greenborough Hospital. There'll be an inquest, and then they'll do a post-mortem. We need to establish exactly what happened to Ronnie, and if necessary, bring the person who caused his death to justice.'

'But Ronnie's body?' Clay looked upset.

'We need to trace his family before we can tell you that, sir,' she said.

Brodie stood up. 'What my brother is trying to say is if no one claims him, we'll take care of the funeral. We appreciated the work he did for us, and we'll miss him.'

'That's good to hear, sir. We'll be in touch very soon.' Nikki glanced at Joseph and they headed for the door.

Nikki was about to open it when Brodie said, 'There is one person you might like to talk to, Inspector.'

Nikki turned. 'Yes?'

'The curate at St Saviour's in Helmsley Street. Think his name is Leon something. He helps some of the migrants who are struggling. He runs a food bank and some other church-based stuff. He visited Ronnie when he got poorly last winter, brought him food and things. Try him.'

'We will,' Nikki said. 'Thank you.'

* * *

They were back at the caravan park, which to Joseph looked more like a gypsy encampment. It was hard to believe that

Ronnie Tyrrell had lived here, apparently quite content, for seven or eight years. There had to be a story there, but he had a feeling it was going to be difficult to unearth.

John Carson was standing almost exactly where they had left him. He seemed deep in thought. He jumped when they approached.

'Sorry. I was miles away.'

'Actually, I think you were right here.' Joseph smiled. 'Engrossed in what might have happened.'

'That's true. I'll tell you more when forensics has finished, but I have a pretty clear picture of where the fire started, and possibly how.'

Joseph looked at the smouldering remains and wondered how on earth he could tell anything from such a mess. 'Go on.'

'He wasn't alone. I can see the remains of two glasses, one close to the bed area and one further down, closer to the kitchen. The whisky bottle was most likely almost empty. If it had been full, the intense heat from the fire would have blown it, but it was intact. That indicates he had a visitor, and they polished off a goodly portion of a bottle of scotch — expensive malt, to be precise.'

'We need to talk to everyone here,' Nikki said. 'Someone must have seen if Ronnie had a visitor, especially if he was almost a recluse. A visitor would have been noticed.'

'I think you'll find that uniform are already on that,' John said.

'But he wasn't a drinker, or so his boss says,' Nikki mused. 'So why down half a bottle of scotch?'

'I suppose it may not have been full to start with.' John shrugged. 'Possibly he didn't drink as a rule, but maybe he and his visitor had something to celebrate. We'll probably never know for sure.'

'Unless we catch the arsonist and he tells us,' Joseph said. He really didn't want to have to look at more charred bodies. He'd done enough of that on Special Ops. The unforgettable smell of burnt flesh. He hastily pushed the memory away.

John was still staring at the remains. 'From the burn pattern, working from the least damaged area to the most damaged, the fire originated in the lounge area, just outside the kitchen. That area burned fiercely because of the fuel load there.'

'Fuel load?' asked Nikki.

'Amount of material, furnishings — basically stuff that fed the fire. There was probably a couch, curtains, cushions, books, papers, clothes, and the fire-setter would have used an accelerant of some sort. Examination of the residue will tell us if that's the case.' John flexed his shoulders. 'Your forensics people have been very thorough, and because a life was lost, fire and rescue will send an investigator.' A small smile played about his lips. 'My successor.'

'Is he good?' asked Nikki.

'*She* is very good. One of the only female fire-investigation officers in the country. You'll have all the answers, DI Galena, but not immediately. It takes time.'

'I know you said you never assume anything, John, but without holding you to it, what does your professional instinct tell you?' Joseph wondered if they were thinking along the same lines.

John Carson took a deep breath. 'Ronnie lets in a visitor. Visitor brings bottle of scotch. Ronnie, unused to heavy drinking, gets tipsy. Visitor suggests he lie down. He gets onto his bed, maybe he even nods off. His visitor has come prepared, goes to the loo or maybe the kitchen on some pretext, and starts his fire. He allows it to get a hold, then escapes, locking the door behind him. Ronnie wakes and rushes to the door, but too late, and he perishes.'

This was the scenario Joseph had envisaged. 'Ronnie's caravan was in a quiet secluded spot in the corner, with a hedge forming a barrier along one side. If not many people were around, he could have got out pretty well unnoticed.'

'Someone saw him though, didn't they?' Nikki added. 'Let's hope they got a really good look.' She looked at John. 'Is this what all those practice attempts were preparing for? Killing Ronnie Tyrrell?'

John Carson ran a hand across his forehead. 'Too soon for that question, Inspector, but maybe. The thing is, I can tell you how it happened, but as to *why*, and *who* did it, that's far from easy to discover.' He gave them a tired smile. 'However, I'm certain that you *will* find him. I can see from your faces that you know exactly how ruthless this man is. You'll do everything you can.'

'You're right there, John. By the way, it looks like we are going to be picking your brains for as long as it takes to get him, so it's Nikki and Joseph, okay?'

John smiled. 'Feels a little odd, after all the years of formality, but that's great.'

'There's little more we can do here, so we'll let you get on. Will you join us at the station when you're through?' Nikki said.

'I'll see you there.' He paused. 'One thing is bothering me slightly . . . This kind of thing generally happens at night, so why risk doing it in broad daylight?'

'And would you drink whisky at eleven in the morning? Especially if you're not a heavy drinker?' added Nikki.

'And,' Joseph said, 'how did the killer know that Ronnie would be here and not working? Apparently he worked all hours.'

They looked at each other. 'More questions than answers, it seems,' John said. 'I think your part is far more complicated than mine.'

Joseph felt inclined to agree.

CHAPTER FOUR

As soon as he got home, he removed all his clothing and walked naked through his flat to the wet room. For all he knew, he may have stood for hours beneath the scalding shower. He felt numb inside, almost as though he'd been given some drug that quashed all emotion.

He finally turned off the water, stepped from the shower and wrapped himself in two big bath sheets. When his teeth began to chatter, he knew he was going into shock. He hurried down to the kitchen, took a half bottle of brandy from the cupboard and splashed a big measure into a mug.

He sipped the brandy, felt it burn his throat and only then allowed himself to sink to the floor. What had he expected to feel? Elation? Euphoria? Instead, he felt sick. He drew the towels tight around him, and gulped more brandy.

He'd been seen. But so what? He'd done nothing to conceal his presence at Mud Town. Day and night, people came and went through the site. Shift workers with odd hours. New faces appeared and disappeared. Who recalled them? Who cared about them? No one, which was why Tyrrell had loved it so much. One more face among many. So he was surprised by just how many men had run to try and save Tyrrell. He had stood at a distance and watched for a few minutes. One man actually risked his life, wrestling with a heavy gas bottle to free it from the burning caravan before it exploded. How could he do that for someone who must have been almost a stranger to him? Others, in similar circumstances, would run, flee to save their own skins. Why are we so different when it comes to the things that really matter? To life or death. Fight or flight?

He tipped back the last of the brandy and exhaled. Tyrrell was dead. Now he had to move on.

The cold he felt seemed to come from deep inside him. He turned the central heating as high as it would go, certain that he'd never be warm again. Then he remembered the fire, and the way the flames burst forth as they found something new to devour. The breathtaking heat that hit you like a physical force and seared right into you. There was something hypnotic and quite beautiful in its greedy progress, yet it frightened him too.

He pulled on fresh clothes, and threw what he'd been wearing into the washing machine. But even as he watched them spin, the acrid stench of smoke lingered on.

An hour later, he was back in the shower, scrubbing himself raw, trying to rid his hair of the cloying smell of burning. It wasn't meant to be like this. Tears mingled with the water pouring over his face. He must find a way to get over it. He had to finish what he'd started, and there was still a long, long way to go.

* * *

'Who's she?' Nikki nudged Joseph and pointed to the smartly dressed woman talking to Cameron Walker.

'I think her name's Laura Archer. She's taken over from Richard Foley while he's on leave. She's the Saltern-le-Fen psychologist. Rumour has it that Richard is taking a post abroad and she'll be covering the whole division.'

'Ah. I've heard that DI Jackman thinks pretty highly of her.' Nikki pulled a face. 'But I liked Richard Foley. He never overdramatised. I'll be sorry if he leaves permanently.'

'Hey, why not ask her what makes an arsonist tick?' Joseph said. 'Might help. I know very little about the subject, and that's not good.'

'You're right.' Nikki rubbed her hands together. 'This could be quite a fortuitous meeting.' She hurried across to where Cam and the psychologist were still in earnest conversation and held out her hand. 'DI Nikki Galena. And you're Laura Archer? Your reputation precedes you, Laura.'

Cam rolled his eyes. 'Watch out, Laura, she wants something. I've seen this before.'

'Rats! Thank you, *Acting* Superintendent Walker, for blowing my cover. But yes,' she became serious, 'I do need your help.'

'Well, if I can. I'm finished here, so . . . ?'

Nikki noted her clear blue eyes and light brown, perfectly styled hair. Nikki decided she herself needed a makeover. Badly. 'My office?'

'Lead on.' The smile showed even teeth. Skin, clear and smooth. Nikki sighed inwardly. Not fair. Not fair at all.

Joseph joined them in her office. 'Cat's bringing in drinks. I hope you drink coffee, Laura?'

'Anything, thank you. I've noticed that there's not a lot of difference between tea and coffee with these police station vending machines.'

'Ah, but we're different. We have a *proper* coffee machine.' Joseph smiled.

'Now you're talking!' Laura looked to Nikki. 'So, what's the problem you need help with?'

'We have a fire-setter, an arsonist . . . a pyromaniac? I'm not sure what to call him. He's killed someone.'

Laura frowned. 'I'm sorry to hear that. But you aren't talking about a pyromaniac. They're very rare, and they have a serious mental health issue. It's an impulse control disorder. They light fires with no obvious motive. It's a compulsion, like kleptomania. They can't stop themselves.'

DC Cat Cullen entered, bearing a tray with coffee in three white china cups.

'We don't always get such service, but you're a guest.' Joseph grinned at Cat, who made a sarcastic bobbing curtsy and backed out of the room.

'Are you sure you're police officers?' Laura looked from Nikki and Joseph to the china cups. 'Extraordinary.'

'We inherited the coffee machine and everything that goes with it from someone we cared about.' Nikki spoke sadly, then roused herself. 'So, what have we got, Laura? An arsonist?'

'Tell me exactly what's happened so far.'

Between them, she and Joseph recounted the incidents, as well as the fire investigator's fears.

'From what you tell me, I'd say this is certainly the work of an arsonist. We classify them according to the motives that drive them, which can be excitement, vandalism, revenge, concealment of a crime, profit, terrorism or extremism, or no discernible motive at all, which often means complex mental illness. You need to discover the reason behind this behaviour.' She sipped her coffee. 'They're very complicated people, Inspector. Somewhat like serial killers, they can be organised or disorganised. If you're unlucky enough to have an organised one, he may be unusually clever. He — for it's almost always a man — leaves little or no physical or forensic evidence, uses elaborate incendiary devices, adopts a methodical approach to the setting of the fire, often with considerable study beforehand, and is of above average intelligence.' She paused. 'And he dislikes people.'

'And the disorganised one?' Joseph asked.

'He'll use anything that comes to hand — matches, lighter fluid, petrol. He's likely to be rather chaotic and would probably not even think about whether he'd left fingerprints or footprints. Unlike his organised counterpart, he's asocial, in other words he's socially inadequate.'

Nikki frowned. 'I'm not sure about our man. We'll need to see what forensics and our fire investigator come up with.'

Laura set down her cup. 'I'm happy to help. Give me the findings and I'll try to build you a list of characteristics, a sort of profile, if you like.'

27

'That would be a real help, Laura. As soon as we have the reports, we'll send them over to you. You're based in Saltern, aren't you?'

'I'm here in Greenborough this week, so I'll call by, but here's my card. Ring me any time.'

Nikki thanked her. Feeling distinctly envious, she watched Laura leave her office. She glanced at Joseph, wondering what he saw. Joseph, however, was staring intently at the notes he'd made.

'The motive could be revenge, don't you think?' he said. 'I mean, he doesn't fit most of the other categories. Think of those practice fires. This was planned, wasn't it? An intentional murder?'

Laura forgotten, Nikki nodded vigorously. 'Absolutely. But why Ronnie? We need to know more about his past. Let's speak to Cat, see if she's come up with anything.'

Outside in the office, Cat Cullen was squinting at her monitor screen and muttering.

'Doesn't look very hopeful, Cat,' Nikki said. 'Ronnie Tyrrell?

'Ronnie bloody-never-set-a-foot-wrong Tyrrell. Yes, ma'am.'

'Ah. But anything else? Personal life?'

'Didn't have one. Local boy. Average pupil, left school, went to work on the land, disappeared for two years, came back, went to the Fairweathers and stayed there until he fried, er, died. End of life-story.'

'Family?'

'Moved down to the West Country, but Ronnie didn't go with them. I found an address but it's way out of date. The people who live there now had never heard of the Tyrrells and had no idea how we could contact them.'

Something from this very ordinary life struck Nikki. 'Disappeared for two years? What's that all about?'

'Beats me, but I'll stick with it.' Cat glanced to the empty desk facing her own. 'Ben should be back in shortly. I'll get him to help me try and trace the parents, if that's okay, ma'am?'

DC Ben Radley — Cat's boyfriend of the past eighteen months — was a bloodhound when it came to tracking people. 'That's fine, Cat. We need to tell this man's parents. They have a right to know what happened to their son, even if they were estranged. And I don't want them reading about it in the papers or seeing it on the news.'

Cat nodded. 'We'll find them, ma'am.'

Nikki looked at Joseph. 'And we should go and see that curate, the one Brodie Fairweather mentioned. Where did he say St Saviours was?'

'Helmsley Street, west end of town.'

'Let's go pay him a call.'

* * *

Joseph held open the big oak door. As she went in, Nikki whispered, 'What does curate mean?'

'As far as I recall, he's a sort of assistant to the vicar. I think "curate" means being responsible for the cure or care of the souls in his parish.'

'So are they ordained?'

'Yes, but they always have an assisting role.'

Nikki looked around the big church, a little overawed by its sheer size. She had driven past it many times, but had never really noticed it, let alone been inside. It wasn't ornately decorated, but the soaring arches and the carved wooden screens were magnificent.

A well-built young man with wavy, corn-blond hair strode towards them. Nikki thought he looked more like a boxer than a cleric.

'I was told to expect you. I'm Leon Martin.' He ushered them into a small vestry to one side of the chancel, and pulled some plastic chairs from a stack in the corner. 'How can I help?'

Nikki sat down. 'I understand you knew Ronnie Tyrrell?'

The curate frowned. '*Knew?*'

'He was killed earlier today. We believe he was murdered,' Joseph said simply.

Leon Martin closed his eyes and murmured a few words under his breath. 'Dead? Murdered? Not Ronnie, can't be. He's such a . . . a quiet man. And he owns next to nothing, certainly nothing worth stealing. Who would want to kill him?'

There was a long silence while Nikki and Joseph gave the curate time to assimilate what they had just told him. Nikki asked, 'We understand that Ronnie disappeared for two years when he was younger. Can you shed any light on what that was about?'

Leon brushed his fringe from his face. It was a tired gesture. 'It was a family thing. He had a sister, a really bright girl. She went to university and everything, and Ronnie's father wanted him to do the same. But Ronnie just wasn't academic. All he wanted to do was work on the land, and they fell out. In the end it got so bad he just took off.' Leon frowned. 'As far as I remember, the parents moved to the Exeter area, to be nearer the daughter, and Ronnie distanced himself from them. I don't know exactly where he went, but I know the whole time he was away, he worked in agriculture.'

'So, no deep, dark secrets, just a family disagreement,' Joseph murmured.

'As far as I know, Ronnie had no dark secrets. He was just a young man who wanted a simple life. It was so much against his parents' wishes that he lost them forever.'

'Forever?' asked Nikki.

'They died in a coach accident a few years ago. They were going on a cruise and the bus that was ferrying them to the port crashed.'

'And how did Ronnie take that?' she asked.

'He didn't say as much, but I think he'd always hoped for a reconciliation at some point. He was very low for a while, and losing touch with his sister didn't help. I don't think they ever met up again. Then Ronnie found out that she'd arranged their parents' funeral without telling him, so . . .' Leon sighed.

'Nice woman!' Joseph said.

Leon shrugged. 'It happens.'

'Wasn't there a will?' said Nikki. 'Didn't they leave him anything? After all, he was their son.'

'He never mentioned any money. And he didn't change the way he lived, so I can't think there was anything for Ronnie.' He shook his head. 'So sad.'

'You've been a great help, thank you.' Nikki was glad to get up from the uncomfortable chair.

'How did he die, Inspector? Quickly, I hope,' Leon asked.

Nikki hesitated. 'There's no easy way to say this, Leon. You'll see it in the papers anyway. He burned to death. In his caravan.'

The curate's face turned quite grey. 'Oh, my Lord! That poor man!'

On their way out, down the nave, Joseph asked the curate how he had met Ronnie. 'Was he religious?'

Leon laughed, a little sadly. 'Ronnie was an atheist. I met him through some migrants. They had nowhere to live so Ronnie spoke to the Fairweather brothers and got them a van in Mud Town. It wasn't the Ritz, but it was warm and dry and relatively clean. He didn't believe in God, officers, but he was a good man, and very kind.'

Nikki suddenly remembered Niall's problem. 'Forgive me for asking this. It's a completely different issue, but have you heard of a religious cult that calls itself the New Order Luciferians?'

Leon's hand flew to the crucifix at his neck. 'I can assure you they're definitely not a religious group!' His voice trembled with anger. 'But you'll have to talk to the Reverend Taylor about that. He knows more than I do.'

The young curate suddenly became distant, even cold. Nikki and Joseph thanked him and left.

'You certainly rattled him by mentioning those satanists, didn't you?' said Joseph, unlocking the car.

'Understandable, I suppose.' Nikki opened the passenger door. 'Bit like telling an Arsenal supporter you fancy Chelsea's chances.'

'Mmm, I think not. He got upset and then he clammed up. Maybe we *should* talk to Reverend what's his name?'

'Taylor. Yes, I think we should, but not now. We have the death of a quiet man to investigate.'

CHAPTER FIVE

By the end of the day, they had built up a pretty solid picture of the late Ronnie Tyrrell, and it left them all at a loss as to why this unremarkable man had been murdered in such a violent manner.

Ben tossed his pen onto his desk. 'There's nothing here. Nothing at all. We've confirmed everything the curate told you, including the deaths of the parents, and the insensitive sister.'

'Who, by the way,' added Cat, 'is at present in the Philippines doing climate change studies with the Department of Earth Sciences from Durham University. So it's unlikely she nipped back to cremate her beloved brother.'

'None of the workers at Mud Town have a word to say against him. The guy who saw a stranger leaving just before the fire took hold is devastated that he didn't take more notice. His description is hazy, to say the least,' Dave Harris chipped in. 'Male. Dark padded jacket, jeans and dark hair. He's not even too sure about the hair colour.'

Dave, who had been part of the team for years, had retired. Then, to Nikki's delight, he had come back as a civilian interviewing officer. His local knowledge and contacts were invaluable. He had spent some time up at Mud Town, chatting to the shocked residents.

'I spoke to a man named Alexis, who'd been there longer than anyone. I asked him if anyone on the site had a grudge against Ronnie, and he laughed at me. He said Ronnie didn't have an enemy in the world.'

'He had *one* alright,' grumbled Cat. 'A particularly nasty bastard.'

They all stared at the photograph of the burnt-out remains of the caravan on the whiteboard. It was sobering to think that a life could be extinguished, reduced to a charred nightmare, in minutes.

'Could it have been a case of mistaken identity?' asked Ben.

Nikki shook her head. 'He sat and talked to Ronnie, and even drank with him before he killed him. I just can't see that.'

'Ronnie *has* to have a secret somewhere in his sad life,' Joseph said. 'No matter what everyone says about him being such an innocent. This screams revenge. But revenge for what?'

'We need to dig deeper. Make some more calls, talk to more people, go back further, and,' Nikki looked to Cat and Ben, 'find out where he was in those two missing years.' She stretched. 'But that's for tomorrow. Home now. We'll pick it up again in the morning.'

The team were busy pulling on jackets and heading off when Nikki heard her office phone ringing. She caught Rory just before he hung up.

'Nothing of huge importance yet, Nikki. Only I was fascinated by that whisky bottle. It escaped serious damage because the metal strut of the bed protected it. There was still a little residue inside.' He paused. 'Apart from being an unusual brand of whisky, it had traces of a sedative. Mild, but nevertheless it would have slowed his reflexes and made him drowsy.'

'So, he was deliberately incapacitated?'

'Looks that way, doesn't it? So I doubt our killer actually drank any himself. Maybe he just pretended to. Anyway, I'll put this in my report, but I thought I'd give you that little nugget of information straight away.'

'What was the brand of whisky, Rory?'

'It's called Glenfarclas, and at around fifty quid a bottle, I'd bite someone's hand off for a glass of the stuff! Divine!'

She could hear Rory kiss his fingertips. 'Where would you buy it?'

'Definitely a whisky specialist. Online would be my first port of call. Want me to check it out for you? David loves his malt whisky, so he might even know the suppliers.'

'Please. We have precious few leads, so that could be a great help.'

'Now, regarding the wedding . . .'

'Oh, count us in! Can't wait.'

'Just one little thing . . .'

Nikki wondered what was coming next, and made herself ready.

'Since we're holding it in a Second World War air base, we thought it would be such fun if the guests all dressed in thirties and forties' wartime outfits.'

'Bloody hell, Rory! Can you see me in fancy dress?'

A low chuckle rumbled down the phone. 'I thought maybe you'd like to be a land girl. Or maybe a factory worker? Bright red lipstick, an overall and hair all shooshed up in a red and white spotty scarf. Lovely!'

'I hate to waste that gold-leaf, deckle-edged invitation, but really. Land Army? For goodness sake, Rory!'

'Air-raid warden?'

'Go away, Wilkinson. Go back to your cadavers and tell *them* your bright ideas.'

'I already have. Consensus of opinion was a resounding, "go for it!" Night night, fair lady!'

Nikki stared at the humming receiver and shook her head. No way.

'What's that look for?' Joseph stood in her doorway, head to one side.

'Rory Wilkinson! You'll never believe this, but he wants all his wedding guests, and that includes us, to wear Second World War outfits!'

'Really? Well, what a great idea! I think I'll go as a fighter pilot. I fancy that. Very smart!'

'Joseph?' Nikki looked at him in horror. 'You *are* joking, aren't you?'

He looked at her innocently. 'No. Hey, you could be a—'

'I've just been told, thank you. A Land Army girl. Or maybe a munitions factory worker. Wonderful!'

'I was thinking more of one of those gorgeous army drivers.' He grinned broadly. 'I love a woman in uniform.'

'Go take a hike, Easter! I'm not dressing up!' She stopped. 'Oh, damn! I was supposed to go to mother's this afternoon! With all this happening, I completely forgot.'

'Ring her now. Ask her if she fancies a takeaway. We can pick one up and go straight there.'

Nikki made the call. 'She'd love one. She especially fancies Chinese, if that's okay?'

'Excellent. Shall we leave your car here and go in mine for once?'

'Why not? I'll get my coat.'

* * *

Eve Anderson was in good form. 'I knew something serious had come up when you didn't ring me, and you'd be in touch when you could. The fern garden isn't going anywhere.'

They sat around the kitchen table with their meal.

Nikki loved her mother's new home. The converted chapel had been beautifully designed and crafted by her mother's old friend Jenny, who had sadly fallen victim to a ruthless murderer the previous year. Eve had inherited the house and was endeavouring to make it every bit as special as her dear friend had intended.

'We had an arsonist once, when I was stationed in Buckinghamshire,' Eve said. 'Turned out to be one of the fire crew.'

Nikki raised her eyebrows. 'That's unbelievable.'

'Apparently not,' said Eve. 'There've been a lot of cases over the years. Men who want to be seen as a hero, start the fire, then wade in to put it out. They're usually desperate for praise or recognition.'

Joseph smiled. 'Who needs a psychologist when we have Eve?'

'Cheeky! It was just such a shock when we heard it was one of our own RAF firefighters, the guys that are supposed to protect us. We were all fascinated to know why.'

'And your man? What was his problem?' Nikki asked.

'He'd been constantly overlooked for promotion, his wife had left him, and he couldn't take the rejection.'

'So in the end, he lost everything.' Nikki shook her head. 'I'm assuming he was prosecuted?'

'Oh yes, he was. It was a sad case, although thank God he never hurt anyone.'

'But he could have! It would have only taken a strong breeze, or the wind to change, or for the flames to find something inflammable that he didn't know about. It doesn't bear thinking about.' A glance at her mother told Nikki it was time to change the subject. Eve herself had been trapped on a burning ship when she was an RAF officer. She never talked about it.

'So, is the fern garden nearly done?' Nikki asked.

'Getting there. I've ordered a garden seat to go at the back, with a trellis arch over it. Years ago, I saw a Victorian one in some stately home, and these modern reproductions are lovely. It will be somewhere to sit and have a cuppa in between weeding and hoeing.'

'You are enjoying this, aren't you, Eve?' Joseph smiled at her.

'It was Jenny's brainchild, her project. I want it to be perfect, in her memory.' She drew in a long breath. 'I still expect to see her walking through the lounge, or sitting by the fire. I miss her terribly.' She sat up straighter. 'And that brings me to another subject. I'm glad you've both come here tonight, because I want to run something past you.'

Nikki laid her fork down. 'This sounds serious.'

'You remember Wendy Avery, one of my other friends?'

'Of course!' Nikki said. 'One of Charlie's Angels, as I recall.'

'Well, she had a water tank burst in her home a few days ago, and now she's got all the workmen organised, she's coming to stay while they sort out the mess.'

Joseph nodded. 'Excellent idea. I liked Wendy, a no-nonsense kind of woman.'

'Indeed. But the thing is, I'm thinking of asking her if she'd like to move in here permanently. There's plenty of room. In fact, although the old place is a dream home, it's far too big for one batty old woman.' She looked at Nikki. 'Of course, when something happens to one or both of us, it'll come to you as part of your inheritance—'

'Mum! Don't even go there! This is your home. You do as you wish with it. Whatever makes you happy, and for what it's worth, I think it'd be fantastic if Wendy came here.'

Eve exhaled. 'What a relief! I've been wondering if I was doing the right thing.'

'Great idea,' added Joseph. 'And it'll be a relief for Nikki, knowing you're not alone out here.'

It was true. Monks Lantern was an attractive property, lying well back off the road in a small village. Nikki had been a copper for far too long not to know that it was a prime target for burglars. Having Wendy here would make a big difference. 'Do you think she'll agree?'

'Her husband died years ago and she's rattling around in her house just like me. And we've always got on well. Plus she loves this place. Let's just say I think she'll give it serious consideration.'

'Then I hope that she says yes.' Nikki started to clear the plates, then paused and looked at her mother knowingly. 'Er . . . is the fact that you are both alone in big houses the only reason for this radical decision?'

Eve bit her lip. 'You're an astute woman, Nikki Galena! I hadn't intended to mention any other reason.' She sat back in her chair and stared at Nikki. 'Since that last business, I don't know, somehow I've just felt on edge. I've never felt like it before. For the first time I've found myself checking the shadows, looking hard at strangers.'

Joseph placed a hand on her arm. 'For heaven's sake, Eve, it's hardly surprising, is it? You and your friends' lives were all threatened, and hell, you were kidnapped! But it *is* all over. You and your amazing team put an end to it, forever.'

'But did we? I can't help thinking that the few of us that are left are still vulnerable.'

'I'm sure that's not the case. You had assurances from people in very high places, as I recall.'

'Oh, I know. I'm probably just being paranoid. Perhaps it takes time to get back on an even keel after something terrible happens. I've thrown myself into everything I possibly can in Beech Lacey, and I love this village.' She laughed. 'Maybe I'm just getting old. Whatever, it would be nice to have someone here of an evening.'

'Then let's hope Wendy feels the same. When is she arriving?'

'Tomorrow morning. She only lives just outside Greenborough, so as soon as she's set her workmen to task, she'll be driving over.'

'Then ask her straight away, Mum. Don't beat about the bush. And tell us what she says, won't you?' Hearing her mother express feelings of insecurity was something new, and Nikki didn't like it.

'Eve?' Joseph said. 'If anything bothers you, you have our mobile numbers, and you have Cameron Walker's as well. He only lives five minutes away. You ring us, day or night, understand?'

'Oh, now I've worried you! I'm becoming a dotty old lady, let's leave it at that. Forget my ramblings. You two have enough to worry about if you have a fire-setter in the area. Catch him, Nikki. Believe me, there is nothing more terrifying than fire. I should know.'

On the drive back across the darkened Fens, Nikki anxiously scanned the horizon. Somewhere out there was their fire-setter. When and where would he strike again?

CHAPTER SIX

The following morning, PC Yvonne Collins strode down Ferry Street and stopped outside an imposing Georgian house. She missed Niall, her old crewmate, but was delighted that he'd made sergeant. Now she was solo again, and it felt strange. In a year, she'd be retiring. She'd spent all her working life in the force, and wondered what she would do. She lived alone with her rescue dog, Hobo, and there were days when the prospect of not turning out for work each day was daunting.

Yvonne had a good neighbour, a retired schoolteacher called Ray. He looked after Hobo while she was on shift. She knew that retirement hadn't suited Ray at all, he'd gone from healthy and active to quite ill.

Yvonne set aside her thoughts, and recalled the reason for her visit to Ferry Street.

Satanists? In Greenborough? What crap! About as likely as Yvonne herself performing in a pole-dancing club! This town had its problems, like any other, but in the main the people here were decent. The thought of a satanic church in Greenborough was laughable. According to Niall, DS Easter suspected it was a front for something else, and she thought that was probably true. Now she was about to get inside and take a look around. She didn't expect to see horned demons lurking in the cupboards, but over the years she'd learned that keeping your eyes open often revealed small clues that later proved vital. Yvonne was good at spotting those, often things that didn't make sense at first glance.

She was carrying a folder containing a series of mugshots of local youths who'd fallen foul of the law. She was here today ostensibly to try and identify some of the gang who'd threatened the "satanists." It was her excuse for getting inside the Black House and asking some questions.

The door was opened by a tall, willowy woman of around thirty. She had long brown hair caught back in a ponytail, revealing an angular, rather distinctive face.

Yvonne smiled and produced her warrant card. 'There was a disturbance here the other evening, and we are anxious to find the young men behind it. Could I come in?'

The woman stood back and held the door open. 'My husband told me about it, Officer, although thankfully I wasn't here at the time. I hate violence.'

'And you are?'

'Corinne Black. My husband is Giles Black. He was with the group that were attacked.'

'Is he here, Mrs Black? I really do need to speak to him.'

'No, I'm sorry, he's in a business meeting in Lincoln today, but his brother Tom is here, he was also in the group at the time. Perhaps he can help you.' She led Yvonne into a spacious lounge and asked her to take a seat while she went to find Tom.

Yvonne looked around. Everything in the room gave the impression of a successful, well-off family that liked to socialise. The decor was expensive, with quality furniture arranged just so, and rich drapes at the windows. She looked down at her sensible shoes, and the thick pile cream carpet, and hoped she hadn't left any footprints. The framed photos that seemed to decorate every available surface were mostly taken at classy venues, dinner parties or corporate functions. In almost every shot, copious quantities of alcohol were being consumed.

'Constable Collins? I'm Tom Black, how kind of you to take our little fracas so seriously!'

He pumped Yvonne's hand enthusiastically.

'Yes, I'm really impressed,' he added and gestured to the sofa. 'Please take a seat and tell me how I can help you.'

Tom Black was around thirty, with a neat, close-clipped beard, black hair and very dark eyes. He put Yvonne in mind of the actor who played Merlin. Oh, what was his name?

'We were told that a group of people were leaving a meeting here, and were heckled and physically jostled by a gang of foul-mouthed youths. Is that right?'

''Fraid so. No one was actually injured. We were just pushed around a bit and had obscenities yelled at us.'

'I have some photographs here. Perhaps you'd take a look and see if any of the faces seem familiar.' She handed him the mugshots.

He looked at them in silence and then drew a long breath. 'It was dark and, frankly, they all looked the same. Dreary street clothes and hoodies pulled down to shield their faces. Mind you, this one does look a bit like the one who spat at me.'

Yvonne nodded and stared at the picture. 'Very likely. He's fond of that little trick.'

'Nice.' He grimaced.

Yvonne offered him a half smile. 'Actually, this one really is a lost cause. I've tried to help him, given him every chance, but nothing works. Basically, he's a very angry, very unpleasant young man.'

'Sorry, but he's the only one I would even hazard a guess at identifying.' Tom Black handed her back the photos. 'But if you leave me the pictures, I could ask my brother when he returns. He actually got in between one of them and a friend of ours, so maybe he saw his face.'

'That's fine, I can come back when he's here. I need these to show someone else.' She didn't, but she wasn't leaving them here. 'Can I ask you something, sir?'

This seemed to amuse him. 'Ask away, Officer.'

'About the meeting. What sort of meeting was it? Only I'm getting conflicting reports and I want to get it right. Is the group religious by nature?'

'Can I get you some tea, officer? Then I'll explain.'

With or without hemlock? 'That would be lovely,' she said. 'Milk no sugar, please.'

While he was out of the room, Yvonne continued her appraisal, but nothing odd showed itself. She would like to see more of the place. It was very big, and she guessed she had been shown into the part reserved for 'outsiders,' like the parlours of old without the dust sheets. On the other hand, Tom Black seemed very personable, polite without being condescending, and he was certainly not trying to hurry her out. *I'm probably about to be fed a well-rehearsed spiel about the goings on at the Black House meetings. Or am I just becoming even more of a crusty old cynic?*

He returned with her drink, and she accepted it gratefully. Real tea, no less, served in a cup with a saucer. She herself always made tea in a pot with loose leaf tea, and heartily disliked the weak concoction made by speed-dunking a bag of floor sweepings.

Tom sat down in a deep armchair opposite her and smiled. 'Okay, PC Collins. Go for it.'

Yvonne suddenly felt rather silly. 'Well, I did hear that your group are satanists.'

'Not exactly, but not too far from that, I suppose. We are Luciferians.'

'Is that a bona fide religion?'

Tom laughed. 'I'd say it's a religion for the irreligious. And no, we're not devil worshippers. We regard Lucifer as the bringer of light. And you will no doubt be delighted to hear that we're strict advocates of law and order. We shun violence and all criminal activities.'

'Refreshing to hear.' Yvonne hoped he wouldn't think she was being sarcastic. 'So why do we have such a different idea when we hear talk of Satan?'

'Satanists have very different beliefs, but even they are misunderstood. All those hammy films from the sixties and seventies didn't help. Modern satanism is a kind of umbrella term for a variety of different beliefs and practices that are essentially nonconformist.' He sat back. 'But I'm sure you don't really want a lecture on belief systems, do you?'

'I need to know why those youths saw fit to attack you, so, no, I don't need a masterclass. But I do want to know what I'm dealing with.'

'We are no threat to anyone, Officer. But we don't want to be intimidated through people's ignorance.'

The darkly handsome young man had considerable charisma. Yvonne guessed that a younger woman might well have gone home and dreamt about those eyes.

'It *is* ignorance that drove those young men to heckle us,' Tom said quietly. 'They have a picture created from the fears of dogmatic religion. It's made of all the diabolical trappings bestowed upon Satan and glorified by heavy metal bands and horror films. We can't blame them for believing it, but we do condemn their unthinking acceptance of all that rubbish. We believe in respecting those who deserve respect, and we never interfere with people who cause us no problem. Sadly, we are not always shown the same courtesy.'

Tom Black was very persuasive.

'This house, sir? Is it your family home?'

Tom nodded. 'My ancestors made their money when Greenborough was a thriving wool town, and all their descendants have been blessed with good business sense. My grandfather, being somewhat egocentric, changed the name of this house to the Black House.' He looked at her, and smiled. 'Sorry, no dark, malevolent connotations. It's just our family name, like Smith, Brown or Green.'

That was her next question answered.

'How long have you been a Luciferian, Mr Black?'

'Since I was around nine or ten, although both my brother and I took a long time to fully commit to it.'

'And your parents? Do they still live here?'

'No. They moved to America many years ago. They were avid followers of a man named Anton Szandor LaVey, an American author and occultist. He was the man who wrote *The Satanic Bible*. That wasn't for us, so they left us the Black House and moved to the States.'

'Tom?' Corinne Black poked her head around the door. 'Paris on the phone for you. Can you come?'

Tom Black stood up. 'Duty calls, Officer. But, please come back and speak to Giles. He'll be here after four.' The dark eyes glinted mischievously. 'Although maybe you have all you need now?'

'Touché!' thought Yvonne. 'Yes, thank you, but I'll still pop back later, if that's alright?'

He gave her a polite little bow, shook her hand once again, and hurried from the room.

Yvonne walked back down Ferry Street, thinking over their conversation. She was normally a very good judge of character, but Tom Black confused her. He seemed to her to be sincere, yet there was something about the Black House that bothered her. She couldn't work out what it was.

One of those small details. When he extended his arm to shake her hand, his shirt cuff had ridden up a little, exposing a small tattoo just above his wrist. It was a complex design of twisted flames, forming a scarlet, orange and yellow fireball. A symbol of his religion or something else? Maybe she was reading too much into it because they were all on high alert for fire-setters.

Yvonne nearly stopped, beset by an overwhelming urge to get straight back inside the Black House.

CHAPTER SEVEN

No fires had swept through any part of Greenborough during the night. Nikki was relieved, but she didn't believe they'd heard the last of their arsonist. No one had been able to trace where Ronnie Tyrrell was for those two missing years. She had pinned her hopes on some official job, but they had checked his national insurance number and employment record, and it seemed he must have been working cash in hand.

She left Cat still trying to dig up something useful on those years, and got the others looking into Ronnie the person. Their best bet had been Leon the curate, and she had frightened him into silence when she mentioned satanists. 'You have a big gob, Nikki Galena!' she muttered to herself.

'No one is disputing that, I'll bet.' Joseph chuckled from the doorway.

'Shut up, Easter! I'll tell you when I need help beating myself up.'

'Sorry, I'm sure. I bring a message from Rory.'

She looked up hopefully.

'He says the full forensic report will take a while, but he wanted you to know that they've confirmed that an accelerant was used in the caravan. Our arsonist appears to have packed a whole handful of Zip firelighters and a couple of lighter fuel-soaked rags down the side of the bench seat, close to the kitchen area, and sprayed lighter fuel around.'

'Exactly where John Carson suggested.' Nikki looked angrily at Joseph. 'It confirms that we're looking for a cold-blooded murderer.'

'Something we already knew, but as you say, now it's official.'

'Okay, back to Mud Town. Someone else *must* have seen that stranger, or seen his car parked close by. These workers do shifts. If we go at a different time of day we might hit on someone who wasn't there for our initial visit.'

'Worth a try. I'll get a car and see you downstairs.'

The enormity of what the arsonist had done struck her with greater force. The hate, the total lack of compassion that would lead someone to deliberately consign another human being to such a terrible death was impossible to take in. She must talk to Laura Archer again soon. She needed to get inside this killer's head.

She walked down the stairs, deep in thought. Maybe it really was a single act of revenge? Had Ronnie Tyrrell, in his short life, done something that had aroused enough bad feeling to warrant his horrible, painful demise? Quiet, kind Ronnie. He had been a sad man too. Denied permission to do the only thing he wanted, bullied by his parents and abandoned by his only sibling, and finally cut off financially, if the curate was correct. They needed to find his parents' executor in order to clarify that.

'When you've finished thinking,' Joseph stood with the door of a fleet car wide open, 'your carriage awaits.'

'Sorry. Just trying to get a handle on the arsonist's motive, and coming up empty.'

'Too soon for that. We need to know an awful lot more about Ronnie Tyrrell first.'

She climbed in and fastened her safety belt. 'Then foot down, Lewis Hamilton. Let's go find someone who spent time with him.'

* * *

'Try Justina Mekas. Last caravan on the right. She works a night shift, so you might not have spoken to her before.' Alexis sat on the step of his caravan and pulled off mud-caked boots. 'I've often seen her talking to Ronnie, and I think he might have helped her with her English when she first arrived. She's Lithuanian.'

Joseph thanked him and they tramped through the muddy encampment towards Justina's van. He hated to think what it must be like to live here all year round. It was autumn now, although it seemed as if the seasons had blended into one grey nothing. There should have been orange and scarlet leaves glowing against crisp blue skies. Instead, they hung, damp and decaying, decimated by high winds and constant drizzly rain. He could only imagine the sea of mud in January when they brought the sugar beet harvest in. Then, great self-propelled harvesters lumbered up and down the endless fields, piled the beets into mountains of big ugly roots, and fleets of lorries carted tons of them from the fields. Lanes became impassable and handwritten signs indicating "Mud on Road" sprang up everywhere.

Nikki knocked on the door and they stood back and waited. Joseph did not expect a welcome. Many Eastern Europeans came from places where the police were not to be trusted, were even feared.

Evidently they had just woken her. One hand held a thick fleecy dressing gown to her thin body, and the other grasped the door handle, ready to shut it fast.

Joseph introduced himself and Nikki, and smiled reassuringly. 'It's about Ronnie.'

Her narrow face relaxed. She took a step back and held the door open for them. 'I'm glad you've come.'

They walked into a blast of warm air. Joseph guessed that Justina felt the cold after a long night shift.

He looked around. The space was cramped and airless, her things utilitarian, just the basic necessities. Apart from a framed photograph of two young children, there were no ornaments or decorations. Even so, the single berth caravan was neat and clean.

She pointed to a narrow bench alongside the table. They slid in and sat down.

'I wanted to come to see you after they told me what had happened.' Justina brushed a long strand of pale blonde hair away from her face. 'But I don't like going into police station.'

'No matter, we are here now.' Nikki looked at Justina with interest. 'You were Ronnie's friend?'

She shrugged. 'Maybe. I don't know. He was kind to me and he helped me, so I suppose we were friends.'

Joseph realised it would be hard for a woman on her own to trust anyone in this harsh, alien world. He pointed to the photograph. 'Your children?'

A quiet pride replaced the apathy on her face. 'Yes, mine. Home with grandparents.'

'You work for their futures?' he asked.

'I work to keep them alive.' She looked him in the eye. 'But you want to know about Ronnie, not me.'

He nodded and looked down. Not his business.

'Were you out when the incident happened, Justina?' asked Nikki.

'I had to work long shift. What do you say? Back to back. I never got home until late that evening. They told me then.'

Joseph knew not to rush her, but he was curious to know why she said she'd wanted to see them.

'Had Ronnie seemed worried at all of late? Nervous? Or different in any way?' Nikki was asking.

'No. Ronnie was just Ronnie. He wasn't different.'

Joseph leant forward. 'Justina, we've been told that when he was young, he ran away for two years. We believe he couldn't cope with the pressure his father put on him to go to university. Did he ever tell you where he went?'

The woman's eyes narrowed. 'His father was unkind man. You do not force your children to do things they are not happy with. He should have been pleased that his son had a passion, no matter what it was.'

So, thought Joseph, *she does know about Ronnie's past. Maybe she knows more than Leon the curate.* 'I heard his father left him with nothing when he died.'

Justina's face hardened to granite. Joseph suspected she'd been fonder of Ronnie than she was prepared to admit. 'He told you that?' he asked.

She nodded sadly. 'The sister — the cow — she took it all.'

'Couldn't he have contested the will?' asked Nikki.

'He said that he would not . . . how do you say it? Not give her the . . . the pleasure?'

'The satisfaction,' Joseph said.

She nodded. 'That's right. That's what he said.'

'I suppose he resented the sister after that,' said Nikki thoughtfully.

'Not really.' She gave a hint of a smile. 'Not easy for a man like Ronnie. He wasn't like me. I am suspicious of everyone. I give you my respect after a long time only, but Ronnie only saw good. It would have been difficult for Ronnie to hate his sister for long.' She paused. 'It takes a lot of energy to hate someone. You have to give a big part of your life to dark thoughts. Ronnie didn't do that. All he said was that he hoped the money did her no good at all. And that was it.'

In the stuffy caravan, a silence fell. Then Nikki asked, 'Where did he go when he ran away?'

The hint of a smile widened. 'He never went anywhere,' Justina said. 'Ronnie thought it was very funny. He had another of your sayings. Hiding, but right under your nose?'

'Hiding in plain sight?'

She nodded. 'Plain sight, that's right. His father used to have small boat moored on the river quite close to their home. There was a jetty and a little boathouse. The boat had gone, but boathouse still there. Ronnie lived there.'

'But how did he live? How did he support himself?' Nikki asked.

'The farmer who owned the land around the Tyrrells's home had a lot of land in the area, and he had had big argument with the father many years before. He gave Ronnie work, and he taught him a lot. Ronnie only moved on when farmer sick and die.' Her English faltered.

'So he was right here all the time?' Nikki asked.

Justina's grin was wide and open now. She beamed at them. 'Right here.'

But it doesn't solve our problem, thought Joseph. 'And he never mentioned anything during that time that might have been traumatic? Upsetting?'

'He said it was best time of his life, so no, nothing bad happened.' The sadness returned. 'He was a good man, and I miss him. Please find who did that to him, and lock him up.'

'We'd like nothing better, I assure you.' Nikki nodded seriously.

End of story. But it was no story at all. Joseph glanced at Nikki and saw from her puzzled expression that she was thinking the same. Was Ronnie's killer a psychopath? Was it just a random murder with no motive at all?

They thanked Justina and walked slowly back to the car.

'A madman?' Nikki whispered almost to herself. 'I'm inclined to think not. There's something we're not seeing, isn't there? Something we, and probably a lot of other people, don't know about.'

'But how do we find it?' Joseph said.

'Like we always do. We dig deeper, and keep on digging.'

* * *

John Carson pored over the notes he'd made the night before. He felt uncomfortable about this particular fire-setter, and he wasn't quite sure why. He'd headed up, and solved, hundreds of fire investigations. Each one was different — the conditions, circumstances and motives. Different methods, different targets and very different outcomes.

Nearly all of them were intended as an assault on property. It was rare to find a case of murder by arson. But that was what had happened in Mud Town. From the information he and Rory Wilkinson had provided, Nikki Galena would have a nearly perfect picture of *what* happened in that caravan, and *how*. This time, however, John wanted to help her discover *why*. He felt oddly responsible. Although he had reported his suspicions to Cam Walker, he should not have procrastinated as he had, he should have mentioned his concerns sooner. After only the second small fire, he had known they were dealing with a beginner who aspired to bigger things. Now a man was dead because he, John, had held back.

Well, there was nothing to be gained by sitting around and feeling guilty. The best he could do now was to see if there was something about this fire that only he could discover, some small factor that might help trace the arsonist.

John gathered up his papers and notes and pushed them into his old briefcase. He would go back to the scene of the crime.

* * *

While Nikki reported to Superintendent Cameron Walker, Joseph continued a search he had begun the day before. He couldn't believe there were satanists in Greenborough, but there might well be a criminal group operating. He had come across secret societies before, and they usually meant trouble.

'You look deep in thought, Sarge.' Ben was leaning on the doorframe at the entrance to Joseph's tiny office.

'I'm thinking about secret societies.'

Ben grinned. 'My favourite subject. Ever read *Foucault's Pendulum*?'

'I have. Did you enjoy it?'

'Loved it, even more than *The Name of the Rose*.' Ben came in, and in the absence of another chair, perched on the edge of the desk. 'So what are you thinking? Something sinister lurking down our back streets?'

'It appears to be operating from one of the more upmarket areas actually.'

Ben frowned. 'You're saying this is for real?'

'Maybe. Or I could be allowing my overactive imagination to run riot. Whatever, I'm pretty sure the group aren't satanists, whatever people say.'

'Unlikely.' Ben looked thoughtful, 'Although there are a lot of weird groups springing up these days. Must be the times we're living in. Hey! Maybe we have an underground sector of the Illuminati!'

Joseph looked at Ben with interest. 'You seem to have a rather worryingly good knowledge of secret societies, my friend. Who are the Illuminati anyway?'

'No one knows if they even exist, but they're supposed to be overlords, controlling world affairs — world leaders, politicians, religious leaders. There are videos on YouTube all about it.' Ben paused. 'In my opinion, people are so disenchanted with the politicians and, despite our so-called democracy, having no control over their lives that they buy into the conspiracy theories.'

'I see,' Joseph said. 'Well, I'm not suggesting we are hosting some cult that belongs in a Dan Brown thriller, not a known group anyway. But I do wonder if this religious cult thing might be a cover for something else. There have been several cases reported recently around the country, where a collection of powerful business people have used that kind of cover to manipulate money illegally.'

'Want me to check it out?' asked Ben eagerly.

'Niall has Yvonne Collins making some enquiries, but you can follow up whatever she comes back with, if you'd like to. Tracing the arsonist comes first, of course.'

'Will do, Sarge.' He looked less excited. 'That's what I came to see you about. I'm afraid we've run into a brick wall with Ronnie's past history.'

Joseph sighed. 'That doesn't surprise me. I'm wondering if there *is* anything to find.'

Ben shifted on the edge of the desk. 'The evidence doesn't point to a random attack, Sarge. It was definitely premeditated.'

'Oh yes, but was Ronnie Tyrrell chosen simply because he was a loner living among people who don't particularly welcome strangers or the police?'

'You mean, was he just a pawn? The arsonist was just going for a more advanced level of arson attack? One that involved a human victim?' Ben frowned.

'It's a possibility, isn't it?'

Ben puffed out his cheeks. 'It is, I suppose. Though I don't quite go along with that. I don't know why either, especially when we haven't found any reason for it in Ronnie's life. But I'm pretty sure he was targeted for who he was.'

'That's what the boss feels too,' Joseph said. 'I'm just playing devil's advocate.'

'Sarge?'

Both men looked up to see Cat in the doorway, looking worried.

'Fire and rescue have just notified us. There's another fire. This time it's on a small industrial estate. One of the units has gone up.'

Joseph jumped up. 'Where?'

'It's about two miles outside town on the old Wash Road. The Fenlander Enterprise Park.'

'I know it. Cat, go get Nikki. She's with the super. We need to check this out ourselves.' He snatched up his jacket from the back of his chair, and added, 'Any report of fatalities?'

'We have very little yet, Sarge.' Cat ran her hand through her spiky hair. 'It's only just been reported.'

'Do we know what kind of unit it is?' Joseph asked, aware of the highly flammable stuff used in some small industrial businesses.

'Something to do with greetings cards, I think,' called back Cat, on her way to the super's office.

Joseph groaned. Paper and card. Not good. But at least it wasn't the welding shop that worked out of the Fenlander Park. With their oxyacetylene welding kits, it could be catastrophic. He just hoped that this unit was some distance from there. 'Ben, you and Cat hold the fort here and we'll keep you informed of what we find. Tell Nikki I'll be in the car!'

CHAPTER EIGHT

They didn't need directions. The tall plume of smoke was visible for miles across the flat land.

Joseph swept into the car park and brought the car to a halt as near as he could get to one of the fire appliances. They jumped out.

Even though they were some way away from the burning unit, the heat and fumes hit them. All around was the sound of roaring and crackling. Nikki looked out for the incident commander, but instead saw the tall silhouette of John Carson, staring at the flames as they climbed hungrily into the sky.

'Is he telepathic?' she murmured to Joseph.

'He has contacts, Nikki. He told me. Friends at the fire station.'

'Or he listens in to our emergency radio wavelengths.' She pulled at Joseph's arm and they hurried across to where he stood.

'John! Do we have another one? Is it our guy again?' Nikki called out.

He turned, startled, and then looked back to where the fire crew were running in another hose. 'Oh, without a doubt. They've got a fight on their hands with the gusty wind. The units around have all been evacuated, but they are struggling to stop it spreading.' He glanced at Nikki. 'And we should get further back ourselves. If the wind changes direction, we could be in trouble.'

Back nearer the vehicles, Joseph asked, 'Have they told you anything yet?'

'They reckon it's really lucky that no one was working there today. It was all locked up. The people from the next door unit said the owner's gone to a trade fair in Birmingham.'

'Thank heavens for that.' Nikki sighed. 'But why are you so sure it's the work of our arsonist, John?'

'I've been asking around. Someone saw a stranger coming from around the back of the unit earlier this morning. There's no access or exits from there, it's just a fenced-in yard. No one would have had any business there, and with the unit closed today, it sounds suspicious.' He looked at her rather sadly. 'And I *know* this was started deliberately. There was nothing highly combustible in there. No fuels, gases, nothing like that. Paper and card cause what we call class A fires. They're organic material and water extinguishes them easily. The speed this fire took hold, plus the fact that witnesses said it seemed to have had two separate points of origin, lead me to believe an accelerant was used.'

Before Nikki could answer, Joseph touched her arm and pointed.

Several of the fire crew were shouting. Suddenly fire officers were running towards the blazing unit.

Nikki held her breath. Then she heard the fateful words, 'They've found someone inside!'

Joseph closed his eyes, and his grip tightened on her arm.

'Oh Lord! Not another one,' she said. 'No one could have survived that, could they?'

'Poor devil.' John shook his head.

'I thought it was closed and the owner away,' she whispered.

'That's probably true,' Joseph said. 'We don't know who the victim is, do we? They may be completely unconnected to the business. We'll have to wait till the fire's brought under control and the investigators and forensics can get in.'

Nikki drew in a long breath. 'Then we should go and talk to some of the other people who work here. Find out all we can about this company.'

'Right.' Joseph looked across to where a crowd of people had gathered behind a cordon. 'And I suggest we call for some assistance. There are a lot of small businesses operating from here. We could do with some help.'

'Ring in now. I'll go make a start. John? Want to come?'

John shook his head. 'I'll stay here for now. I'll have a chat with the incident commander later. I'll find out all I can that might help you.'

'Okay. Oh, and John, did you get the name of the person who saw that stranger leaving the scene?'

John took a folded sheet of paper from his pocket. 'Jack Pontin. He works over at the Solway windows and conservatory unit opposite. Ah, that's him.' He pointed towards the crowd. 'The man in the orange sweatshirt.'

Nikki walked over to where Jack Pontin stood staring in horrified disbelief at what remained of the little greeting card factory.

'I can't believe it! Mel and Dev are the nicest couple. They'll be devastated when they get back from Birmingham.'

'What are their full names, sir? And the name of the company?'

'Melissa and Devlin Daley, Officer. They're locals, live on the London Road, but I don't know the number. Their business is called "Melissa's Wishes." They make specialist personalised greeting cards. It's a mail order company.' He paused and grimaced. 'Or was.'

'But they were away today? Do they often close on a week day?'

'It was only because of the trade fair in Birmingham. They're usually here all hours.'

'What about staff? Do they employ many people?'

Jack Pontin shook his head. 'It's a family business. Just them, and sometimes Melissa's sister Clary helps out. She's an artist, pretty good too.'

'But she wasn't working either?'

'The place was closed when I came in this morning, and I haven't seen anyone go in all day. I see a lot from here, and although I have had customers, I reckon I'd have seen Clary. She has long ginger hair, really striking.'

'And the man you saw coming from the back of the unit? When was that?'

'About fifteen minutes before we noticed smoke coming from under the doors.' He looked at her apologetically. 'And my description won't help much, because I was doing some calculations at the time and barely noticed him. It wasn't till later that I wondered what anyone could have been doing around the back.'

'What do you remember about him?' asked Nikki.

'He was average height, indigo denim jeans and a black padded jacket.'

'Hair colour?'

'Brownish, I think, and I suppose he was around my age, that's late twenties.'

Could describe half the male population of the Fens, thought Nikki. 'Better than nothing, sir. At least you *did* notice him. That could be very important indeed.'

The man looked slightly relieved. He asked, 'I heard someone say they found a body inside? Is that true?'

Nikki was noncommittal. 'Nothing is confirmed, sir. It'll be a while before anyone can get in there to tell us.'

'But if it's true, who is it?'

Nikki was asking herself the same question. 'We're going to need a statement from you, sir, if that's alright?'

'For what it's worth, sure.' His eyes had never left the burning building. 'They put everything they had into that place. Now look at it.'

A woman suddenly pushed her way through the crowd. 'Are you the police?' she asked Nikki bluntly. She looked very pale.

'I'm DI Nikki Galena. Can I help you?'

The woman bit anxiously on her bottom lip. 'Everyone's saying that the Daleys are both in Birmingham, but I swear I saw Melissa here earlier.'

An icy finger traced a path down Nikki's spine.

Jack Pontin stared at the woman. 'But Dev told me they were going to the trade fair, first thing this morning.'

'I know! He told me that too, and that Clary was going with them, but I saw Mel. I know I did.'

'Hold on. Who are you?' Nikki asked. 'When did you think you saw her?'

'I'm Helen Hawker, and I work in the Cane Furniture Company unit, close to the entrance. Mel and I are friends, have been since school days.'

'Okay, Helen. When and where did you see her?' Nikki hoped she was wrong.

'I was on the phone to one of our clients. It must have been about two hours ago, I suppose. She was hurrying in on foot, almost running. I'd have gone after her, in case something was wrong, but I was taking an important order and got tied up.' She pushed her hair from her face. 'I went down a bit later but it was all locked up, so I thought maybe she'd called back to pick something up, and had gone again.' She wrung her hands. 'You don't think she was . . . was still in there, do you?'

'Helen, we know nothing yet, so please don't get too upset.' She touched the woman's arm. 'Can you tell me what number their house is in London Road?'

'201. But they're saying there's a body!' Her voice rose to a wail. 'If it's Melissa, I'll never forgive myself!'

Nikki turned to Jack Pontin. 'Can you look after Helen for me? I need to talk to my colleagues.' She touched Helen's arm. 'It's not your fault, okay? As you said, Melissa probably just called in and went out again. Let's not assume the worst.'

Nikki didn't believe a word of it, but she had to say something.

She ran to where Joseph stood talking to one of the fire crew.

'There *is* a body,' he said in a low voice.

'A woman?'

'Too badly burnt to tell,' the young fireman said. 'And I mean badly damaged. One of the nastiest I've seen since I joined Blue Watch.'

'How about the fire? Is it under control?' she asked.

'Yep. At last. But it'll burn for a good while yet. Luckily we managed to contain it to the one building, with just a bit of minor damage to the unit next door — superficial smoke damage, nothing structural.'

Nikki thanked him and drew Joseph away to a quiet corner of the car park. 'Someone saw the owner, Melissa Daley, hurrying towards the unit about two hours ago. They didn't see her leave.'

'Are they sure?' Joseph said. 'Everyone I've spoken to said she and her husband were in Birmingham.'

'We need to get a mobile number for Devlin Daley, but we can't tell him what's happened and then let him drive back. I suggest we get the West Midland Police to help out. He needs to be told before he hears about it on the news, and we need to know if his wife and sister-in-law are with him.'

'I'll get Ben to sort that straight away.' Joseph pulled out his mobile. 'Cat can do a search on their address and get round to their house and check it out. We can leave an officer there, in case they come back early for any reason.'

'They live in London Road. The woman said it was number 201. I'll go back and see if she has a contact number for Melissa. She said they were old friends.'

Joseph nodded. While he spoke to Ben, Nikki hurried back to find Helen Hawker.

Having procured the mobile number for Melissa, Nikki now had to deal with it. It was always difficult, but this time it seemed particularly hard. After a moment or two of deliberation, she made up her mind and called.

Nikki was taken aback when a woman answered, sounding suspicious. 'Yes? Who is this?'

'Melissa Daley? This is DI Nikki Galena, Fenland Constabulary.'

'The police?'

'Mrs Daley, can I ask where you are, please? And are you alone?'

There was a pause, then Melissa, sounding shaky, said, 'Has something happened?'

'Mrs Daley, please just tell me, are you at home? And are you alone?'

'I'm at home, yes.'

'Now listen to me carefully. There will be someone with you very shortly, but can you confirm where Mr Daley is today? It's most important.'

'Oh God! Dev! He's had an accident, hasn't he?'

Nikki was starting to wish she'd gone about this differently. 'No, no, not at all. Just tell me, is he in Birmingham today?'

'Yes! Why, is he alright? Has something terrible happened there? Oh, is it terrorist attack? Please God, no!'

'Mrs Devlin, *nothing* has happened in Birmingham, I assure you. There's been a fire on the industrial estate and we want to know that you and your husband are safe.'

Nikki heard a long drawn out sigh. 'Oh, yes, yes, I'm safe. Dev left early this morning and he rang me to say he'd arrived safely. I had a migraine and couldn't face the journey. But the unit? Is it badly damaged?'

Nikki heaved a sigh of relief. This was not the time to tell this woman of the complete destruction of her place of work, or about the body. 'We don't have full details yet, Mrs Daley, but we'll keep you informed.'

'I should go immediately, shouldn't I? Oh, there's a police car drawing up outside now.'

Now Melissa Daley sounded less fraught, Nikki decided to leave the rest to Cat. There was just one big question that still needed an answer. 'You have a sister, Clary?'

'Yes, Clary was going today too, but she pulled out at the last minute. Nothing unusual there, she's an artist. Sometimes she just does that if she needs to paint.'

'Would you be kind enough to give her contact details to the officer who has just arrived, please? And thank you for your help. I'm sorry to have alarmed you.'

Nikki ended the call. Clary? Could she be the one in the unit? And why had Melissa not mentioned calling in there earlier? If she had such a bad migraine, would she be *running* into the Fenlander Park? Most people with migraines could hardly stand, let alone hurry. Confused, Nikki looked around for Joseph. She needed to throw this lot at him and see what he made of it.

CHAPTER NINE

'So what did our friend the flat-foot want?' Giles Black flopped down into one of the big soft sofas.

'You'll find out for yourself, brother. PC Yvonne Collins is coming back to speak to you.' Tom Black grinned.

'Oh dear, didn't your boyish charm work this time? You're not losing your touch, are you?'

'She was a very pleasant woman, actually, though not the best actor. I certainly didn't buy her story about tracking down the yob that spat at me, but she was nice all the same.'

'So why was she here? You can't tell me that the police are really interested in that stupid little affair. Checking us out, do you think?' Giles kicked off his shoes and stretched out his long legs in front of him.

'Certainly was, but all done nice and politely.' He laughed. 'I think she quite liked me, so that's a good start.'

'Then I'll do my best not to make her change that opinion. By the time she leaves, I'll have her believing that our whole family are warm-hearted, honest, community-spirited citizens.'

Tom raised his eyebrows. 'Don't go completely overboard, Giles! She's no fool. And don't be deceived by the old-school policewoman routine. I'm betting she's as sharp as a knife. She has shrewd eyes. And she misses nothing, believe me!'

'Trust me, little brother. I'll be the perfect gentleman.'

Tom looked unconvinced. 'So, how did the meeting go?'

'Pretty good. I reckon I've pulled in another high-profile interested party, so long as our figures reflect my erudite and convincing spiel.' Giles looked smug.

'Indeed they do, unless you've overdone the sales pitch.'

Giles looked at his brother reproachfully. 'As if! I was simply brilliant. Lucifer himself would be proud of me, even if my brother isn't.'

'I know you, Giles. Your enthusiasm is admirable, but you do tend to get carried away.' Tom disliked having to play spoilsport, the one who always pulled in the reins, and right now, however nice PC Collins was, he really didn't want her as a permanent fixture in his sitting room. 'I'm sure you did a great job today, Giles. Now just be polite to the copper, and send her on her way happy, okay?'

Giles gave a stiff little bow. 'Consider her gone.'

* * *

The day was drawing to a close, but John Carson was still at the scene of the fire. Melissa's Wishes was now little more than a smouldering pile of twisted metal, partially burned debris and ash — a dream destroyed. He hoped they were well insured and would have the heart to begin again. He supposed that would depend on who had died in the conflagration. Before she left, Nikki had told him that both the owners were accounted for, but a relative of theirs who helped out occasionally was not. John had briefly been allowed to see the body when the forensic team arrived, and he was certain that it was a woman, but because of the extensive burning, even he had to admit he could be wrong.

He spent some time walking around, talking to the people who had seen the fire from the start. Many had rushed out to try to help, but were beaten back by the ferocity of the blaze as well as the locked doors. He had listened to several comments that all pointed to arson. Those people who did manage to look through the stockroom windows described some of the flames as blue. The material in that unit was not the kind to release a blue flame unless an accelerant had been used. John was sure that when forensics searched the debris, they would find residue of an alcohol-based accelerant.

He made himself consider the body. It wasn't a pleasant task, even for someone with his experience. The skeletal structure was largely intact, and the body had assumed the pugilists' stance, arms raised in defence like a boxer in the ring. He knew this happened because, as the body burns, the muscles contract and the flexor muscles, which are stronger, overpower the extensor muscles, drawing it into a foetal position.

John knew that although it looked horrible, this could aid identification. The hands tightened into fists, and this sometimes protected the pads of the fingertips from extensive burns, so fingerprints were found. This could be important if the DNA in the burnt bones was too degraded to use. That, and the teeth. Many dental features survive intact while other parts of the body do not.

They could identify the person quite quickly, as long as they had a possible victim in mind for reference. Maybe this relative? John was overcome by sadness. Losing your business was one thing, but to lose a loved one at the same time . . . He had seen it before, and it was heartrending. He'd also seen homeless people who'd found their way into a building to sleep and perished trying to get warm. He doubted this was the case here.

John stared up into the rapidly darkening sky. Really, he should let it all go. He was retired. He was getting old. He should be walking his dog, the one he hadn't got around to buying yet. He should be playing bowls, planning river cruises for the "mature" single. Anything other than this!

John turned his back on the scene and walked to his car. One day he'd do all those things — perhaps. But right now this particular case needed his input, and he had a feeling that somehow he'd play a pivotal role in catching the man behind it. So, he'd better get his head back into gear and offer the police some creative support, before senility set in.

* * *

Yvonne decided to call in at the Black House on her way home. The place drew her back, fascinated her, and so did Tom Black. He had undeniable charisma, and she had warmed to him. She parked outside, convinced that even if he turned out to be a devil-worshipping con man, she'd still find it hard to dislike him.

'You're getting soft, Yvonne Collins. Time to retire,' she whispered to herself. 'Either that, or he really does have demonic powers and he has you mesmerised.'

Mrs Black once again opened the door. With a resigned smile, she beckoned Yvonne in. 'He's in his study. He said he'll see you there.'

Giles Black beamed in welcome. 'My brother told me how kind you've been over that nasty little contretemps with those unpleasant youths.' He pointed to an oxblood leather chair. 'Sit down, Officer. Can I offer you a drink? I'm sure you must be off duty by now.'

'Driving, sir, regretfully.'

'Mind if I have one? Had a bit of a day.'

'Please, go ahead.'

'So, tea or coffee?'

'Neither, sir, thank you. I've just got a couple of questions and I'll be on my way.' She produced the photos.

'That one.' There was no hesitation. He pointed to the same face his brother had. 'Nasty piece of work. As Max Ehrmann so rightly said, "Avoid loud and aggressive persons, for they are a vexation to the spirit." And that young man vexed my spirit exceedingly.'

'I'll be speaking to him, sir, be assured.' She paused. 'But I'm concerned that this won't be the only time something like this happens here. Your brother Tom explained about you being Luciferians, and he told me a little about your beliefs, but I'm afraid the street kids won't appreciate the difference between yourselves and devil-worshipping black magic groups.' She looked directly at him. 'If you continue to hold meetings, I'm not sure how we can protect you.'

Giles looked hurt. 'Our meetings are perfectly peaceful. Just once a month, and on our special celebration days. You can't expect us to abandon them, can you?'

'No, of course not, sir. I just wondered if they could be kept a little more low key? Change the dates, maybe? If the gangs don't know when they are, they won't be lying in wait when you come out. That, or let us know in advance, and we'll try to keep an eye open for trouble. Not that I can promise much, with our budgets cut as they are.'

'We'll survive, Officer. I really appreciate your concern. Part of our teaching is about balancing dark and light, so we'll find a way, don't you worry.'

'I do hope so.' Yvonne wasn't convinced. Giles was a showman, she could see, all smooth talk. He didn't attract her like his brother had. Tom had seemed more genuine, despite the silver tongue.

While they talked, she tried to memorise all the things on display in this rather impressive office. She filed everything away in her mind, to be considered later, hoping to notice something that would tell her these people were not what they seemed. 'Do you have many members in your group, Mr Black?'

'Around fifty, give or take. But we are growing, and more followers are joining us all the time.'

'What do you offer these followers, if you don't mind me asking?' Yvonne was curious.

Giles settled back in his chair. 'Hope, PC Collins. We reject dogma. The "official" religions have been the cause of wars and devastation throughout history. Instead, we offer an ethical life that supports creativity, success, freedom, excellence, individuality and enjoyment. What more can you ask for? We believe that we human beings are masters of this planet. We don't believe in Lucifer as a God, but rather as an enlightened being that can teach us wisdom. We are subservient to no one.'

'So, you don't worship Satan, as has been suggested?'

He laughed. 'Sorry to disappoint, but ask any Luciferian, or anyone from the Church of Satan for that matter, and they'd tell you that worshipping an evil entity is deranged. We're certainly not psychopaths. Far from it.'

Yvonne suddenly wanted out of this place. He seemed to be sincere, but something told her it was a well-rehearsed spiel. He'd done his homework, she'd say that much. But if he had something criminal to hide, he would have.

'Have I converted you?'

'Not exactly, though I can see its appeal,' Yvonne said diplomatically.

'You could do worse, Officer. It can be very lucrative.'

Thanks, chum, but I'll survive on my police pension if it's all the same. Yvonne smiled. 'Thank you for your time, Mr Black. You've been most helpful, and I'll keep you posted about the result of my interview with the youth who attacked you.' She stood up, and accepted the outstretched hand.

As she shook it, she saw the tiny flame orange tattoo, the fireball. A family thing? Or something else?

She climbed back into her car and pulled out her notebook. While it was fresh in her mind, she made a drawing of the tattoo that both brothers sported on their arm. Yet another late-night search on Google. That, and a quick check on what Luciferians believed in.

Were they really so benign?

* * *

Melissa Daley had insisted on going to the Fenlander Enterprise Park to see for herself exactly what had happened. Her visit lasted just moments, and then she turned her back. Cat and Ben escorted her home in tears.

Nikki and Joseph arrived to find her still sobbing.

Cat nodded towards the door and Nikki followed her out into the hall. 'I can't trace the sister, boss. I've tried her home and her studio, and, zilch.' Cat kept her voice down. 'Melissa doesn't know about the dead person found inside her unit. We decided to wait until the husband gets back. He's en route and should be here quite shortly.'

'I agree, but I do need to talk to her. A witness, a friend who knows her well, saw her hurrying into the estate not long before the fire. I have to know what that was all about.'

'She's well upset. I'd be very surprised if she had anything to do with the fire.'

Nikki felt the same. Melissa was certainly not crying crocodile tears. 'Maybe I'll have another word with this friend of hers before I wade in and cause more havoc.' She went outside, found the number for Helen Hawker, and called her.

'Helen, I have to ask this. Are you absolutely certain it was Melissa that you saw?'

'Oh yes. Mel has a very distinctive jacket. It's a sort of long parka coat in bright tomato red, with a rusty coloured fur-lined hood. And she always wears jeans and trainers. It was Mel, I'm certain of it.'

'Without appearing rude, can I ask if you have good long distance vision?'

Helen paused. 'Fairly good, although I do wear distance glasses to drive. But it was Mel, honestly.'

Nikki thanked her and rang off. A slight doubt niggled at her. If Helen had been dealing with a client, she wouldn't have had time to put her distance glasses on. Could she have been mistaken and seen another woman in a red coat? She would need to tread carefully.

Back in the lounge, she debated as to whether she should broach the subject or wait for Devlin to arrive. The fact was, someone had died in that fire, and that meant murder.

'Mrs Daley, I'm sorry to have to ask questions at such a difficult time, but I'm afraid I have no choice.'

Melissa looked up and dabbed at her eyes. 'Whatever I can tell you, although I don't know how I can help.'

'You never went into the unit this morning? Not at any time?'

Melissa looked confused. 'No, I told you, I had a migraine. I get really bad ones, they knock me off my feet.'

Nikki looked at her eyes. They were not just red from crying, and they had dark rings underneath. She wasn't lying. 'This might seem very odd, Mrs Daley, but I understand you own a red parka coat, with a fur-trimmed hood?'

'Yes. What's this all about?'

'Please, bear with me. Can I see it?'

For a moment, Nikki thought Melissa was going to object, then she stood up and went out into the hall. 'It's here. Although why on earth you want to . . . oh.' She stopped, staring at the clothes hooks beside the front door. 'It's gone.' Then she rolled her eyes. 'Clary! She's always taking my things. I swear she lives in a world of her own.'

Nikki's heart sank. Helen Hawker must have seen Clary, not Melissa. 'Excuse me for one minute, please. I need to have a word with my colleague.'

She beckoned to Joseph and hurried outside. There, she told him what she believed.

'It's still not absolute proof that it is Clary in that building. She could have called in, then left again. I know it's a long shot, but until we have evidence . . .' Joseph shrugged. 'So what do we tell Melissa?'

'I think it's time to tell her that someone died in the fire, and as her sister is not answering her phone, we have cause for concern,' Nikki said.

Joseph frowned. 'Before the husband returns?'

Just then, a car swung into the drive and a man jumped out, staring anxiously at the police vehicles.

'Police? What on earth is going on? Mel? Is my wife alright?'

'Mr Daley? Devlin Daley?'

'Yes, yes. What's happened?'

Joseph stepped forward. 'Your wife is fine. She's indoors waiting for you, sir. But there's been an incident at the industrial estate where you have your business premises. A fire.'

Devlin Daley froze for a second, then ran past them into the house.

Joseph squeezed Nikki's arm. 'Give them a minute. This is pretty awful news, without the coming bombshell. Let Ben and Cat get the first part out of the way, and then we'll do the deed.'

Nikki nodded. It would give her breathing space to decide what to say. She sighed. Whatever words she used would cause anguish.

After a short wait, they went inside.

Very gently, Nikki explained what they'd found, and their fears for Clary. Dev shook his head vehemently.

'It won't be Clary. You'd have to know her to understand. She flits from here to there with no regard for time, or for letting you know what she's doing. She sometimes paints all night and sleeps all day. She disappears for days on end. She misses meals.' He threw up his hands. 'She'll be somewhere, but she won't have gone to the unit. She helps us out sometimes when we're busy, but she hates it. She can't stand formal nine-to-five hours, she's too creative, too carefree.'

'And she doesn't have a key to the unit,' Melissa added calmly.

Joseph's look said, Damn! We got it wrong.

'How many keys are there, please?' Nikki asked.

Dev answered. 'Three. We have one each, and there's a spare.'

Nikki asked to see them, and Dev went off to the kitchen. He came back with two sets of keys.

'Mine, and the spare. Where's yours, Mel?'

'In my coat pocke—' She fell silent.

Nikki's eyes narrowed. 'The red coat? The one that Clary took last time she was here?'

Melissa nodded mutely.

Dev drew in a loud breath. 'She took your coat? When?'

'Last night, I suppose. I never noticed, with the migraine and everything.'

'Mrs Daley, a woman who was mistakenly identified as you was seen heading for the unit, just before the fire. She was wearing a red parka with a fur-trimmed hood, jeans and trainers.' Nikki hated having to say this. 'And now we know that she had possession of the key, we have to consider the possibility that she did go there.'

In a strangled voice, Melissa said, 'This can't be happening. Oh please, not Clary!'

Hugging his wife, Dev kept saying, 'But she'd have no reason to go there! Why? It doesn't make sense.'

Nothing makes sense, thought Nikki. *Is Clary going to be another Ronnie?*

'Sergeant Easter and I need to get the investigation under way. Cat and Ben will wait with you till the family liaison officer gets here. Will you be alright?' Nikki looked anxiously at the stunned couple.

Dev made a visible effort to pull himself together. 'We'll be fine. We don't need any help, honestly. There's nothing we can do until the morning, is there? I mean, we don't know for certain yet, about our Clary, do we?'

'You will let us know, DI Galena, won't you? *Whatever* you discover.' Melissa's expression was almost childlike.

'The moment we know something, we'll come and see you, I promise.'

Cat went with them to the door. 'We'll hang on in case they change their minds about support. I'll make them a cuppa, and we'll try to convince them that having someone here would really help.'

'Yes, if you would, Cat. Just do what you can. The shock won't have hit them yet.'

'Do you think it's Clary, ma'am?' Cat asked.

'I'd say so, wouldn't you?'

'Sadly, yes,' Cat said. 'The coat, the keys. Who else?'

'Speaking of keys, did Melissa give you any spares for Clary's home and studio? We'll need something with her

DNA on it, or failing that, her fingerprints, and I don't want to trash the place.'

Cat reached into her pocket. 'I've given her a receipt for these. The Yale is the front door, and the big long key is her studio.' She handed Nikki a sheet of paper. 'Address. You'll need that.'

'Don't stay too late,' Nikki said, 'and update me if anything of interest comes to light.'

'Wilco, boss.'

* * *

Joseph and Nikki knocked and rang the doorbell, but there was no reply. Nikki hesitated, then slid the key into the lock.

Clary's place was an old Victorian property on the edge of town. There were stained-glass windows on either side of the front door, and the entrance hall was tiled. The hall was papered in a heavy, dark, William Morris pattern, and Joseph whispered, 'Acanthus. My elderly aunt had it. Always hated it.'

Nikki kept expecting to see an aspidistra in a ceramic jardinière, or a fringed lampshade over an ornate china lamp. It was like walking into the past.

'Odd.' Joseph stared around. 'She's an artist, but there are no paintings.'

Nikki felt as if she had no business being there. What if Clary *had* just taken off? She wouldn't be pleased to return and find two strangers nosing through her home. 'Let's get a hairbrush, or a toothbrush, and find something from the kitchen that'll have her fingerprints on, and get out of here. This place gives me the creeps. I'd never believe a young artist lived here. It's like a mausoleum.'

They collected a few kitchen items and found a hairbrush in her bedroom, which smelt of rose and lavender potpourri and candle wax.

'We'd better check the studio before we go. Cat says it's down the garden.'

73

Joseph selected the right key and located an outside light switch. They fought their way through a maze of overgrown shrubs and bushes to Clary's studio.

It was a large, modern construction, clearly purpose-built, with high angled windows to let in maximum light. Joseph opened the door and switched on the lights.

'Oh! What a difference! This is amazing!' he exclaimed.

Nikki stepped inside. This woman's passion for painting seemed to seep into her like a physical thing. There were easels, tables, a computer and printers, long shallow drawers that contained pictures, sketches and computer printouts, and artists' materials. The smells of linseed oil, turpentine and drying paint mingled with that of dust. One of the walls had canvasses stacked against it. Joseph carefully pulled some of them forward. 'Her work is incredible,' he murmured. 'I'd buy one of these if I could afford it.'

Nikki stared at a canvas exploding with purples and reds, and wasn't so sure.

Joseph smiled at her. 'Don't try to ask what it means, it's beyond words — that's why she paints. Take a look at some of these and tell me if anything appeals, even if you don't know why.'

Frowning, Nikki moved from one to another. Then she smiled. 'I like this.'

Joseph placed a hand on her shoulder and squeezed lightly. 'Why?'

'Does it matter? I just like it.'

'Right answer. That's what it's all about. You've made a connection with what the artist was feeling, without the use of words, or even conscious thought. It just touches something in you.'

Nikki looked at the painting. It had no real form to it, but it made her think of mist rising over the marshes on a warm summer morning. Soon the haze would clear to reveal a blue sky and the silvery shining waters of the Wash. It signified hope, and it made her want to laugh and cry at the same time. Never before had she felt so moved by a picture. Actually, she couldn't remember ever really *looking* at a picture before, other than photos. This was *not* what Nikki Galena was all about.

She shook her head as if to clear it. 'We need to go.'

Joseph nodded. Reluctantly, he turned his back on the paintings, switched off the lights and they left. 'I'd have put an alarm on this lot,' he said. 'This work is special, it needs protecting.'

Nikki silently agreed. She just hoped that the work would not find itself in money-grabbing galleries and on collectors' walls. When artists died, their work went up in value.

* * *

This time he had been physically sick. As before, he had showered, and then showered again, but still the smell of burning clung to him. Now he was going around adding drops of essential oils to little ceramic burners with candles beneath them. These had a more concentrated perfume than the incense sticks he normally used. After the first fire, he realised that he had to be careful not to use too much cologne after his shower. The last thing he wanted was to draw attention to himself at work. Luckily he was working mostly alone at the moment, and that was fine with him.

He wasn't a big drinker, but he knew what he liked, and he liked the best. Tonight, to steady his nerves, he chose a very expensive brandy that he'd been keeping for a number of years. He opened the dusty bottle and sat at the kitchen table, sipping slowly. It was time to re-evaluate. He stared at the polished wood surface of the table and made a mental list.

Had today's operation been successful? Yes, absolutely, although he hadn't been in complete control. For the first time, he had had to contend with a wind, and he had miscalculated. Others could have been hurt, and that was not his intention. He had a very clear-cut plan to stick to, and wanted no collateral damage.

Had he done anything to draw attention to himself? He didn't think so. He'd been careful to avoid the few CCTV cameras that he knew about. He would have been seen by the workers, but he was an ordinary man of unremarkable appearance.

Was the next stage in place? Yes. He could now concentrate exclusively on that.

Was there anything that would give him away if he was questioned? He closed his eyes and thought hard. He was sure that no one apart from him could smell that stink of burning, so his house was fine. He kept nothing on the premises that could incriminate him, nothing in his garage or his car. All the materials he used were kept in a safe place.

Finally, was he mentally prepared for phase three? The alcohol warmed the back of his throat and he shuddered. This time, at least, he hadn't sat on the floor and gone into shock. He'd recovered sooner. So, yes, he was ready. This had to be done, and he would carry it through to the bitter end.

CHAPTER TEN

The CID room was buzzing with activity. Nikki had taken the morning meeting, reported to Cam Walker, and was behind her desk by ten fifteen.

Rory had found a fingerprint and tied it immediately to one lifted from a glass fruit juice bottle that Joseph had removed from the rubbish bin at Clary's house. They had positively identified their second victim as Clary Sargeant, single woman, age twenty-nine, artist, of Dover Lane, Greenborough.

Her sister had been told, and was understandably devastated. Luckily her husband, Devlin Daley, was more composed and offered to help in any way he could. Cat had returned from talking to them, and assured Nikki that neither could explain why Clary would have gone to the unit. They could come up with absolutely no one who hated her enough to want to kill her. She was a free spirit, creative and quite naïve. People who appreciated her work were totally in awe of her, but apparently Clary was unaware of this. She simply *needed* to paint. Other people's opinions about her work didn't seem to register, or matter.

Joseph looked up from a copy of Cat's notes. 'I keep thinking about all that talent, just gone. It's such a terrible waste.'

He seemed to have taken Clary's death personally, and Nikki understood why. She had seen him react to the paintings. Indeed, she too was haunted by the one that made her think of a misty morning.

'I've been thinking about her work,' he went on. 'It's almost as if two different people were painting. Some of the more powerful pieces were full of rage. Then, some of the others were exquisitely beautiful and calming.'

'We all have moods and emotional ups and downs. If you're a sensitive artist, that must be magnified a hundredfold,' Nikki said.

Joseph grinned. 'Rather profound — for Nikki Galena.'

'Bollocks.'

'That's more like it.' He chuckled.

Nikki stretched. 'So, once again we need to dig into someone's past. What's the betting we find another great big zero, just like Ronnie Tyrrell?'

Joseph glanced through her office door and across to the murder room, where two sets of pictures were decorating the whiteboard.

Ronnie Tyrrell and Clary Sargeant. Their post-mortem photos turned Nikki's stomach every time she saw them. Then, a photo of each as she preferred to think of them. Ronnie's was an enlargement of a rather poor driving licence photo, and Clary's was a shot that her sister had taken. It showed an auburn-haired beauty looking mesmerised by something off-camera.

'We have to discover if there is a connection between them, don't we?' Joseph murmured. 'Although I can't see it myself. They're polar opposites — the farm worker and the sensitive artist. What could be more different?'

'But are they so different?' Nikki pondered. 'They were both loners. Neither had many friends, or so we're told. They were similar ages and they came from the same neighbourhood.'

'Neither had been in trouble with the law,' continued Joseph, 'and both died at the hands of an arsonist. I see your point. They do have similarities.'

'But that's not enough, is it?'

'No, not nearly enough. But it's a start. I'll get the team to begin working on Clary's past. At least this time we have some close relatives to work with.'

'Send Cat and Ben. I think they've built up a pretty good relationship with the Daleys.'

'Okay. We need a picture of Clary, from her childhood. Then we can crosscheck it against Ronnie's history and see if we come up with any matches.'

Nikki moved a pile of reports to one side. 'I want to go and talk to John Carson. While the others are checking out the victims, we should be hunting for the arsonist, and John could help us a great deal there.'

'And so could Laura Archer. Let's gather some info from John and then take it to Laura for her assessment. Didn't she say she's working in Greenborough this week?'

Nikki nodded. Her stomach had tightened when Joseph suggested visiting that much too beautiful woman. Come on, Nikki Galena, she thought. Just get over it! Laura was a damned good psychologist, and they needed every bit of help they could get. 'Good plan,' she said, pushing away the image of cornflower blue eyes and immaculate clothes.

'Did you know that Laura Archer and DI Jackman from Saltern-le-Fen are an item?' Joseph said suddenly.

Wanting to shout hallelujah, Nikki somehow managed to keep her voice even. 'Really? No, I hadn't heard that.'

'Mmm, for the last six months, apparently. He's a really nice guy, and very good-looking. I bet they make a pretty striking couple.'

Nikki felt utterly ashamed of herself. Was she going to start feeling jealous every time an attractive woman appeared? They were happy, both of them. It was just that there were times when she wondered what a lovely man like Joseph saw in her. She was certainly not beautiful, and not always the nicest person to be around, but that didn't seem to matter to him. She shouldn't question it. She must learn to give thanks and enjoy what they had.

'Joseph? How come you know this, and I don't?'

'Because I listen to the mess-room gossips, and you don't.' He beamed at her. 'Knowledge is power.'

She coughed. 'Right, well, back to work. I'll ring John, and you rally the troops, okay?'

Joseph stood up. 'Roger. I'm on it.' He left her office.

Was that a smile on his face?

* * *

Joseph was still smiling when he walked into the CID room. Poor Nikki! She should know by now that there was only one woman in his life. If she lived to be a hundred, Nikki Galena would never believe that she was a very attractive woman. He wasn't the only one to think that either. He remembered his old army mate, Vinnie Silver. But that was part of what made her so special. Nikki had no awareness of herself as a woman.

Joseph found Ben deep in conversation with PC Yvonne Collins. He was willing to bet they were talking about the dark doings in the Black House.

'Anything tasty, Vonnie?' he asked.

Instead of the expected cutting remark, she said, 'Frankly, I'm puzzled. I'm usually so certain about people, and I don't like the feeling.'

She told him about her two visits. 'All I can say is that I feel uncomfortable about this group, and I'm normally right about these things.'

'I'll go along with that,' Ben said. 'I wouldn't ever disregard one of Vonnie's hunches.'

'What do we know about the Black family, apart from their odd taste in religion?' Joseph asked.

Ben folded his arms. 'There are four of them living in the Black House — Giles and his wife Corinne, his brother Tom, and their younger sister, Olivia. Corinne doesn't work, Olivia suffers from some illness that prevents her from working, and the Black brothers buy and sell. That's not financial trading, but actual commodities. Their business seems to thrive on finding products that certain people need, and then sourcing suppliers who want to sell. They buy in bulk so they can charge knockdown prices. By the look of it, it's a very lucrative business.'

'Is it kosher?' asked Joseph.

Ben nodded. 'I've not gone in too deeply, but it seems to be.'

'There's family money in that house too,' added Yvonne. 'A lot of it. Tom Black told me that the whole family, going back generations, have always been good with money.'

'Did you meet the younger sister, Vonnie?' Joseph asked.

'No, I didn't, although I noticed an oxygen cylinder in the hall. Maybe she's bedridden.'

'Or doesn't like talking to the police,' added Ben wryly.

Joseph looked at Yvonne. 'Keep chipping away, Vonnie. Ben? I need you to get back on the arson case. Can you, Cat and Dave do a wholesale assault on Clary Sergeant's past? Everything you can think of — schools, clubs, medical history, workplaces, friends, interests, the whole works. And you can start by going back to the Daleys and getting their slant on Clary and her childhood, okay?'

'Wilco, Sarge, but I'll keep an eye on the Blacks in my spare time, if that's okay?'

'Fine, but just prioritise.'

'Don't worry, I will.' Ben went to find Dave and Cat.

Back in his tiny office, Joseph googled Clary Sergeant. He wanted to know more about her career as an artist. He found that she exhibited under the name Clary Sage, and it seemed that her work was highly sought after by certain collectors. The odd thing was, she didn't seem to have an agent or a particular gallery to promote her work. It just seemed to turn up at different galleries, and there was no mention of price. He would have to ask her sister about it. Her studio had contained perhaps fifty or sixty finished works, but none were labelled or packed for delivery. He wondered again what would become of the canvasses, and if it was true that an artist was worth more to collectors after their death. Only very high-profile artists, he guessed, those whose work already commanded very high prices. He couldn't imagine Clary selling her work even for what it was worth. Then again, she had died very young and unexpectedly, *and* was a murder victim. The publicity might cause dealers and collectors to grab hold of everything they could, especially the greedy, profiteering ones. Joseph heaved a sigh, sad that Clary Sage would make no more amazing artwork.

He stared at the screen and wondered why he felt so strongly about this woman's pictures. They had affected him deeply, and for one of them to have made a profound impression on Nikki spoke volumes. But even so, he was surprised that it bothered him so much.

'I've got hold of John,' Nikki called over to him. 'He's over at the morgue, talking to Rory. Why don't we go meet him there?'

'Good idea. We can also see if Rory has anything to add at the same time.'

* * *

Some police officers were attracted to the morgue. Not Nikki. If it were not for Rory's black, camp humour she'd have avoided it as much as possible. She would never understand how Rory felt so at home there.

He was on good form today. 'Welcome, children, to my humble abode!'

'Rory. John. We do meet in the nicest places,' Nikki said dryly, looking at anything but the charred remains of Clary Sargeant.

'I hope you are not being derogatory about my glorious domain.' Rory's eyes bulged.

'Moi?' Nikki asked.

Rory snorted. 'Anyway, no matter. Let me tell you what dear John and I have gleaned from this sad situation. Gather round, cherubs.'

Nikki and Joseph moved closer to the table.

'This poor lass was undoubtedly murdered. Her hands and feet had been bound tightly with heavy-duty adhesive tape. There was residue of the melted plastic and adhesive still in situ where she lay.'

'Was she sedated before this happened? I remember Ronnie was given something in his drink,' Nikki said.

'I don't think so. We have nothing to go on really, but there's no supporting evidence to say that was the case this time,' Rory said sadly.

'And I have ascertained that a considerable amount of accelerant was used, most likely petrol, as we found the remains of a can at the back of the unit,' John added. 'Plus, forensics checked the ashes and debris, and found no sign of a key. That tells us that Clary let her killer in, and he locked the unit behind him when he left — after he lit the fire.'

Nikki shivered. 'That poor woman. I just can't believe anyone could deliberately do such a thing.'

Rory shook his head. 'Dear heart, I've seen all manner of horrors that so-called human beings are capable of inflicting. This is just one of many.'

'There was burnt evidence of that red coat you mentioned, Nikki,' John said. 'So when the witness recognised Melissa's parka, she was correct. It just wasn't Melissa that was wearing it.'

'I wonder if the killer was actually after Melissa, or Clary?' Joseph asked.

'It had to be Clary,' Nikki said. 'He lured her there somehow. And she let him in. So she had to know him, surely? Would she allow a stranger inside when she was alone?'

'I doubt it. Unless he watched her unlock the door, then pushed her inside and overpowered her.' Joseph was staring at what had once been a talented artist. 'That's a possibility.'

'We'll probably never know.' John looked gaunt. 'Unless he's one of those people who's proud of what they've done. In that case he'll tell you in detail, when you catch him.'

'And if he does, I may not be able to stop myself wrapping my hands around his throat,' Nikki growled. 'He's murdered two quiet, law-abiding people, and he's done it in a horrific manner. I want to know why!'

'Have you found any sort of connection between them?' asked John.

'Not yet, but as they say, it's early days. The team are on it now.' Nikki walked across the big, sterile room and flopped into a chair. 'John? Do you think this man really is a beginner who's learning a trade? Or should we be checking his MO against known arsonists?'

John gave a tired laugh. 'I know the MO of every arsonist and fire-setter we've ever had in this county. And believe me, this is a new kid on the block.'

'Then in that case, we have no idea where he'll strike next.' Joseph rubbed his temple. 'We need to know why he killed Ronnie and Clary, then perhaps we'll have a chance to pinpoint other possible targets.'

Nikki heaved a sigh. 'And where the hell do we start?'

'We already have,' Joseph said quietly. 'The team are trying to find what links the two victims, and it has to be something from their past. We'll find it, Nikki.'

She was sure he was right, but would they find it before the next poor soul went up in flames? 'Can you help us, John? Can you think of something that might tell us what kind of man this is? Apart from a heartless beast, that is.'

John thought for a moment. 'He's not particularly well-organised. Some fire-setters are very methodical. Others use quite sophisticated methods, and even carefully constructed incendiary devices. He's nowhere near that level yet, but he does seem to understand the principles. He knows what will burn and what may inhibit the fire. But,' he sighed, 'I don't know what makes me think so, I don't think he's actually getting a kick from this. In fact, I get the feeling he isn't your average arsonist.'

Nikki groaned. 'Oh hell! Just what I needed to hear! We've got an enigma, a one-off. Someone we'll never get a profile on, because they don't fit an arsonist's job description! Bugger!'

John threw her an apologetic smile. 'Sorry. But this could help, although I don't know how. There was a puddle of fresh vomit in the area just outside the back door. I'm thinking it was our killer.'

She stared at him. 'He threw up?'

'Quite possibly.' John looked across to Rory. 'And our good pathologist here tells me you can lift DNA from vomit.'

Rory beamed. 'And the good pathologist also bagged and tagged it. In a very short time, we'll have some results for you to play with.'

'Really?' Nikki brightened. 'So even if he's not on file, we'll have something, should we apprehend a suspect. Cool!'

'Not *if*, but when,' Joseph said. 'That's a real something — as long as it *is* the killer's.'

John chipped in. 'I checked with the fire crews, and no member of the public went round there after the fire started, and none of the firefighters upchucked either.'

Nikki frowned. 'So he does the deed, then is sick. How odd. I thought it was supposed to elicit a thrill, sometimes even sexual arousal?'

'Thrill, yes. That's fairly common in arson. Especially in the juvenile/young adult bracket, and those rarely hurt people. Sexual arousal is rare, and usually those are opportunists who just start small fires with available materials, nothing like this man.'

'If he hates what he's doing so badly that it makes him sick, why use this way of killing?' Joseph looked perplexed.

Nikki narrowed her eyes. 'Maybe, if we can work that out, it'll get us on track.' She had the feeling that this was very important indeed. 'Time we took it to Laura Archer, I think. Thank you, Rory, thank you, John. We'll tie up again later.'

Rory tutted. 'Always in such a rush! And I *so* wanted to talk about Second World War costumes!'

John looked perplexed.

'Take no notice, John,' Nikki said. 'He's clearly not well!'

* * *

Laura Archer listened intently to everything Nikki had to say. When she'd finished, Laura was silent.

After a while, she said, 'I'm afraid I agree with your investigator, John Carson, about this man. He's not conforming to any known behaviour patterns, or the classifications I told you about the other day. I'm wondering if it has some other cause, like a religious mania. That would explain his *need* to use fire, even though it repelled him.'

Joseph puffed out his cheeks. 'Phew. As in committing his victims to a fiery demise? Condemning them to the fires of hell? Like a punishment for something?'

'Kind of, although I was thinking more that a lot of beliefs consider fire to be cleansing. It purifies. It purges.'

Nikki tried to keep up. 'So was he trying to "save" his victims? Or punish them?'

Laura continued. 'The bible is littered with references to baptism with fire. Then there's the sacrifices, the burnt offerings.'

'And the reference to God's "fiery law," where all the chaff is burnt away, leaving only righteousness.'

Joseph had looked grave as he spoke. Nikki wondered where that had come from. Joseph wasn't religious, but sometimes he surprised her with his knowledge of such matters.

'Exactly, and fire is often considered a powerfully good thing. Think of sending fallen Norse warriors to Valhalla — in a burning burial ship. Or the funeral pyres on the banks of the Ganges. The Hindus believe that burning the deceased in a holy place will allow their souls to be transported straight to heaven.'

'So, we could be looking for a religious zealot?' Nikki's heart sank. This complicated things. She liked straightforward — a crime of passion, a violent reaction to a perceived injury. Simple revenge that was in some way understandable. A kicking back, even if it were done illegally. The unhinged mind baffled her.

She looked from Joseph, in deep thought, to Laura, who was clearly considering possibilities, and was mighty glad she had them both on board.

'There's one other explanation,' Laura said softly. 'Maybe the excitement was so intense that it made him sick.'

'Like an over-excited child?' Nikki asked, remembering her darling Hannah as a little one. She frequently threw up when she knew they were going to a special treat.

'Yes. Intense excitement or stress can cause the same reaction in susceptible adults. That type of arsonist will almost certainly stay around to watch the whole debacle. He will be in the crowd that gathers. He won't be able to leave until the inferno — the result of his handiwork — has abated.' Her expression grew darker. 'And by then, he will almost certainly be planning his next fire.'

Nikki put her elbows on the desk, clasped her hands together and rested her chin on them. She sighed. 'I have to stop him. I don't want more people dying and more buildings destroyed. Now I'm not sure what I'm looking for.'

'John said he mingled with the crowd after the fire,' Joseph said. 'He was looking for someone who might have been the arsonist. He spoke to workers from the estate, and none of them saw a stranger there. John would have spotted an arsonist. He knew exactly what he was looking for. He's certain the man started the fire, locked the door, was sick, then got away as quickly as possible.'

'And that brings us back to someone who *has* to use fire in order to kill for some as yet unknown reason,' Nikki concluded.

Laura nodded. 'Looks that way. If it helps, I'll look out some historical case studies that show a similar pattern. There might be a clue as to why he needs to use fire.'

'I'd be grateful, Laura. In my book, this makes him all the more dangerous. Fanatics, extremists and the barking mad, excuse the terminology, all make me very nervous indeed.'

'You'd be a fool not to feel that way,' said Joseph solemnly.

'Okay, well, until we know more, nothing for it but to help the others look into Clary's past,' Nikki smiled at Laura, 'and wait for your thoughts on why our man is using fire as a lethal weapon.'

CHAPTER ELEVEN

Yvonne stared at the computer screen, looking at tattoo designs featuring fire. She'd never have imagined there could be so many. Flames, fireballs, volcanoes, burning trees, fire demons and dragons, phoenixes, Molotov cocktails and fire-fighters. Some covered huge areas of the body and were more like monster graphic designs, and others were smaller and more symbolic, but there were none that looked like those on the Black brothers' wrists.

It looked as though her next stop would be the local tattoo parlours, but first she wanted to delve a little deeper into the Luciferian faith, if you could call it that.

There was a considerable amount of information about it. Yvonne was surprised to read that alternative religions were rather in vogue, especially those centring on Satan. She scrolled through article after article, coming to the conclusion that Luciferians were probably the best of the bunch. She read one in depth, a paper on the similarities and differences between Luciferians and satanists. It was almost word for word what the Blacks had told her. Yvonne frowned. Had they just quoted chunks of the research at her? Once again, she didn't know whether she was being strung along by a couple of sharp conmen, or given an honest introduction to what they truly believed. Giles had tried, fleetingly, to recruit her, offering a lucrative future. But recruit her into what? A religion? Or a shady business venture?

Yvonne chuckled to herself. Surely even Giles Black wouldn't try to rope a police officer into the fold? The smile faded when she recalled those police officers who'd been happy to take back-handers or join certain underground groups. She thought of the Masons. They certainly looked after their own. Perhaps it wasn't quite so strange after all.

She decided it was time to hit the tattoo parlours. Her first stop would be the Inksmith Studio in Godolphin Alley. It was run by a rather exotic woman called Phoebe and known to be the cleanest and most upmarket in the area. If Phoebe couldn't help her, then her task would be more difficult.

Phoebe took a few minutes out from her latest creation, a rather splendid wolf's head surrounded by stars, to take a look at Yvonne's sketch.

'It's not a standard, that's for sure. And it's not one of ours.' She handed it back to Yvonne. 'Try Alvie, down in Rock Lane. There's something about it that makes me think of his style.'

Yvonne walked down the one way street that led to Rock Lane. It was cobbled and hard on the feet, even with her tough shoes. Alvie's place was distinctly more backstreet, frankly pretty seedy, but Phoebe had called Alvie "a master of inking the skin."

She glanced at some of the designs on show in the rather grimy window, wondering why people felt the need to decorate themselves in this way. You got fed up with wallpaper, so you changed it. You'd had enough of one particular picture on your wall, so you put another up, but you couldn't do that with your body. People changed. Tastes changed. Lovers changed. But that tat you got for a dare when you were legless one night was forever, unless you fancied paying for laser surgery.

She pushed open the door and went in.

A young man and a middle-aged woman looked up. She was glad to be wearing her uniform. At least they wouldn't believe she was coming in for a bit of skin art before she got too wrinkly.

'Is Alvie around?'

'He's out back. He won't be long.' The lad gave her a friendly grin. 'He's just finishing a bit of work on my mate.'

Well, I really hope he's pleased with it, thought Yvonne, *because there's no going back if he hates it.* She took a seat, wondering privately if the rather ordinary woman was there for a bit of decoration for herself, or also waiting for someone. Yvonne looked around. It was much cleaner inside, and there was an up-to-date hygiene certificate on the wall. Could she imagine Tom and Giles Black coming here? Another question with no answer. If you wanted a discreet tattoo, you had to go somewhere, and maybe a parlour down a quiet alley was better than the one close to the busy high street.

It wasn't long before a door opened and a short, stocky lad came out with the tattooist. Yvonne stared at the young man and wondered if there was much skin left to tattoo. The boy was one big illustration! Yvonne turned to his friend and said, 'A bit of work! You were kidding, weren't you?'

'He's addicted.'

Yvonne scratched her head. 'You mean that, don't you?'

'Well, maybe it's called an obsession, I dunno. I just know he spends all his wages on them.'

'But not you?' Yvonne looked at the boy's clear, unmarked skin.

'No fear! Don't like pain! And me mum would kill me.'

'Clever woman your mum. Stay as you are, lad. One day you'll be glad you did.'

After the young men had left, she showed Alvie her design.

'Oh yes, that's one of mine.' Alvie had long dark hair scraped back into a tight ponytail and a close-clipped dark beard. He looked rather devilish himself, and that was without the gothic tattoos on his own arms.

'Can you tell me what it signifies, please?'

'It's a private design, Officer. She gave me a drawing, and I made a transfer up for her.'

'Her?'

'Yep. It was a woman came to me first, and then several others came for identical tats.'

'And the meaning?'

'No idea. They wouldn't tell me, and believe me, I did ask.'

'Can you tell its origins? You know, like some are Celtic or some are Maori.'

Alvie stared at the picture. 'No, it has no traditional origin that I know of. Sorry, Officer, can't tell you any more I'm afraid.'

Yvonne left, no more enlightened than when she went in, except for the fact that a woman had ordered them. Corinne? Surely not Olivia? She was sick, wasn't she? Or maybe it wasn't a Black at all.

She walked back to the main road, still wondering what was going on in the Black House.

* * *

At around three p.m., Nikki's phone rang. 'Mum! I was just thinking about you. Has Wendy decided whether to join you at Monks Lantern?'

'That's why I'm ringing, Nikki. Yes, she thinks it's a great idea. As do I. The more I consider it, the happier I feel. Knowing that you and Joseph feel the same makes it all the better.'

'Fantastic news! I can't wait to tell Joseph.'

'It's strange, you know.' Eve sounded serious now. 'She feels as I do, about being unsettled and jumpy. And I've never heard Wendy admit to something like that before. She has nerves of steel. We saw some terrible things while in the military — and we've both seen friends and colleagues die, sometimes right in front of us. We talked about it last night, and came to the conclusion that neither of us wanted to admit, not even to ourselves, that we were badly affected by losing Jenny and Anne. More than we expected.'

'Have you heard from your other old friends, Lou and Rene, Mum? Do they feel the same?'

'We're having a get-together here at Monks Lantern at the weekend. They'd love to see you again, if you can get free, even just for a little while.'

'We'll make it, one way or another. I'd love to see them again myself. You have a great group of buddies there.'

'I'm just sad we're so depleted. You would have loved Jenny. Anne too, but Jenny was a force of nature. I miss her, Nikki, and I always will.' She sighed. 'And yes, we all feel edgy, even stoic Lou and gung-ho Rene.'

Nikki didn't like to say, but they were all getting to an age when things often did start to worry people more. However, these were no ordinary women. Each one had served their country in a high-level role, and they all had a barrel-load of courage. It was odd that every one of them felt so uneasy. 'It'll be good for you all to get together again. You can talk it through, and maybe come up with some constructive ideas about how to overcome it.'

'And maybe we can bounce it off you and Joseph?' Eve asked.

'Absolutely — arsonist permitting,' Nikki said grimly.

'There was another fire, wasn't there? I heard about it on the radio,' said Eve. 'Same man?'

'We think so — well, no, we are certain about it.'

'Stay safe, sweetheart. No heroics — promise?'

Nikki laughed. 'We'll do what we have to do, as always, Mum, and that's what you would do in the same circumstances.'

'Okay, okay. Actually, I'm starting to see the error of my ways. It's gardening for me from now on, and Wendy is dead keen to help out, thank heavens! She's found some old maps and plans relating to Monks Lantern and the original layout around here, so we already have another project to tackle when the fern garden is complete.'

'Good to hear. And, Mum? I'm thrilled about Wendy moving in, I really am.'

'I know you are, Nikki. The one thing I do not want to be is a burden. I'd feel awful if you were worrying about me.'

'What crap! You couldn't be a burden if you tried! A pain in the arse, possibly, especially when you go all Secret Squirrel on me, but a burden? No way!'

They laughed, and then Nikki ended the call, greatly relieved. Her mother was an enigma. She was a wonderfully brave woman, but nevertheless, alone in the big converted chapel on the edge of a rural village, she was vulnerable. Having two ageing Amazons living at Monks Lantern evened up the odds considerably.

Nikki stood up and went to find Joseph, glad to be passing on some good news for a change.

* * *

Giles and Tom Black sat at the bottom of Olivia's bed and set out the chess pieces on the board.

Olivia watched her brothers commence their game. Because of their surname, both brothers wanted the black pieces, and the game always began with good-natured bickering.

They had done this since their childhood, and she suspected they always would.

She played occasionally, but today her breathing was difficult, so she lay back and enjoyed her brothers' company. Her asthma came and went. Yesterday she had overtaxed herself, and today she was paying for it. At least this time she hadn't ended up in A&E.

Olivia sighed softly.

'Okay, sis?' asked Tom.

She nodded. It had been a sigh of contentment. She knew how lucky she was. She had two brothers who cared about her, who provided enough money that she didn't have to work. Whatever it was they did, Giles and Tom were certainly passionate about it. Over the last few years they had been increasingly busy. More people came and went. Olivia kept herself to herself. It was her brothers' business, and it seemed to be bringing in more money than ever before.

Olivia had spent all of her short working life in advertising. When she first gave up her job, she had worried about the strain she was putting on the Black family coffers. Giles and Tom had assured her that she wouldn't have to worry about money. They had plans, they said. "Lucifer will provide." And then they laughed. It was their stock response whenever she asked.

Because of her illness, Olivia led a strange, insular life, but it suited her. She no longer enjoyed going out, except for the occasional trip to the Café des Amis with an old friend. She hated television, with its endless stories of misery and violence, so she watched films online. She read. Books freed her from the asthma and its cylinders of oxygen.

She watched her brothers at their game, deep in concentration, and thanked — Lucifer? She was lucky, and that was all she knew for sure.

* * *

'Different schools, different GPs, different social class, different everything!' Cat threw down her pen and stared angrily at the monitor screen. 'Four hours of solid searching and I've come up empty.'

'Same here,' sighed Ben.

'Me too,' grumbled Dave. 'It's so disheartening.'

Cat leaned back and stretched her arms. 'God, I'm stiff! Staring at a computer screen all day doesn't do a lot for the posture.' She glanced at the clock. It was almost time to pack it in for the day, but she had really wanted to find something, *anything*, no matter how tenuous, to link Clary with Ronnie.

Ben stood up. 'The Daleys couldn't have been more helpful, but nothing they gave us had the slightest connection with Ronnie. I'm beginning to think there isn't one. Maybe he had a different reason for killing each of them.'

Dave nodded slowly. 'So you're suggesting there's no connection at all?'

'Well, it would explain the total absence of a link. Suppose he's very religious. Maybe at one time or another each of them insulted his beliefs, so he made them pay.'

'Okay,' said Cat. 'Let's take one of them — I'd suggest Clary, as we know more about her — and make a list of her known friends and associates, then see if any of them crop up among the people that Ronnie was connected to.' Cat flopped back down into her chair. 'I'm game to give it another hour. How about you guys?'

'All I've got on is a microwave meal and a glass of beer,' said Dave, sounding forlorn, 'and maybe a box-set binge if I stay awake long enough. Count me in.'

'And since you're cooking tonight, Cat Cullen, I have little option but to stay too.' Ben laughed. 'Let's start matching!'

* * *

From her office, Nikki could see the others still hard at it. She smiled. The team were everything a DI could ask for — loyal, enthusiastic and dedicated. Cat and Ben could both have gone for their detective sergeant's exams by now, and sailed through. And Dave hadn't needed to come back after his official retirement, but they all felt a responsibility towards the team. Nikki wasn't sure how long things could continue like this. Changes were happening in the force, things she had no control over. But she would go down fighting, and she was pretty sure she'd have her team alongside her.

Joseph nodded towards the CID room. 'Looks like my plans for an early, relaxed meal tonight have just gone out the window. We can hardly bog off and leave them slaving, can we?'

'Have you ever had the feeling you're wasting your time?' Nikki said.

Joseph squinted at her. 'As in?'

'As in we are barking loudly up the wrong bloody tree.'

'All we can do at this stage is follow procedure,' said Joseph. 'Check and recheck everything we know about our two victims and the people around them and try to make connections. We've already dealt with the forensic evidence, the little there was of it. We've sought professional help in fire forensics *and* psychology. What more can we do?'

'You are so bloody reasonable, Joseph Easter!'

'But you love me,' he whispered.

She glanced towards the open door, and gave him a slow smile.

They saw Dave approach and looked quickly away from each other.

'Ma'am. Sarge. We've found just one name that connects our two victims. It probably doesn't mean anything, but we thought you should know.'

'Who is it?' asked Joseph quickly.

'The curate at St Saviours. Leon Martin.'

Nikki glanced at Joseph. 'The man who was so upset when I mentioned satanists in Greenborough.'

'And one of the few people who really knew something about Ronnie Tyrrell,' Joseph added.

There was a moment's silence as they all digested this. Then Nikki said, 'We mustn't let our suspicions about our killer being on some religious crusade run riot just yet, but all the same, I think we need to speak to him.' She smiled at Dave. 'Well done, guys. Now you really should all get off home. Joseph and I will call on the curate.'

* * *

Leon Martin sat down hard in the front pew and stared at the altar. 'Clary? But why?' Nikki and Joseph were silent. 'She was . . . how can I put it? Almost otherworldly. She was different to anyone I've ever met.'

'You knew her well?' asked Nikki.

'Not well, but now I wish I'd made more effort to spend some time with her. Her paintings were astonishing.'

'I wouldn't have had you down as a contemporary art fan,' Joseph said. 'I'd have thought you preferred a more classic style.'

'Oh, Clary could paint anything, Sergeant. That's where I met her. Someone had talked her into giving an informal talk to an art class at the church hall. She showed them some of her paintings. Her heart was in modern stuff, but she did some beautiful landscape work too. Now all that wonderful talent . . .' He shook his head.

'We agree,' Joseph said. 'We saw her work. A terrible waste.'

'Leon, can you think of a single connection between Clary and Ronnie Tyrrell?' Nikki asked.

The curate puffed out his cheeks. 'None that I can think of. Ronnie certainly never mentioned her, even in passing.' He paused. 'But he did like art. He knew something about it too. When you saw him in that caravan in Mud Town, you forgot that he came from a good family and could have gone to university if he'd had the inclination.'

'Do you think he could have met Clary because of their shared interest?'

Leon shook his head. 'No. I say that because I actually have a small painting of Clary's. It hangs in my little cottage. Ronnie commented on it one day when he visited me, but he said he didn't recognise the artist.'

'You're lucky to have one of her pictures,' Joseph said.

'I'll treasure it. It's even more precious because it was a present.' Leon shrugged. 'She was like that. When she was at the church hall I just happened to mention that I liked it, and two days later she turned up here and gave it to me. She said things should always find their way to people who would love them.'

'She seemed to be a very gentle, rather fey sort of person, yet some of her modern paintings are very powerful, and quite dark,' Joseph said.

'I never saw any of those, she certainly didn't bring them to the art class. A talented artist can paint out their anger and sadness on the canvas, you know. I just wish everyone could rid themselves of their negative emotions like that, instead of fighting.'

Life isn't as simple as that, thought Nikki. Her job had taught her that much. 'Leon, is there anyone around here who might be fascinated by fire in a biblical way? As in quoting scriptures about cleansing, or purifying with fire?'

'Heavens, no! As far as I know, the only people around here who can quote the scriptures are the vicar and me! Greenborough isn't exactly heathen, but it's not very holy, either.'

She nodded. 'I thought that was probably the case.'

'Can I help in any other way, Officers?'

'Just keep your ears open, and contact us immediately if you hear any talk about either of the two deaths, or about fire.' Nikki couldn't think of any further questions. Dinner was calling. In fact, she was starving. 'We appreciate your time, Leon.' She handed him her card, and they made their way back down the aisle of the big church. This time she'd managed to avoid all mention of the dark arts.

CHAPTER TWELVE

Around three a.m., the phone rang. Nikki recognised the voice of Danny the night-shift sergeant.

'Car fire this time, ma'am. Driver still inside. It might not be connected to your case, but I thought you might like to check it out,' Danny said.

'Where?' asked Nikki groggily, trying to nudge Joseph awake.

'Whistlepenny Woods. The car park closest to the fishing lake.'

'Thanks, Danny. We'll take a look. With that maniac out there, we can't afford to leave it.'

'Thought as much, ma'am. Fire service got there pretty smartish, but there's not much left of the driver.'

'Lovely. Thanks for that.'

'Pleasure.'

'Another one?' Joseph was out of bed, searching for his clothes.

'Car fire close to Whistlepenny Woods. Danny isn't sure if it's connected or not.'

'Bet it is.' Joseph pulled on his chinos. 'That little conservation area is well off the road. It's the perfect spot to torch a vehicle.'

'*And* the driver,' added Nikki flatly.

'Rory won't like this at all. Don't think he'll be wanting more crispy critters.'

'Can't say I'm too keen myself.' Nikki pulled on a thick sweater. 'I'll be mighty glad when we don't have to look at burnt bodies anymore.'

They drove towards Whistlepenny Woods, watching the flashing lights of the emergency vehicles across the fields.

'Bit of a déjà vu scenario, isn't it?' Joseph said as they drew up.

'Complete with resident fire investigator, retired, Mr John Carson,' commented Nikki.

'That guy can't ever sleep, can he? He's always first at the scene.'

They hurried across to where John stood talking to the fire crew.

'You guys are being kept busy at the moment,' Joseph said to one of the firefighters.

Josh Kent looked at the car. 'The fires I can contend with, no problem. I really enjoy the battle. But finding another human being inside, that's the bit I don't like.'

There was little left of the front of the car. The back seats, although badly burnt, were still recognisable, and some of the original paintwork was left on the boot lid — about eighteen inches of a blistered red. It was almost impossible to recognise the make of the vehicle, and the driver was in a worse state.

Nikki's stomach lurched.

'You okay?' She felt Joseph's hand on her arm.

She took a long, deep breath and fought down the rising nausea. 'Just not good with this sort of thing.'

She was glad that Joseph made no attempt to shield her from the sight. It would mean she wasn't up to the job, which was far from being true.

'You'd have to be some kind of weirdo to be alright seeing something like this.' Joseph stared at the car and its blackened occupant. He turned to John Carson.

'What have we got this time, John? What do the fire boys say?'

John beckoned them to a distance from the fire crew.

'This time we differ, I'm afraid.' He rubbed his eyes.

'What are the known facts?' asked Nikki.

John's hand dropped from his face. 'There was an anonymous call to fire and rescue. They'd just been out to a false alarm at a cottage close by, so responded almost at once. They said that the front of the car was already an inferno, but they got to work fast and brought it under control. The driver was probably dead before they arrived.'

'How does your opinion differ?' Joseph asked.

'They found evidence of fire-starting materials in the boot. They are pretty sure the dead man is your arsonist.'

Nikki glanced at Joseph and then back to John. 'But you disagree? Why?'

John shrugged. The hollow eyes and haunted expression of total exhaustion were hard to miss.

'I think this is a ploy to throw you off the scent. Yes, there are incendiary materials in the boot, but I think they were put there deliberately, so you believed your investigation was over.'

'How come the front of the car burned so quickly, John?' Nikki asked.

'Accelerant. Petrol, most likely. The fire crew think he was preparing some sort of Molotov cocktail. They found the remains of a glass bottle in what's left of the passenger footwell. They reckon he either had an accident, or maybe decided he'd had enough and took his own life.'

'And *you* think the accelerant was poured over the body and the front of the car,' Joseph said.

'I do. I'm sure of it,' John said.

'Was the car locked?'

'No, but the key was in the ignition. That's one reason they think it was suicide, or an accident on the part of the driver.'

Nikki frowned. 'If the driver was already dead, or unconscious, the killer wouldn't need to lock him in and take the keys, as he did with Clary. He could afford to leave them behind.'

'Exactly,' said John. He drew his coat around him. 'Plus, I've been working out the timings. I think that 999 call was made *before* the car was set alight. I believe our killer wanted the fire crew to get to the boot area in time, and find the incriminating evidence. I wouldn't be surprised if the false alarm call to the cottage was made by the killer too, in order to bring a fire tender to the area.'

'And who's the driver?'

'Who indeed? A male, but that's all we know.'

'And the car? The rear number plate is still legible. I'll have a look.' Joseph checked his smartphone. 'Stolen earlier today, from a Greenborough supermarket car park. Owner reported it immediately.'

'Hope it's fully insured,' muttered John. He turned to Nikki. 'I know I'm right about this.'

Nikki nodded. 'Don't worry, John, I'm with you. It's all too staged, too unlikely. We can check those 999 calls. It's easy to tell a genuine caller, and all calls are recorded so we can certainly calculate the timing.'

'And why a stolen car?' added Joseph. 'If he was ending it all, why not use his own car? He wouldn't be needing it any more, would he?'

'He might have done that to make identifying him more difficult for us,' Nikki guessed. 'But we need forensics, that's for sure. And we need to know who that is in the driver's seat. This is a crime scene, folks.'

'I'll ring, shall I?' Joseph took out his phone again. 'Rory won't thank us, but needs must and all that.'

'Go for it.' Nikki suddenly felt very tired. Unless they were wrong, and all the firemen were right, the killer was playing with them. He was getting bolder and more organised. 'I'm guessing there was no puddle of vomit this time, John?'

John shook his head. 'None noted.'

Yes, he was toughening up. Another bad sign.

* * *

The sun wouldn't rise until around seven, so the forensic team had to work using portable lamps.

Rory Wilkinson was indeed less than impressed by the state of the new candidate for his mortuary, and he told them so at every available opportunity.

Nikki had asked uniform to cordon off a large area around the car. When daylight arrived, she wanted every inch combed for evidence left behind by whoever had set the fire. Naturally, the fire service had washed clean the area close to the vehicle when they hosed down the blaze, but it was still worth examining the area. Had the killer driven to meet his victim? If so there might be evidence of another vehicle. The ground was damp from a shower of rain earlier that night, so any recent tracks would show. Had he really been so bold? Or would his nervous stomach have reacted once more?

Nikki stood quietly, thinking the whole thing through. The fire chief had made it quite clear that he believed she was wasting resources. He was certain that the dead man was the arsonist, and she had to admit he put up a convincing argument. Now she was not quite so certain that John was right, but deep down she trusted him. She knew the value of a man who'd worked with fire his entire lifetime. *Think, Nikki Galena. Facts are what you need, and facts alone.*

She walked back towards where Joseph stood talking with a couple of uniformed PCs. 'There's little more we can do here. Let's go home, grab a shower and some breakfast, and wait for the evidence to filter in.'

Joseph nodded. 'We may get a call about a missing person to follow up on. Rory has just told me that the driver was wearing a ring, an old one from the look of it. He said he'd know more after he'd had one of his lab technicians examine it.'

'Good, so we have a starting point. Not much, but it's something.' She yawned. 'Let's get out of here. I need to get into a nice hot shower and get rid of the smell of burning.'

'Me too. It's getting like Groundhog Day, washing the smell of smoke from your hair.'

Nikki wondered if the killer felt the same, if he was still alive and hadn't fried in that burnt-out car.

* * *

After breakfast, Eve and Wendy got out all the old plans and maps for the land where Monks Lantern sat.

'So, we have a graveyard, or a defunct graveyard, just beyond the far wall. Jenny told me she owned that piece of land, but it's so overgrown that she wasn't sure what to do with it.' Eve peered closer at the land registry documents. 'I'm pretty sure she didn't know it was a graveyard.'

'She would have loved that idea!' Wendy laughed. 'Anything quirky.'

'We need to look up the rules and regulations regarding disused graves. I'm pretty sure that there'll be things we can do, but they'll need official approval.' Eve poured more coffee. Already she knew she'd done the right thing by asking Wendy to come and live with her. The odd feeling of nervousness had dissipated almost overnight. They would have some good times in the old chapel.

'The main thing is, what should we use that area for?' ruminated Wendy, brushing her dark hair away from her face.

'I have no idea.' Eve smiled at her friend, noticing that she too looked much more relaxed than when she arrived. She was a tall woman, with athletic good looks. Even in her gardening clothes, up to her neck in nettles, Wendy Avery managed to look elegant. 'What *do* you do with a spare graveyard?'

'How about a tranquil garden? It already has some lovely trees. We could add a water feature, do some sensitive planting, and make it into a natural, peaceful place.'

'Nice idea. It would be appropriate too.' Eve liked the thought a lot. 'By the look of the plans, there's a pathway leading away from it down the side of the property to the road. 'What say we allow the local village people to use it too, when it's all finished?'

'As long as they respect it, I think that's a lovely idea. I can already see the over-sixties club using it for their Tai Chi class.'

'And the art group! How lovely to be able to do plant and tree studies outside in the fresh air.' Eve beamed. 'As soon as we get the fern garden finished, we'll make some enquiries about how to proceed.'

'Smashing! Can't wait.' Wendy smiled at Eve. 'I do appreciate this, Eve, really I do. My moving here, I mean. I was starting to think that I only had the downhill slope to look forward to, and after what happened to Anne and Jenny, well . . .'

'Me too, Wendy. And believe me, having you here is a godsend. I was starting to think some very dark thoughts.'

'Dreams featuring Zimmer frames?'

'And stairlifts!' Eve shivered. 'Now we have a reason to be cheerful!'

'So what do we do? We decide to revamp a graveyard! Now that's a *really* cheerful thought!' Wendy grinned at her.

'It's not *what* we're doing, is it? We've both led active lives, on the go twenty-four seven, sometimes living close to the edge. Retirement and a life of leisure doesn't suit people like us. Do you know, I'd even given up my pastel painting, and I loved that. If it hadn't been for the fact that I promised Jenny to finish her fern garden, and then got caught up with finding out about plants and things, I might have been on the slippery slope to resignation and apathy.'

'I know what you're saying. Now we have a new project, we'll get our mojo back in no time.' Wendy gathered up the breakfast dishes. 'Come to think of it, my friend's son is in the church. Maybe he knows the rights and wrongs of dealing with disused resting places. I need to ring her and let her know I'm on the move. so I'll ask her to have a word with him.'

'Excellent. And in the meantime?'

'Back to Jenny's ferns, I guess.'

* * *

John Carson stared at the burnt-out vehicle. Most people would see a bewildering mess, but to him it was a puzzle to be solved logically. Earlier in his career as an investigator, he'd taken a great interest in vehicle fire investigation, and he knew that there were hundreds of different factors to take into consideration. He started by studying the heat patterns.

He checked the melted rubber and plastic, and the oxidising metal. It was clear to John that this fire hadn't been started by accident. In the front of the vehicle he found localised burn patterns, and distinct marks where an accelerant had been deliberately poured and splashed. If someone sitting in the driving seat had leant over towards the passenger well to fill a glass bottle, and accidentally dropped it, the petrol wouldn't have collected in puddles or sprayed the driver. And naturally, the moment something went wrong he would have leapt from the car. John knew he hadn't been wearing a safety belt. He certainly wouldn't have sat there waiting for the fire to consume him.

The driver's corpse had been removed and taken to the mortuary. A little later, the car itself would be taken to a specialist car pound for further inspection. But John was certain he'd got it right. The driver had been drugged or knocked unconscious, and then placed inside the car, which was set alight. But not before a 999 call had been made.

John stood back and surveyed the scene for one last time. The timing had been perfect. In another few minutes, all trace of the fire-setter's kit in the boot would have been gone. As it was, it was easily identifiable. And the fire and rescue guys were convinced that it was the arsonist who had perished. Exactly as the killer intended.

CHAPTER THIRTEEN

At four p.m., Nikki took a call from a distraught young woman, worried sick about her husband, Harry. The previous night, he had gone for a lads' night out and hadn't returned home. She had rung his friends and his family and the local hospitals, but no one had seen him since he left a public house in Greenborough town centre.

Normally the disappearance of a healthy young male with no mental health problems would have been of no interest to CID, but right now, Nikki was very interested indeed. It was the first lead they had.

'Joseph! Get a car, would you? We have a call to make.'

* * *

Elaine and Harry Moore lived in a two-bedroomed terraced house in a quiet cul-de-sac on the outskirts of Greenborough. Inside, Nikki and Joseph found a neat, well-kept home with little sayings stencilled on the walls.

Nikki stared at one of these, *Learn from yesterday, Live for today, and Hope for tomorrow*, and her throat dried up. Although she wanted to know who had died in that car, she prayed it wasn't Harry Moore. The whole house shone with love and happiness, and she didn't want to be the one to bring it crashing down.

'He never does anything without ringing me, never!' Elaine sniffed. 'I know something terrible has happened to him. It would take something really awful to stop him getting in touch.'

Her sister, Denise, was with her and she clasped her sister's hand. 'He's a treasure, Inspector. He adores Elaine, and he'd never leave her to worry about him like this.'

'You say he was out with friends?' asked Joseph.

'It was a bit of a celebration.' Elaine blew her nose. 'His best friend, Lance, has been accepted into the air force, so they were having a get-together in the Britannia.'

'And his friends saw him leave?'

'At ten, Inspector. He never stays out too late when I'm on my own.' She swallowed noisily. 'And that's the last they saw of him.'

'We'll be trying to trace his movements on CCTV, Elaine, but at the moment we have nothing to offer you.' Nikki tried to sound calm, but she was desperate to flee that love-filled room. The cushions with hearts on them, the smiling photographs, the single red rose in a bud vase, were just too perfect, but all Nikki saw was a blackened corpse in a torched car.

'We always thought the police took no notice of missing persons,' said Denise, 'but you've been really kind.'

Was this the time to tell them Harry might be dead? Nikki glanced at Joseph. He gave her an almost imperceptible nod.

She took a breath. 'I don't want to scare you unnecessarily, Elaine, but a man was killed last night, so we are taking every report of a missing person very seriously.'

The two women gasped.

'Harry? My Harry? Oh no!'

'Please, Mrs Moore, we are by no means sure that it is your husband, but we really need to know something about him, if you think you're up to helping us.' Joseph spoke softly.

Denise got up and went to the fireplace. She removed a photograph from the mantelpiece and handed it to Nikki, 'Harry. Is this the dead man?'

I wish I knew, thought Nikki. 'Could we borrow this? We'll return it to you, of course.'

'But is it him?' Denise demanded.

'He was very badly injured, I'm afraid,' Joseph said. 'But as it's an ongoing investigation, we really can't say at present. I'm very sorry, but our hands are tied. I've already said more than I should, but we understand your concerns about Harry.' He gave them a smile full of compassion. 'Can I ask you some questions about him? I'll be as brief as possible, I promise.'

Both women nodded mutely. Nikki was very glad to have Joseph beside her. He managed situations like this very well.

'Does Harry have any distinguishing marks?' asked Joseph. 'Tattoos, maybe?'

They'd be of no help at all in identifying their body, but Nikki realised that Joseph was just working his way to other features that might help.

'No, he never liked tattoos,' Elaine said softly. 'And he has no birthmarks or anything like that.'

Nikki noticed Denise watching them suspiciously. She got the feeling she'd picked up on just how "badly injured" their dead man was.

'One of his front teeth is a crown,' said Denise, not taking her eyes off Nikki. 'If that helps?'

Nikki nodded silently. Yes, Denise understood all right. Maybe she was thinking of an accident on the railway line, or a horrific car crash.

'And one of his big toes has a metal pin through it,' she added pointedly.

'Thank you,' Nikki said. That was exactly what they wanted. Now she needed to get hold of Rory, fast. She stood up, still holding the photograph. 'Mrs Moore, we'll be in touch the moment we know anything definite, I promise.' She turned to the sister. 'Can you stay here with Elaine?'

Denise nodded. 'Of course. But you won't keep us waiting any longer than you have to, will you? You can see the state of her.'

Joseph touched her arm. 'You have our word. The minute we know. Okay?'

Outside in the car, Nikki phoned Rory, but he wasn't answering. She left a message and hung up. 'Damn! Oh well, we'd better get back to base and hope he contacts us soon.'

* * *

This time it had been a very different experience. He couldn't work out why.

It had been the simplest of fires to set, but the most difficult to get right because of the problem of timing. As it was, he had pulled it off perfectly. He just wondered if the police would pick up on his subtle "hint" as to who the driver might be. Not that it really mattered, but it might buy him a little breathing space.

He had originally planned to conduct his campaign over a much longer period, maybe even a month. But after the first fire, he knew that if he were to ever complete what he had to do, he would need to work as fast as possible and get it over with. He couldn't fail her, he just couldn't. It was unthinkable.

He should get himself some supper, he supposed, but since the work had begun, he'd lost his appetite for cooked food. He couldn't even face toast. Now he was living on sandwiches, cereal, salad and fruit.

The previous day he had passed a fast food outlet in the shopping centre. The smell of barbequed ribs had turned his stomach, and he'd been forced to run to the gents. He sat with his supper of cornflakes and began to consider the next stage. The actual setting of the fires had been textbook, and he'd found it exhilarating, exciting, but his reaction to what he was doing shocked and surprised him. He closed his eyes for a moment, and vowed that it wouldn't stop him from seeing it through to the bitter end.

* * *

Nikki waited at the station, refusing to leave until they knew the identity of the man in that burnt-out car. Rory had been called out on an emergency, but had texted her to say he would contact her as soon as he returned.

Joseph went to find some food, and they sat in her office and shared a KFC meal for two.

'Wish I'd known. I'd have joined you.' Cameron Walker strolled into the office and pinched a chip from Nikki's box.

'It wasn't planned,' Joseph said. 'We're waiting for a possible ID on the body.' He offered Cam a piece of chicken.

'I'll wait with you then. It's a bad business, and between you and me, upstairs are putting pressure on me to clear it up, pronto.' Nikki opened her mouth to speak and he held up his hand. 'But don't worry, I've told them to back off and let us do what we have to. Maybe it's because I'm the new kid in town, but I seem to have got away with it — so far.' He grinned.

'How are you finding it here, Cam?' asked Nikki.

'Bit of a culture shock to say the least. Last night I almost threw in the towel. I had some spotty kid who'd never seen the inside of a uniform lecturing me on the use of reasonable force. He kept talking about human rights. Can you believe it? After all the years I've done! I felt like using a bit of reasonable force on him.'

'It's a different world, my friend, and in my opinion the best time to be a police officer is long gone.' Nikki broke into a smile. 'But we just keep our heads down and carry on regardless.'

Cam laughed. 'It's the only way. And I'll cover your backs as best I can.'

At last, Nikki's phone rang.

Rory sounded harassed. 'Not one of my best days, dear heart. A particularly traumatic infant death, then I broke down on the way back. Still, something good comes out of every situation and the man from Green Flag was gorgeous!'

'I'm telling David!'

'Do! He'd agree with me, I know. But I imagine you need some information on your car driver.'

'Yes, Rory. We have two things that might help with identifying him. One is a metal pin in his big toe, and the other a crowned front tooth.'

The line fell silent, then Rory said, 'In that case, this is not your man. Definitely no pinned toes. Actually there was very little at all left of his feet, but the pin would have needed crematorium level heat to break it down, and there was nothing in the residue. Sorry, Nikki, back to the drawing board for you.'

'Does the body have any particular distinguishing features that might help us if we do get another lead?'

'Funnily enough, yes. I was just going to tell you. He'd suffered a fractured lower jaw in the not too distant past, and there was a small titanium plate still in situ. That should help considerably, I imagine.'

Nikki thanked him, relieved for Elaine Moore's sake, but disappointed too. 'Sorry, guys. It's not the man we thought it was.'

Joseph shrugged. 'Well, someone will be delighted by the news, although Harry Moore is still unaccounted for. Shall I ring her?'

'Please, Joseph. She might not know where he is, but at least she has hope now.'

While Joseph made the call, Cameron said, 'Have you any feelings about this man, Nikki? Anything about his MO speak to you?'

Nikki inhaled. 'To be honest, Cam, I'm really stumped. John Carson too, *and* Laura Archer. He's not your textbook arsonist at all. Laura's checking out case histories for us, and John is spending every waking hour at the scenes of the crimes, but this killer is definitely not following the Dummy's Guide to arson attacks.'

About to answer, Cam stopped, listening to Joseph talking animatedly with Elaine, or possibly her sister.

'Hold on! Slow down. Now say that again.'

Nikki stared at him, wondering what was coming next. She saw him scribbling notes while he listened. She mouthed, 'Loudspeaker!'

Joseph turned it on and they heard Denise's anxious voice. 'He was in hospital all the time. He'd been given something, some drug, and he couldn't even tell them his name, that's why he hadn't got in touch. But that's not the worry now, he's much better. It's his friend, it's Jez. He's still missing.'

'Okay,' said Joseph calmly. 'Who is Jez?'

'Jeremy Bedford. Everyone calls him Jez. He left the pub at the same time as Harry, but Harry can't remember what happened to them after that. Now we hear that Jez didn't get home either, and he wasn't admitted to hospital with Harry.'

Joseph took down Jez's address and contact details. 'Do you know him personally, Denise?'

'Not well, but I've met him several times.'

'Can you describe him for me?'

'Tall, about six foot two, well-built, dark curly hair,' she paused. 'He was mugged about six months ago, Sergeant. They broke his right wrist and his jaw.'

Joseph closed his eyes. 'Thank you, Denise. I'm really pleased that Harry's been found. Do give our best to Elaine.'

'But Jez?'

'We'll follow it up, I assure you, and you'll be kept informed.'

'Oh, I do so hope it's not him, Sergeant. He's such a gentle man. A lovely guy.'

Nikki felt a pang of sorrow. Sometimes they had some really gutty jobs to do. She picked up the phone and rang Rory.

'Missing me already? It must be almost fifteen minutes since we last spoke.'

Nikki didn't feel like laughing. 'We might have an ID, Rory. Has our man suffered a broken wrist in the past?'

'Not that we noticed, but the bones were very badly degraded. Let me take another look for you. Can you hold on?'

Nikki waited.

It was nearly ten minutes before he was back on the line. 'It's almost imperceptible through the charring, but the right wrist does show a probable fracture through the scaphoid, and possibly an avulsion fracture around the head of the humerus. Tomorrow I'll get some in-depth work done on it and confirm. Meanwhile, I need sustenance and a relaxing, bubbly bath! I'm exhausted, darling! Au revoir!'

Nikki hung up. 'I think we have another unpleasant job to do before we get home tonight, Joseph.'

He looked at the address. 'Another local. 1 Rain Bridge Lane, out near the recreation park. Single man — oh hell, he still lives with his parents. This is going to be a really tough one.'

Cam stood up. 'I'll get a liaison officer to meet you there. You can't leave them alone with news like this.'

'Thank you, Cam, we appreciate it.' Nikki looked at Joseph. 'And we need to get hold of the others who were at this "lads' night out." How many blokes do you know who'd walk out on an evening's piss-up with their best mates and go home early?'

'Good point. Someone or something lured them out. I'll put a note on Cat's desk. First thing tomorrow morning she can get a list of names and addresses from Elaine Moore and chase them up.' He sighed. 'I guess we can't put this off any longer, can we?'

Without a word, Nikki stood up and pulled on her jacket.

CHAPTER FOURTEEN

One Rain Bridge Lane was the only house with lights burning in all the windows. It was a semi-detached house in a pleasant road where people looked after their gardens and, with one or two exceptions, kept their homes in good order.

A man answered the door almost at once. When he saw their warrant cards, his face fell.

'You've found him, haven't you?' His voice was gravelly and his words clipped. Nikki guessed he already knew his son was dead.

'Can we come in, sir?' She kept her voice neutral.

In silence he held the door back, and led the way through the hall to where his wife waited in a brightly decorated kitchen.

Nikki noted the plants filling the windowsill. The fridge door was covered in little magnets from holiday places and days out. It was a cheerful room, and they obviously spent a lot of their time in it.

'This is Marion, my wife.' A small woman with a round face sat at the table, looking up at them hopefully.

'Have you got some news?' Her hands were clasped around a mug that declared her to be "The Best Mum in the World."

Nikki took a deep breath. 'Mr and Mrs Bedford, there was a serious incident last night. Now, although we have no firm confirmation as yet that Jeremy was involved, we have to prepare you . . .'

'Jez?' Marion's eyes filled with tears. 'Prepare us?'

'A man died, Mrs Bedford,' Joseph said softly. 'We believe that it might be Jeremy.'

'*Might* be?' Her husband glared at them.

'There was no identification with him—' Joseph began, but Mr Bedford cut him short.

'I'll come with you. Now! I need to know if it's our son! I'll identify him.' Mr Bedford moved to stand behind his wife. His hands gripped her shoulders tightly. 'We *have* to know.'

'Please, sit down, sir. This isn't straightforward.' Nikki looked at them sadly. She knew what they were suffering. She had been there too, when she was told that her own daughter, Hannah, was about to die.

Joseph seemed to know what she was thinking and tactfully took over.

'We believe the man was deliberately killed. It's a serious murder investigation, so we must be careful what we say. As DI Galena said, we can't be sure it's Jeremy, so until we know more, we can only ask for your patience, and give you all the help and support we can.'

'Murder? There's not a soul on this earth would want to murder Jeremy!' Edward said.

'Eddie's right, Officers.' Marion seemed to take heart from this. 'It can't be our Jez. He's our gentle giant. No one would hurt him.'

'Please, will you help us?' Nikki asked. 'Tell us all about him. You say no one would hurt him, but he was mugged a while back, wasn't he?'

'Oh, but that was just terrible bad luck. Wrong place, wrong time. A drug addict tried to steal his wallet and his phone. Jez tried to calm him, but the addict was off his head on something, and really hurt our boy.' Edward flopped into a chair next to his wife. 'He wouldn't hurt a fly, so why would anyone want to kill him? No, it has to be a mistake.'

'I know this is a long shot, but would you still have any of the hospital paperwork from when Jeremy was attacked? A report about follow-up treatment, anything like that?'

Marion Bedford started to rise, but her husband touched her shoulder. 'I'll get it. We always keep our family medical stuff in the sideboard.'

He returned a few minutes later and handed Nikki a sheaf of papers. 'That's everything from the orthopaedic and the dental maxillofacial clinic.'

Nikki glanced down the reports and saw the words *scaphoid* and *avulsion fracture*.

Exactly what Rory had said. It seemed there was little doubt.

The doorbell's tinny melody sounded loud in the small kitchen.

'We've organised some support for you both, sir,' said Joseph, moving towards the door. 'That should be one of our family liaison officers. She'll help you until we have a definitive answer.'

Nikki was pleased to see Sergeant Lucy Wells come through the door. She was a sensitive woman, with many years' experience in dealing with these situations.

'I've been briefed,' she said softly to Nikki. 'Leave it with me.'

'We'll update you the moment we know anything ourselves.' Nikki turned back to the Bedfords, introduced Lucy, and apologised for having to leave so quickly. 'Be assured, we'll do everything we can to get you an answer as soon as we possibly can.'

Outside, she slipped her arm through Joseph's. 'That poor couple.'

'You okay?'

She nodded, but kept her hold on him. 'Just brings back painful memories. You think they'll fade with time, but they don't. Still, thankfully, you do get over them quicker as time passes.'

He slipped his arm around her waist and they walked slowly down Rain Bridge Lane and back to the car.

* * *

It was around midnight when they finally got home, and even then, neither of them could relax.

Nikki felt cold right through to her bones. The autumn nights were chilly now, but she felt as if the cold came from within.

They sat at the old pine kitchen table and sipped hot milky drinks.

Joseph stared into his drink. 'Three local people. All similar ages, all described as quiet, inoffensive, kind, creative, harmless . . . It doesn't make sense, does it?'

Nikki leaned forward, her elbows on the table. 'No, it doesn't. If they were hardened criminals, or were known to support some evil, radical group who'd done something terrible, then I could see that this might be a revenge spree, but not these people.'

'A man who loved the land and lived frugally, a sensitive and otherworldly artist, and a gentle giant who spends his spare time coaching disabled kids in different sports.' He shrugged. 'Why on earth choose them?'

'I still believe, even though there isn't a shred of proof to support it, that they're somehow connected. They have to be.' She looked up. 'What was that about disabled kids?'

'Photos in Mum and Dad Bedford's hall, and certificates too. Jeremy was certainly no hardened criminal.'

'Nor were the others, unless they were the cleverest bunch of con artists ever.'

'I wonder if Curate Leon knew Jeremy? So far he's the only vague connection we have. It's possible, I suppose,' Joseph said.

'We'll ask tomorrow.' Nikki yawned. 'And then it's back to the hunt for the missing bloody link.'

Joseph stood up. 'We'll find it. If there is one at all.'

'But how many more nice quiet people are going to be cremated while we look?' Nikki said. 'We *have* to find the reason why he's doing this. But we're not going to get any further tonight, are we? We need some sleep. We've been on the go since three this morning, that's twenty-one hours. We'll be no good to man or beast unless we recharge.'

* * *

Laura Archer was also awake, sitting up in bed, papers and printouts scattered across the duvet. She had traced back as many case studies as she could find, then emailed her old mentor, Sam Page, and picked his brains. The religious connection kept coming up, and she was beginning to feel that the killer was driven to use fire for a very special reason. He was not an arsonist by choice. It was as if fire was the only way to accomplish his aim — whatever that was.

Laura again read through a case study involving a disturbed young man from a severely dysfunctional family, who had killed ten people in a fire in a residential care home. He had been adamant that they had to be "presented to the living flame, in order to be released." Somehow he believed that he was freeing them from the intolerable suffering of being incarcerated in a home. He couldn't see that they were living mostly happy, socially integrated lives, well looked after and comfortable. According to this young man, "Fire is the only true purifier of the soul, and through fire you will attain enlightenment."

She closed the paper and opened another. This one featured a disturbed youth who wreaked a biblical vengeance on all the people who had bullied him throughout his childhood. He posted a message through their doors, a quotation from Jeremiah. It read: *My wrath will go forth like fire, and burn with none to quench it, because of your evil deeds. Jeremiah 4:4.* No one took the threat seriously, and nine people perished. He set fire to their homes while they were inside.

It occurred to her that their killer was driven by a similar compulsion. He had a deep-seated grievance against each of the dead victims, and the only way for them to atone was to die by fire.

Laura gathered up the papers and put out the light. In her head was the single question: *Why?*

* * *

Cameron Walker, his arm draped across his sleeping wife's shoulders, also lay awake, trying to make sense of his new job.

He had called it culture shock, but it was much more than that. It was a whole different world, and he wasn't sure he wanted to live there. Cam was old school. He'd spent his early years in the force happy to be a "proper copper," and he wanted things to stay that way. They couldn't, of course, but it didn't make him feel any better. He was uneasy about the way things were going — stations closing, fewer officers on the streets, more civilians than police officers, and university graduates fast-tracking directly into the higher ranks.

On the positive side, he had inherited a station with, on the whole, good, honest officers, men and women who felt the way he did — DI Nikki Galena for one. As long as he had her on his side, he would cope.

He eased himself down, trying not to wake Kaye. He hadn't sought this job, but he hated to give up on anything. And there was something rather exhilarating about his new post. He felt a little like a fielder in a cricket match, a go-between, a middleman, re-assembling the information that came down to him from the gold-braided planners until it made sense, and passing it on to the foot soldiers, who would put it into effect.

He put his head down and closed his eyes. His first task was to do everything he could to assist Nikki in her arson case. So far he had held the media at bay, but very soon the sensationalist press would get hold of the story, and they could have mass panic on their hands. He needed to keep a lid on it for as long as possible.

His first week at Greenborough. A baptism of fire!

* * *

Tom Black unlocked the side door to the Black House. Tonight they were holding an extraordinary meeting of the more influential members of their group. Silently, one by one, they slipped into the house and made their way to the Temple.

When Tom had counted eleven nocturnal visitors, he called Giles, and the two of them joined their guests.

The room they called the Temple was Gothic in appearance. This was pure chance. The original architect of the Black House had designed it that way, and it suited them perfectly.

Heavy oak panelling adorned the lower half of the walls. A massive ornate fireplace, where tonight a roaring log fire blazed, took pride of place in the centre of a long wall, lined from floor to ceiling with bookshelves. The other three walls were decorated with large, beautifully painted symbols, each reflected in similar carvings in the floor.

The room was clear of furniture, save for a ring of thirteen high-back chairs. Each chair sat at the point of a strange geometric star, etched into the wooden floor. At the centre of the star was a circle containing the three symbols — an eye, a flaming torch, and the alchemical symbol for sulphur, a kind of cross of Lorraine, a two-barred cross resting on the infinity sign.

When they were all seated, Giles spoke first. 'Brothers and sisters, thank you for coming here tonight at such short notice. I'm sure you are all aware that our scuffle with some of the more unsavoury Greenborough youths has come to the attention of the local police. Since then we have had two visits from an officer called PC Collins, and my brother Tom and myself are of the opinion that she is showing a somewhat unhealthy interest in our gatherings.'

There was a low murmur from the seated group.

Giles held up a hand. 'She's a very pleasant woman, not in any way aggressive or rude, but the fact is, we would rather that she had no call to return.'

'Hear, hear,' said a well-dressed man with iron-grey hair and bushy eyebrows.

'One thing that she did suggest, and we agree, is that we should alter the days and times of our meetings so as to avoid attracting the attention of the youths. We've been keeping to a strict calendar until now, so we need your input as to how we should proceed.'

An elegant woman in her late fifties lifted her hand. 'I presume this doesn't refer to specific festival days like the vernal equinox and Walpurgis Night?'

'Oh no, they'll go ahead as always. It's only our monthly get-togethers that need to vary. Possibly with even an occasional change of venue.'

Tom smiled encouragingly at her. 'Basically, we are trying to keep the police happy and on side. If we are seen to be complying with their suggestions, it will be better for us in the long run.'

'What does your lady police officer think of us, Giles?' asked someone.

'I'm not absolutely sure' he said. 'She's obviously a shrewd, intelligent woman, but we made sure she saw and heard nothing that might give her cause for concern.'

'If you would kindly get your business diaries out, perhaps we could get to work planning a new schedule for the coming months? And when the formalities are over, we might enjoy ourselves for an hour or so before you have to leave. What do you think? We have some very good Pinot Noir and a small late supper laid out for you in the dining room.' Tom smiled around at them.

Giles raised an eyebrow. 'And to follow? Well, that's up to you.'

CHAPTER FIFTEEN

The next day, Rory phoned Nikki to tell her that having consulted the maxilla facial surgeon at Greenborough Hospital, it was confirmed that their latest victim was Jeremy Bedford.

Nikki had already instructed Dave to start formally interviewing the group of young men who'd been out celebrating that night. By eleven o'clock he'd managed to put together a timeline of Jeremy's last evening on earth. All that was left was to talk to Harry Moore. Although he had been discharged from hospital, he was apparently still confused about what had happened. Nikki decided that as Cat had already spent time with Elaine Moore, she should be the one to go and see if Harry remembered anything further.

'What have we got so far, Dave?' Nikki asked.

They all stared at the whiteboard with the photo of the latest victim now added to the rest.

Dave checked with his pocketbook. 'There were six lads. They met at the Britannia public house at around seven thirty and stayed there all evening. According to the others, Harry and Jez were on very good form, and were thoroughly enjoying themselves. Harry said that he needed to get away at around ten, but that was nothing unusual apparently. The others said he worried about his wife being on her own at night.' Dave ran his finger down the page. 'Just before Harry left, Jez received a text. It seemed to upset him, so they said, but he laughed it off. He told Harry he'd leave when he did and walk part of the way home with him. The others stayed until they were thrown out at closing time, which for the Britannia is eleven.'

'Did they say what sort of mood Jez was in when he left?' asked Ben.

'They were pretty rat-arsed by that time, but the general consensus was that something was bothering him, probably the text message.' He looked at Nikki. 'Now it all gets a bit fuzzy. I've been down to your friend Spooky in IT, and she's started a CCTV search right across town. With luck and a fair wind, we might discover how they came to be abducted, if that's what happened.'

'Which way did they head?' asked Joseph.

'They turned left outside the pub, and I've already got them on camera walking towards the high street. I picked them up outside the parish church, and then I lost them. That's the point where Spooky's taken over.'

Nikki was glad it was Spooky tracing Jez and Harry's footsteps. Born in Greenborough, there was little she didn't know about the town, and her IT skills were phenomenal. Nikki tried not to think about what Jez's parents were going through right now. It was just too close to home.

'Keep checking with Spooky, Dave. See what she finds and report back. Meanwhile, we'll have to hope that Harry manages to remember something.' She glanced at the clock. 'Cat should be back soon, so let's keep our fingers crossed.'

'It was a long shot, boss,' Dave said, 'but I asked the lads from the pub if they'd ever heard of either Ronnie Tyrrell or Clary Sargeant. The bloke who's going into the RAF actually knew both of them, though I can't think how that helps. He did a bit of seasonal labour for the Fairweather brothers to earn some cash while he was studying, and he worked with Ronnie for a while. His father has an art and craft gallery in Louth, so he recognised Clary's name from her paintings, and he knew she went by the name Clary Sage. I'm pretty sure that's all there is to it.'

'Sounds innocuous enough, I must say,' said Joseph. 'Greenborough's not exactly a big metropolis. People do know each other.'

Dave nodded. 'The lads are really cut up about their mates. What they just couldn't get their heads around was why anyone would want to hurt Jez Bedford. They reckoned he was the sweetest guy imaginable.'

'Odd word to use, from a group of blokes,' said Ben.

Dave sniffed. 'You say that, but they were sincere, I know it. Jez Bedford seems to have been one of life's good guys. Charity work, fun runs, helped out with disabled kids, spent Christmas dishing out Christmas dinners to the homeless, and he'd spent the last two years doing voluntary work with the Samaritans.'

Ben looked up. 'Do you think this could be our link? All our victims seem to have been do-gooders in some way or another, don't they?'

Nikki thought about it. 'Jez, for sure. Ronnie? Well, yes. As I recall, he was the peacemaker at Mud Town. He helped Justina, the Lithuanian girl, with her English, and he helped another homeless couple find a caravan to live in.'

'Clary? What did she do?' asked Dave.

'She gave away her paintings if someone said they liked them. She gave one to Leon, the curate at St Saviours.' Nikki flipped through her notes. 'And I've heard since that she often gave them to charity auctions. Once she made a whole series of landscapes for the Greenborough hospice, and wouldn't take a penny for them.'

'And don't forget the times she went to local art clubs, all gratis,' Joseph added. 'And her sister said she used to run a class in the psychiatric unit at the hospital, helping people with anger and anxiety problems. So she certainly fits the bill, doesn't she?'

'How on earth can that be a motive for murder? And such a terrible form of murder?' Dave looked bewildered.

'Maybe we should give it to Laura Archer to mull over. I think she's coming in after lunch with her case histories.' Nikki smiled to herself at how blithely she mentioned Laura now.

She glanced up at the wall clock 'I'm going to slip out for an hour, Joseph. Ring me if anything important turns up. I've got something I need to take over to Mum at Beech Lacey. For some reason, I feel I need to see her.'

Joseph nodded. 'Of course. And I know why you're going.'

She raised an eyebrow. 'Really?'

'To check she's not telling porkies. You want to see for yourself that she's no longer anxious and stressed-out.'

'No one likes a smartarse, Easter.'

He looked smug. 'But I'm right, aren't I?'

'As always! It's getting tedious!'

* * *

Nikki parked outside Monks Lantern. There were two other cars there but no sign of Eve, or anyone else for that matter. Having rung the bell and got no reply, she walked around to the fern garden. That was also deserted, but she could hear voices, although she wasn't certain where they were coming from.

'Nikki! Over here!' Her mother's head popped up from the far side of a wall at the bottom of the garden. 'We're in the graveyard!'

'Graveyard? What graveyard?' Nikki was nonplussed. She peered over the wall and saw Wendy waving to her.

'Come and see this, Nikki!'

She pushed her way through an overgrown gateway set in the old stone wall and into a secluded wooded area with a scattering of ancient moss-covered memorials and headstones.

She looked around in surprise. 'Oh, I say! Did you know this was part of your land, Mum?'

'Jenny had said some of the uncultivated land beyond the fence was hers. But it was Wendy and her old maps and land registry documents that proved it was actually a grave-yard belonging to Monks Lantern. It's wonderful, isn't it?'

'I'm not sure,' Nikki replied. 'What the hell are you going to do with it?'

'We're just finding out. Wendy's friend's son knows about this sort of thing. He's going to explain the various options we have, and what's involved.'

Nikki suddenly thought back to a really bad case a few years before. It had involved the old churchyard at St Augustine's which was being cleared and the bodies re-interred elsewhere. She hoped her mother knew what she was setting in motion. 'You should have asked me, Mum. Unfortunately, I'm rather well-acquainted with Section 2 of the Disused Burial Grounds (Amendment) Act of 1981.'

'Oh.' Eve opened her mouth. 'What an idiot I am! Of course you'd know about it.'

'Still, I'd be interested to hear what options there are.'

'Then come and meet Judy and her son.' She hurried off towards the others, with Nikki trotting happily in her wake. She no longer had to worry about her mother's state of mind. Eve was clearly back in command and fully functional again.

She picked her way through the overgrown copse, care-ful not to trip on the brambles. 'Leon! What are you doi—? Oh, of course.'

'DI Galena? Is something wrong?' Leon looked slightly apprehensive.

'Eve is my mother. But do go on.'

'I need to do some research before we even look at the options, ladies. We'll have to find out when it was created and when the last body was interred here. Then I need to know how long the Burial Rights for this plot last.' Leon had a gleam in his eye. He looked around. 'It's a good-sized plot, although not over-populated, and it's very peaceful, isn't it?'

His mother Judy agreed. 'I find something rather com-forting in the way the trees and the plants grow around the old gravestones. Sort of new life springing from where the dead are resting.'

'Been at the sherry again, mother?' Leon grinned at her. 'You don't often wax lyrical about cemeteries.'

'I just happen to think that this is a rather lovely spot, that's all. And don't take the mickey out of your mother, boy! You're not too old or too pious for a clip round the ear.'

'Said in the presence of a police officer too.' Leon winked at Nikki.

'I've been involved with this kind of thing before,' she said. 'If this village comes under the same regs as St Augustine's, you have to wait seventy-five years from the date when the last grave was dug. They needed an order for a Faculty to proceed.'

Leon nodded. 'I would think that's correct, but I've heard of other very different regulations too. I'll do my homework thoroughly, never fear.' He gazed around. 'If it were my responsibility, I think I'd tidy this place up, do some real work on the paths, get the trees and shrubs pruned and maybe do some spring planting — lots of bulbs, daffodils, and crocuses — and keep it as it is.' He looked at Nikki. 'You see, when someone is buried in consecrated ground, I believe that it should be their final resting place, and we should respect that.'

Nikki privately agreed with the curate, but she wasn't sure exactly what Eve and Wendy had in mind when they said it could benefit the community. She looked at her watch. Time to get back. 'Leon, while I have you here, do you know a man called Jeremy, or Jez, Bedford?'

'Of course I do. He's a champion of several of the church charitable causes. Great guy, Jez. Why?'

Nikki drew in a long breath. It was enough for Leon.

'Oh no! Not Jez? Surely not Jez? What is happening here?'

Nikki shook her head. 'We wish we knew, Leon, but we have no idea.'

'How did he die? The same way as the others?'

She hesitated. 'He was found in a stolen car.'

'Set on fire?'

'I'm afraid so.'

His hand went to his crucifix. He murmured a few words. 'I should go and see his parents.'

'I'm sure they'd appreciate that.'

Nikki turned to her mother and told her she had to get back. Before she went, she handed Eve a large envelope. 'I found these in among Dad's old things. There are some photographs and old postcards here that I think you'll appreciate.'

Her mother looked at her quizzically, then accepted them with a smile. 'Thank you, darling. I'll look at them when I go back inside. Take care.'

She kissed Nikki on the cheek.

Nikki climbed back into her car, deep in thought. 'Leon Martin. Three deaths, and only one person who had a connection to them all.'

* * *

Although she was almost forty, Spooky looked like a teenage boy. She kept her dark hair short and tousled, and invariably dressed in rugby shirts, Converse boots and blue jeans. But despite her appearance, she headed up one of the best specialised IT units in the county. They were a civilian firm, but worked for the entire Fenland Constabulary as well as any other force that needed their expertise. Fortunately for Nikki and her team, their unit happened to be based at the Greenborough nick.

CCTV was not Spooky's usual thing. The nick had plenty of civilians or rookie coppers who could easily go through the footage, but Dave had told her how serious this particular investigation was, so she'd taken on the work herself. Besides, she was eager to help out her old friend Nikki in any way she could. Nikki had taken her under her wing when Spooky was a probationer police officer. Then, realising that her real talent lay in technology, she had switched careers midway through her training. Now she was back in the police station, but doing what she loved.

Spooky stared at one of the two screens in front of her. It showed a street view map of Greenborough town, through

360 degrees. Using the directional arrows, she was following the path the two young men had taken after they left the pub. Dave had traced them to the parish church, and she had located four more sightings after that. Now she was trying to predict their route, checking out all available CCTV cameras as she went.

She knew Nikki's team were looking for a meeting with another man, someone who went on to kill one of the lads she was "following."

'Ah. Gotcha again, guys!' She printed off stills from the footage as Harry and Jez made their way down a side road that led to the river. She narrowed her eyes and, knowing where the road went, pulled it up on the map. 'So you have two choices at the T-junction. Left to the river and the main road, and right to West Street and a couple of open air car parks.' She frowned. 'Car parks, I'll bet.'

The two young men went out of the picture, turning right.

Spooky rubbed her eyes. They were meeting someone, she knew it. Their step was deliberate and hurried. No messing around, no kicking cans along the gutter or fooling about, as lads do after a session in the boozer. They had a purpose in mind, and what better place to meet someone than a car park? Dave had mentioned that the dead boy had received a text prior to leaving, and Spooky was pretty sure that the sender of that text was waiting in the West Street Car Park.

Spooky logged into the direct link to the council's Public Space Surveillance CCTV network, and found the car park. 'Shit!' She went from camera to camera, and met with a blank screen each time. In the whole L-shaped area, only two were operational.

She went back to the map and scanned the road they must have walked down. There was one more camera, located close to the entrance to the car park. Spooky held her breath. 'Please. Please . . . yes!' There they were.

The two friends entered the car park and looked around. Across the top of the screen, the seconds ticked by, logged by the camera.

Spooky waited, willing the men not to move out of camera range, and then she saw a car draw up. 'Bingo!' The printer clattered as she printed frame after frame and watched a door open, and the two men climb inside. Then the car drove off, out of the picture.

It was the last image of young Jez Bedford.

Spooky scribbled a note of the make of the car, and picked up the printouts. They had climbed in willingly, so they had to know or trust the driver. 'Big mistake,' she whispered to herself. 'Fatal mistake.'

* * *

Cat met Spooky at the entrance to the CID room, and they went to find Nikki together. 'I hate these baby steps,' muttered Cat. 'This man is so dangerous we need to be making major headway, not picking up a tiny crumb of info here and another there.'

'I suppose we should be grateful they're at least steps in the right direction,' Spooky said.

Cat knocked on Nikki's door and they went in. Cat gestured for Spooky to go first.

'The two men *were* meeting someone.' She placed the sheaf of printouts on Nikki's desk. 'I've identified the car as a Vauxhall Astra.'

Nikki stared at the pictures and exhaled. 'Thank you, Spooky. Forensics have just confirmed that the burnt-out car was an Astra, so the picture is building up.' She looked at Cat. 'Anything from Harry Moore?'

'Sadly, no, although I do know a little more about what happened. The hospital confirmed that he'd been given a drug, similar to the ones they use for oral surgery or minor ops to make you relax and forget the procedure.'

'Like Midazolam or Rohypnol?' asked Nikki.

'Exactly. But he does recall what happened before he was slipped the Mickey Finn. First he told me that Jez asked him to go with him because he thought the man who sent him the text knew something important about someone he once knew, a girl who died.'

'Did he say who the girl was?'

'No. According to Harry, he seemed to be very agitated. He was anxious to meet with the man, but was also suspicious of his motives, hence the need for Harry to go with him.'

'I'm assuming Jeremy's phone was incinerated in the car fire?' asked Spooky.

'Affirmative.' Cat said glumly.

'Shame.'

'Okay, Cat, what happened after they got into the car?' asked Nikki.

'Harry said the man drove them to a small deserted parking area just outside town, and parked up. Jez asked him who he was, and he said he was a journalist who'd stumbled upon a story that might be of interest to Jez. Then he took three bottles of beer from a bag on the passenger seat and passed two of them to Harry. They were pretty well oiled to start with, so neither turned down another drink. Harry remembers being pulled out of the car and hitting the road hard, and then nothing until he woke up in hospital the following day. Even then, he was away with the fairies for hours. Apparently he didn't even know who he was.'

'He was lucky. He could have been cremated along with his friend.' Nikki frowned. 'Actually, that's a point, isn't it? Why not kill them both? Why throw Harry out of the vehicle?'

'Because Jez was his target?' Cat chanced. 'And only Jez.'

'That's what it looks like, doesn't it? He's not just killing people, he's targeting very particular ones.'

'And lucky old Harry wasn't on his list.' Cat paused. 'Maybe Jez's parents would know about this dead girl — the one the alleged journalist had info about? Shall I go and ask them?'

'I don't want to overwhelm them with questions today. They're in a terrible state, as you can imagine. Leave it till tomorrow, but meantime, see if anyone else close to him knows who this girl might be, okay?'

'Sure, boss.' Cat brightened. 'If it wasn't just a lure to get Jez to meet him, this could be the lead we were looking for. The dead girl could be the link, couldn't she? To the other victims?'

'Chase it up, Cat.' Nikki paused. 'Ask the curate, Leon Martin, if Jez ever mentioned a friend who died young. Leon seems to know things about everyone.'

'Well, he *is* a vicar. People talk to them. It's what they do. They listen to people's problems.'

'True, I suppose.'

The boss didn't seem totally convinced. She went on. 'Oh, I did press Harry for a description of the driver of the Vauxhall, but he said they'd had a bit of a skinful by that time. He said he thinks the interior light in the vehicle wasn't on, and the driver's face was obscured by the head rest on his seat.'

'Did he guess at an age?' asked Nikki.

'He guessed he was around the same age as them — late twenties, early thirties. And he had brown hair and dark clothing. Harry really did believe that the man was a journalist, and he thought Jez did too. He said the guy was very convincing, pleasant even. He thanked them for meeting him and said he'd explain everything when they got out of Greenborough.'

Spooky looked puzzled. 'How did he know to bring *three* beers? You'd have thought he'd have insisted that Jez meet him alone, wouldn't you? Harry could have been a major problem and really upset his plans.'

'I wondered that,' said Cat. 'I can only guess he's very well-organised. If he knew Jez was drinking with mates, perhaps he erred on the side of caution. I reckon if Jez had turned up with more than one friend, our killer would never have made contact that night, but as it was just Harry, he took a calculated risk.'

'And it worked.' Nikki sat back in her chair and looked at them. 'Thanks, you two. This all helps to build the bigger picture.'

Cat and Spooky stood up.

'Shout if there's any other way IT can help you,' said Spooky.

133

Nikki smiled. 'Don't worry, I will!'

Cat left the office and returned to her desk, convinced they were finally onto something. That girl. How did she die? Who was she? She'd been important enough to Jeremy Bedford to cause him to leave his drinking pals and rush off into the night to meet a complete stranger in a dark car park. Was that what had happened to Ronnie and Clary?

'That's a thoughtful look.' Ben stood beside her desk, smiling down at her.

'It is, isn't it? And for the first time since we got this case, I think we might be getting somewhere! Grab a seat and I'll explain . . .'

CHAPTER SIXTEEN

The more he thought about his last escapade, the more he realised how lucky he had been to pull it off. But was it luck or perfect planning? The next one should be simpler, more straightforward anyhow. But he mustn't get complacent. He couldn't afford to make mistakes, there was far too much at stake.

He checked his list of the materials he'd need, and made sure everything was in place. Then he went back indoors and checked the timings once more. This next hit should be very different to the others, in every way. It should be spectacular, as long as his weak stomach didn't let him down. At this thought, a tiny whisper of smoke seemed to permeate the air, and made him cough. It had to be this way, there was no other choice, but he hated it.

He went to the kitchen, had a long drink of water and swallowed some paracetamol. Ever since he began this operation he'd been suffering from violent headaches, and they seemed to be getting worse. He assumed it was the stress. Well, he would just have to grin and bear it until the work was done.

He opened the file for his next fire, and checked all the data he'd collected on the comings and goings of his intended victim. He knew it backwards by now, but he needed to make sure every single detail was imprinted in his brain. He unpacked the throwaway PAYG phone from Tesco's and inserted the unregistered sim card. There was a minimal amount of money on it, but it would be plenty for what he needed.

He stood up and paced the room, looking at his watch. Not long now.

* * *

Laura Archer gratefully accepted a coffee from Joseph, and proceeded to explain the case histories she had found.

'I think it's rather as we thought. As I looked further into the slightly stranger cases, I realised that sometimes there are people who don't *choose* to use fire. They *have* to.' She looked at Nikki. 'The definition of an arsonist is someone who intentionally starts a fire in order to damage or destroy something, especially a building, or occasionally take a life. Our guy fits that category except that he's not using the fire as a way of venting his anger, or because he has a desperate urge to set fire to things, or it just makes him feel good. I believe he has an agenda. His victims *have* to be consumed by fire.'

'Without knowing what the agenda is, we have no way of predicting his next move.' Joseph felt as if someone had superglued him to the starting block. He hated just waiting for the next fire.

'For me, it's a real failure. I can't profile someone who doesn't fit into any pattern.' Laura looked as frustrated as he felt. 'I can only reiterate what we already know, that he's becoming more and more organised and cool in his planning. It's just the act of condemning someone to the flames that sickens him.' She shrugged. 'Sorry. I really hoped that I'd be able to help.'

'You are helping, Laura,' said Nikki. 'And we've got another question for you. It's tenuous, but all of our victims are apparently altruistic people. We've heard them described as a charity worker; generous; helping others in whatever way they can; do-gooder; all-round good guy; kind; gentle; quiet; sweet natured, and all the rest. None of them seem to have any faults. Now what the hell do you make of that?'

Laura scratched her head. 'Not a lot, to be honest. Some people who've been damaged by abuse can resent kindness being shown to others, especially if they were let down by the people who were supposed to help them.' She paused. 'Yes, in the context of this particular case, I'd say this was about someone being badly let down.'

'The dead girl.' Nikki and Joseph spoke in unison.

'Dead girl?' Laura looked at them blankly.

Nikki pulled a face. 'Don't ask. That's all we know. Our killer lured Jeremy Bedford into his car by suggesting he knew something about a dead girl from his past.'

Laura sat up straight. 'Then you need to find out all about her. She could be the root cause of why this killer is condemning others to death by fire.'

Nikki nodded. 'The team are on it. I haven't seen them look so enthusiastic for weeks.'

* * *

By four thirty the enthusiasm had waned. Between them, Cat, Ben and Dave had spoken to everyone connected to the three victims. None of them knew anything about a girl who'd died young. From the victims' ages, they calculated that she must have been a teenager when she died, but they could find nothing. They were beginning to think that Harry, still recovering from the powerful drug, had imagined half the things he thought he recalled. In desperation, Cat spoke to him again, and he admitted to feeling very unsure and hazy about some of the things he'd said before. He was also starting to understand what a close call he'd had, and the shock of Jez's terrible death was starting to hit home. Maybe this girl had never existed.

* * *

John Carson had spent the greater part of the day searching through old notebooks and diaries for entries he'd made many years ago regarding one particular case.

It was evening by the time he finally found it.

It was the case of a very disturbed young man who'd declared that he had a calling, a directive from on high to avenge a wrong by means of incineration. He'd apparently stated that he had no choice in the matter, atonement *had* to be made by means of fire. He was physically ill every time he made his "sinners" pay.

John read it for the third time. Voices in his head that he believed to be God had instructed this particular young fire-setter to bring a group of people to justice. It was his task to carry out God's will by the use of cleansing fire. This killing spree had been planned to take place over a period of several weeks. However, the young avenging angel was so distressed by what he was doing that he speeded up the programme in order to get it over with as soon as possible. By the end, he was setting two fires, with two deaths, every night.

This was the only other case John could recall of a reluctant arsonist. Now, he believed they had another one.

John sat down on his sofa and picked up the phone. 'Cameron? I might be wrong here, but I have a very worrying suspicion that your man will strike again tonight. I believe he has changed his initial timetable, and wants this whole business over as soon as possible.'

He replaced the receiver, stood up and took his coat and car keys. He wanted to be out on the streets when the call came. And it *would* come.

* * *

Nikki listened to what Cameron had to say.

'There's not a damn thing we can do to pre-empt this! Hell, we need a break, Cam! We need something to follow up, some lead, but there's nothing. He's a spectre, a bloody angel of death, and only he knows when and where the next strike will be!'

Cam nodded. 'We've got more men and women out on the streets than we've ever had, but how can you watch a whole town, especially when you don't know who or what you're looking for?'

Nikki spread her hands. 'And who's to say he'll target the town again? It could be one of the Greenborough villages, and there are dozens of those. Is it time to go public? Ask for their help? No one wants their home or business destroyed, do they? Surely, with the residents and business people all keeping watch we stand a much better chance of catching the bastard?'

Cameron inhaled. 'I've asked, Nikki, but upstairs are worried about panic, and nuisance and hoax calls jamming the system when we need it open to deal with the real stuff. I'm stuck between a rock and a hard place.'

Nikki groaned. 'I suppose they're right. People will think every drunk on his way home is an arsonist, and there'll be ten calls that all turn out to be a fox trying to get into a chicken run. And that's without the hoaxers and nutters. They'd have a bloody field day!'

'Difficult as it is, we'll just have to be vigilant. The Fenland Constabulary's finest are going to be out there all night long. We have to hope that our man either gets spooked by the unusually heavy police presence, or gets flustered and makes a mistake.'

Nikki wasn't convinced, but there was nothing she could say. 'I'll go tell the team. Joseph and I will remain here, just in case John Carson's right. Maybe he'll be wrong for once, you never know.'

'I'm not going anywhere,' Cam said. 'I'm betting John's hunch is right.'

* * *

Michael Porter threw the greasy frying pan into the old butler sink with the rest of the unwashed pots and dishes. Maybe he'd get around to sorting it tonight, maybe not.

Pushing aside newspapers, biscuit wrappers and empty milk cartons, he cleared a space on the kitchen table big enough for his plate. He'd tidy up a bit after tea. 'And maybe not,' he murmured aloud. The room was a tip, but there was no one else to see it, so what did it matter?

He squeezed tomato ketchup over his bacon, sausage and egg. Vaguely, he wondered how long he could go on living like this before he had a heart attack or a stroke. Not that he really cared. At least, if he didn't die, he'd get fed in hospital, and his laundry done free of charge.

He looked around the massive, cold kitchen, and saw it as it had been when he was a kid. Clean and warm, smelling of real coffee, baking, and wholesome meaty dinners. The rambling old house had always been cluttered, but with things that mattered — a row of Wellies, dog beds, flower vases, fishing rods, cameras and books. Hundreds of books. Now it was cluttered with fast food boxes, beer cans and black sacks that he'd forgotten to put out for the bin men.

Michael was twenty-eight years old but felt sixty. His brother was working in the Middle East, his sister had married and gone to Canada and his parents had died within a month of each other, both from cancer. That left Michael. He had been the youngest, the tearaway. A lovable rogue, according to his mother. A right little tyke was his father's description. His siblings had tolerated him. Now they hated him. For letting the home go to rack and ruin and throwing their inheritance down the proverbial. *Well, tough! You've got lives. All I've got is this desolate ruin in the middle of a muddy fen. You've got people who love you. I've got no one. Even the dog ran away.*

He chewed his cheap sausage and wondered what was in it. Certainly not much meat. Michael picked up a slice of white bread that sat on a pile of junk mail next to his plate, placed the remainder of the sausage in it and folded it over. Maybe the bread and butter would improve the flavour.

It didn't. He shovelled the rest of the food into his mouth and finished the meal. Leaving the plate where it was, he stood up and checked his pockets for spare change. He fished out two pound coins and some assorted silver. Was there enough for a pint down the local? He counted it out, but stopped at just over two quid. He needed another sixty pence for a pint, and he wasn't going to find that, not until Friday.

When the phone rang, he scowled. If it was P-P-bloody-I again, he'd really give them what for!

'Yes?'

'Hello? Michael Porter?'

He didn't recognise the voice. 'Whatever you're selling,' he said, 'I don't want it! When I want something, *I* ring you, not the other way round. Got it?'

'I'm not selling anything, I promise you,' the caller said.

'Then why are you wasting my time?' He switched the phone to loudspeaker so he could hear more clearly.

'I want to talk to you, Michael. Please don't hang up.'

'Talk about what?' Michael felt suddenly uneasy.

'About Mischief Night, ten years ago.'

Michael's mouth went dry. He wanted to throw the phone as far as he could and smash it to pieces.

'I see you know what I'm talking about.'

'Who are you?' Michael managed to growl. 'Who the hell are you?'

'It doesn't matter. All you need to know is that it's time.'

'Time for what?'

'Time to pay.'

There was a long silence. Michael felt the first intimations of real fear. 'Go away. I don't know what you're talking about. You've got the wrong person.'

'Oh no, it's you alright, it's you I want. It's you who has to pay.'

'But . . .'

'It's too late now, Michael Porter. I just wanted to hear your voice before you die.'

'Who are you, for God's sake? And why are you threatening me?'

'Goodbye, Michael. And don't try to escape, because you can't. And before you breathe your last, give a thought to Mischief Night, won't you?'

The line went dead. Michael realised he was shaking.

Then he smelt the burning.

For a moment he froze, rooted to the spot in shock. In his head he still heard that voice. *Mischief Night*. And what was that smell?

He broke from his trance and rushed to the cooker. Had he left hot fat on the lighted hob?

No, of course he hadn't, but for some reason, his brain wasn't functioning properly. He looked around. There was no smoke. He tried to think. Who had that been on the phone? Some lunatic? But he knew about Mischief Night, didn't he? And he knew his name, and his telephone number.

Then he heard a rustling noise. It was coming from the hallway. He pushed open the door and ran into the big hall, but it was empty. The sound must have come from the lounge. He pushed open the door, and screamed.

The far end of the lounge, the window end, was engulfed in flames. The curtains were blazing, dripping what looked like liquid fire onto the carpet. The crackling was fast becoming a steady roar, and Michael ran from the room, slamming the door shut behind him.

He ran into the hall and grabbed the front door handle, but it was locked, and the key was gone. He stared at it. But he always left the key in the lock! Windows? No good. The tiny panes of old glass, in mullions, were nearly all rusted, jammed or screwed shut to stop the drafts.

Michael started to cry with sheer helplessness, then remembered the back door. He'd left it unlocked when he came home. That was his way out.

He flung open the kitchen door and gasped. The flames seemed to reach out towards him.

He hunched over and charged to the back door, threw himself against it, but it held fast. Someone had locked it, from outside.

In panic, he ran back to the hall and raced up the stairs. It might mean broken bones, but he'd jump from one of the tall sash windows on the landing. At least he wouldn't burn to death.

He tried three of the big windows before he realised that they'd all been nailed shut. They had been replaced a few years ago and were made of toughened glass, and he'd never break them.

At that moment he knew his caller had been deadly serious. It really was no use trying to escape.

Or maybe not? The loft hatch! He remembered the funny circular window up there that led to the roof. If he could get through that, there was a slim chance he could shimmy down the drainpipe to safety, like he had when he was a kid.

Michael went back to the upstairs landing and found the pole that released the loft hatch clasp. He pushed it in and turned it, but nothing happened. He tried again, and his heart sank. Whoever wanted him dead had done a very thorough job on the old house.

All around him the fire roared. Things were falling and crashing downstairs, and the staircase was now alight. In a blind panic he ran from the landing. There was only one place to go. He didn't think it would save his life, but it might spare him a little of the agony. As he raced down the narrow corridor to the main bathroom, he suddenly thought, why didn't I dial 999?

He slammed the bathroom door closed, then grabbed his mobile from his pocket. For the first time since his old dog ran away, Michael was pleased that it had. He couldn't have coped if his dog were there too. He could fight back the tears no longer. He knew it was too late now, but he need to hear a human voice. He didn't want to be alone when he died, and before he did, he wanted to tell someone that he was sorry. Sorry for Mischief Night.

CHAPTER SEVENTEEN

'Outskirts of Frampton Village! Nuthatch Lane. An old farmhouse — Rycroft Farm!' Nikki called across the CID room to Joseph.

Nikki knew John Carson would be waiting for them, and when they arrived, she wasn't disappointed. 'You were right,' she said without preamble. 'He struck again.'

If possible, John looked even worse than he had the day before. 'I knew it, but I hoped I would be wrong. And this fire was in a very different league to the others.'

Nikki watched from the safety of the lane as three fire appliances tackled the blaze. There would be little left of Rycroft Farm when the flames had finally been doused.

John sighed. 'This time he secured the old building tighter than a duck's backside. The occupant, one Mr Michael Porter, didn't stand a cat in hell's chance of escaping. Windows nailed or screwed shut, doors locked and barricaded. No way out, I'm afraid.'

'Why didn't the guy notice?' asked Joseph incredulously.

'Sad case. Bit of a recluse. Lost his parents, then his siblings went, and he was left to look after the place. He developed a form of depression, and lost interest in the family home. Everything else, for that matter.'

'How do you know all this, John?' asked Nikki.

'One of the fire crew used to drink with him sometimes, down at the Nightingale Watch. Got to know him pretty well. He felt sorry for the bloke. Josh, the fireman, reckons he wouldn't have noticed if someone had draped multicoloured bunting all over the house. And the killer did a neat job, or so they think from what's left of the window frames.'

'And the occupant?' Nikki really didn't want to know, but had to ask.

'There are some very odd reports coming in, so I think maybe we should wait for the dust to settle, in case I feed you misinformation.'

'He's dead, of course?' Joseph said.

'Yes, I'm afraid so, but I'm told he's not as badly burnt as the other victims.'

Nikki heaved a sigh of relief. The whiteboard in the CID room was making her feel queasy every time she looked at it. 'Come on, John, what are these odd reports? We won't hold you to them.'

'Michael Porter made a 999 call. I don't know exactly what was said, but I'm told you need to hear the recording.' He paused. 'They say he intimated that the killer contacted him, just before the house went up. That's why you need to hear it for yourselves.'

Joseph stared up at the skeletal remains of the old farmhouse. 'Phew! This was some blaze, wasn't it?'

'He set it in at least three different places. And he started the fire at the far end of the house at the farthest point from the kitchen, where Michael apparently spent most of his time. It would have been well underway before Michael had a clue as to what was going on. Then I should think he went to investigate, and our killer took the key from the inside of the back door, locked it from the outside and rolled a heavy stone planter in front of it to barricade it further.' John stared at what was left of Rycroft Farm. 'Most of the windows were those tiny diamond shape mullions, so Michael couldn't even break the glass. Poor guy. He must have been terrified.'

'Did the fire crew find him and get him out?' asked Joseph.

'Yes, although it wasn't easy. They found him in the bathroom, which had a deep roll-top bath. He'd climbed in and pulled wet towels over the top of him, but he still asphyxiated.' John shook his head. 'Luckily, they managed to get his body out before the bathroom floor caved in.'

'We need to hear that 999 call, Joseph,' Nikki said. 'There's nothing we can do here. Uniform has been alerted to set up the crime scene, and it's going to be a long while before it's safe for forensics to get in there. We should get back to base and arrange a door-to-door, although there's not many of those out here on the fen.' She turned to John. 'Are you coming with us?'

He shook his head. 'I'll keep my ears open here, and pass on anything of interest to you.'

'John?' Nikki said.

'Yes?'

'Get some sleep, man! You look like shit. And that's being kind.'

'I'd hate to be on the receiving end of one of your *un*kind observations.' He smiled wearily. 'I'll do as you say — *when* you have this man locked up. Until then, it's power naps for me.'

'Power naps are supposed to supplement a night's sleep, not replace it,' Joseph said. 'You take care now. We need you on the case, not driving your car into a fen ditch because you nodded off.'

'Hear, hear,' Nikki said. 'But keep in touch, okay?'

John saluted. 'Scout's honour.'

'And get some sleep!'

She waited for a reply. None came.

* * *

Joseph made them hot drinks and, together with Cam, they went to listen to Michael Porter's last words.

Nikki steeled herself. She'd listened to messages like this before, mainly with suicide cases, and it was gut-wrenchingly hard to do.

They heard the operator ask, "Which emergency service do you require?"

"The house! It's burning! It's on fire! Oh my God! It's everywhere!"

There were a series of clicks as the connection to the fire control room was made. "Give me your address, sir! Help is on its way."

"Rycroft Farm! Nuthatch Lane! Outside Frampton." There was a bout of coughing. "Please . . ."

"Try to remain calm, sir. Are you inside the building?"

"I can't get out. He . . . he's locked me inside."

Nikki put her hand to her mouth. His terror was palpable.

"Where are you located within the building, sir?"

"The upstairs bathroom." Another hacking cough.

"Get down low to the floor, sir. The smoke is worse higher up. And keep talking to me. We have your location, and appliances will be with you very soon."

"Please listen! There's something I have to say. It's too late to help me, but I'm just so *sorry!*"

"Just keep calm, if you can." The fire control officer was holding it together well. Her voice was steady and soothing.

"I have to tell you . . . about Mischief Night. It was just a bit of fun, honestly." By now he was choking.

"Sir! Are there any towels in the bathroom? If so, soak them in water and wrap them around your face. Then use some to block any gaps around the door, okay? Then get back down on the floor. Can you do that for me?"

Nikki heard a scuffling noise and the sound of running water, then a muffled voice said, "I don't know who he was, or how he knew my number, but he knew about Mischief Night! He knew!" Michael began to cry. "This isn't fair! It wasn't my fault! Please believe me!"

"Hold on, sir! The appliances are in your lane now. They'll get you out. Just stay down."

But they heard nothing more from Michael Porter. The last sounds were the piercing screams of the fire engine sirens.

For a moment, the room was still. Then Cam heaved in a big breath and quietly thanked the officer who had played them the recording. 'Let's go to my office and work out what this tells us.'

He walked from the room. Without a word, Nikki and Joseph got up and followed him.

Inside his office, with the door closed, Cam asked, 'Mischief Night? Was he talking about Halloween?'

'It used to be called that locally, back in the fifties, I think, but it referred to the night before Halloween — 30 October,' said Joseph. 'Knock down Ginger and egging windows.'

'Where my Gran lived, out on the marsh, Mischief Night was around Firework Night,' said Nikki. 'I was never sure why.'

'I think it's the same in Yorkshire,' Cam said. 'The night before Bonfire Night. Just an excuse for kids to be naughty. Trick or treat is nothing new. But what was Porter talking about?'

'Something that happened on a Mischief Night, but when? And what?' Nikki frowned.

'And where?' added Joseph. 'Do you think this is connected to that girl who died young? The one that Harry said was Jez's friend?'

'Kids messing around and one got hurt in some way? It's quite possible.' Cam drew his brows together. 'But if our killer is going after all the kids involved in hurting the girl, they would know each other, wouldn't they? And there doesn't seem to be any connection between them. Ronnie Tyrrell saw one of Clary's paintings, didn't he? But he said he'd never heard of the artist.'

'We've found no connections at all between the three victims.' Nikki pulled a face. 'Not even geographically. They didn't live in the same road as kids. They didn't go to the same schools, churches, youth clubs, they had no connections through work, had different doctors, dentists . . .' She threw up her hands. 'If they'd been in a gang, running riot on Mischief Night, they'd remember each other, especially if something went wrong and one of them got hurt. Hell, if the kid died, they'd certainly remember!'

'And don't forget,' Joseph added. 'Jez said that the girl *died*, not that she was *killed*. So it wasn't necessarily anything suspicious.'

'Well, something happened, didn't it? Porter was eaten up with remorse about it. He had to be, to want to apologise for it in his last moments.' Cam drained his cup and threw it into the bin. 'I think we ought to check for accidents on Mischief Night that occurred as a result of pranksters. We need to go back ten, maybe fifteen years. Anything that involved a girl being injured or killed.'

'Okay, will do, but I'm wondering which date to pick, November fourth or October thirtieth?'

'I guess we'd better go for both.' Joseph shrugged. 'Could be either.'

'And I suppose we need to cover the whole county. We have no idea where this may have happened. It could take time. I'll get the team onto it first thing in the morning.' Nikki yawned. 'We need some sleep, and there's nothing more we can do until the reports from the house to house come in, and we get something from forensics. We should all go home.'

Cam stood up and stretched. 'You won't find me disagreeing, Nikki. I suspect tomorrow will be a very long day.'

* * *

This one had been the easiest of all, and possibly the most disappointing. He wasn't quite sure why.

It had gone off perfectly, and he had to admit that he was beginning to enjoy setting fires. The spectacle, the power of it, filled him with awe. It was like nothing he'd ever encountered before. Nonetheless, something had been missing. He supposed it was the fact that he hadn't been face to face with his victim, just prior to his death. He wouldn't use the phone again. It had distanced him from his target, and he wanted, *needed* to see their terror for himself. He hadn't dared confront Michael Porter in person. He knew Michael had a temper and was strong. Too strong for him. The operation had been an unequivocal success. It was just that it left him feeling empty somehow, let down.

He had had his ritual shower — hair washed twice, clothes changed — but although the stench of burning lingered as it always did and made him slightly nauseous, he felt hollow, unfulfilled.

He poured himself his customary brandy and sat at the kitchen table. After Jeremy Bedford and the stolen car, despite feeling sick as a dog, he'd been elated, high as a kite, manic with delight at what he'd achieved.

Tonight he felt quite different. Sad. He was doing everything he promised, with spectacular success, but he didn't want to go through it all just to feel like a failure in the end. Whatever was to follow, he must make sure to be with the target when the purifying flames did their work. It was worth the nausea, worth the lingering stink of burning on his skin.

He sipped his drink slowly. He would put this one behind him, and move on, because his next fire would be special. He closed his eyes. Yes, very special indeed.

CHAPTER EIGHTEEN

A pale dawn filtered hesitantly through the iron-grey sky. Rory Wilkinson and Ella Jarvis, his SOCO forensic photographer, were picking their way through the blackened debris and rubble that had once been Rycroft Farm.

'I burnt my toast this morning,' grumbled Rory. 'I *knew* it was a bad sign.'

Ella laughed, and choked in a cloud of dust. 'You're lucky you got any breakfast at all, Prof. I got the call and left home straight away.'

'Oh, I couldn't sleep, dear heart. My mind is a veritable turmoil of wedding plans!' He looked up at her from the old metal radiator he was busy inspecting. 'You *are* coming, aren't you?'

'Try and stop me! And I've had an amazing bit of luck with my costume.'

'Oh, do tell!'

'My grandmother was an Ack-Ack girl. She was an anti-aircraft spotter in Second World War with an all-women gun crew on a 3.7 inch gun battery, and I've still got her old uniform. I dug it out of the attic last night, and it fits! Well, sort of.'

'Oh my! That's wonderful! Can't wait to see it.' He turned back to the radiator, an old-style, column cast-iron model. 'Can I have a picture of this, Ella? Especially down the back of it, please.'

Ella took several shots. 'What *is* that?'

'Someone packed newspaper down behind it, a bit of extra fuel to feed the fire. I noticed it on another one too. This place was definitely prepared ahead of time. I suspect we'll find more evidence of this as we move around. I've seen it before, you know.' He pushed his wire-rimmed glasses further up the bridge of his nose, 'I was sent to a devastating fire in what was once an old mental asylum. Gothic Victorian it was, amazing architecture. It had started in the theatre, and I found that all the old radiators had been packed tightly with newspaper, just waiting for a match. The inmates had been planning the fire for months and thought it a great sport. Sadly, one of them died.' He shrugged. 'It was all covered up though. The official verdict was an electrical fault. Supposedly in the best interests of the hospital, the patients and the public. And as I had no proof that it was them that started it, I was forced to back down. Very galling!'

They moved on, into what they believed had been the dining room.

'Looks like this place was full of clutter even before the arsonist started work.' Ella took a shot of what appeared to be a heap of old saucepans and kitchenware, alongside the twisted remains of an ancient treadle sewing machine. 'Just a dumping ground for unwanted stuff.'

'Most of this place was neglected beyond redemption. I think the lone occupant had given up a long time ago.' Rory stared at the stinking, sodden mess that had once been a chaise longue. 'I'd like to have seen this place fifty years ago.'

'So there was just one victim?' asked Ella.

'As with all the other fires. A single victim. Trapped, and with no way of getting out. In this case, the firefighters removed the body to prevent it being totally cremated. He's back at the morgue now, and I'd appreciate your expertise in photographing him.'

Ella grimaced. 'Can't wait.'

'Actually there's something very interesting about the body, and I'd like to see if you notice what it is.'

'Don't be enigmatic, Prof. I haven't had breakfast yet.'

'I'm *always* enigmatic,' Rory said smugly.

By the time they had finished, Rory had discovered a number of extra little helpers that had fuelled the fire.

Ella checked the shots in her camera. 'I'm amazed. One, at the fact that not everything burns, even in this kind of house fire. And two, at the kind of things you knew to look for.'

'Oh, there are always snippets of unburnt evidence. Ask John Carson, or the new fire investigator. She should have a ball when she gets here.' He looked around. 'And odd things seem to escape the fire altogether, like this.' He pointed to an umbrella stand close to the door. One side was scorched, the other looked wet but undamaged. 'And he had to use things that had no smell, didn't he? He could hardly splash a spot of turps around, or sprinkle some lighter fuel. Anyone with a nose would notice that.'

'But cotton balls soaked in petroleum jelly? And the lint that collects in your tumble dryer? For heavens' sake! Who'd have thought *that* would be so flammable.'

'That fluff can be explosively flammable if it consists of fibres that are entirely cotton.' Rory looked at the evidence bag in his hand. It contained a tiny, wet piece of lint residue that he'd found wedged into the springs of a sofa. 'He'd probably been collecting it for months. And the wood shavings — they have a great surface-to-air ratio for combustion.'

'That means he broke in while the owner was out and did all this prep, ready for the big finale?'

'One nasty, callous person, my dear. Can you imagine actually going round screwing windows shut, and locking every possible way out, so that some poor soul would burn to death? It's inconceivable.'

'Is he insane, Prof? Or eaten up with a desire for revenge? Or both?'

'A terrible trauma can trigger this kind of behaviour, although it's rare. Oddly, arsonists don't usually attempt to hurt people, just property. It's the fire they're after, and the power to destroy things. People usually get caught up in those fires purely accidentally. This man is a cold-blooded murderer, nothing less.'

Ella shivered. 'Well, I guess it's time to go and meet his victim.'

Rory nodded and began to pick his way towards the gap where the front door had once stood. 'Mr Michael Porter awaits his last formal photograph. After you, dear heart, and I can't wait to see you in your ATS uniform! Roll on next month!'

* * *

Eve and Wendy were both early risers. Years in the military had seen to that, and neither woman was comfortable with lying in bed. At six forty-five they were walking around the garden, enjoying the freshness of the early autumn morning.

Jenny's fern garden was finally looking as it should, with just the garden seat still to come.

'She'd love this, wouldn't she?' said Wendy softly.

'It's as near to her plans as I could make it, so, yes, I think she would. And I think she'd be pretty shocked that this old fogey was capable of it.' Eve laughed. 'She always said I'd never make a gardener, but for once, I've proved her wrong.'

'And you love it too, don't you?'

Eve thought for a moment. 'Yes, I do. I can see now what people get out of planting and sowing and tending their plants. Sounds daft, I suppose, but after the kind of life we've led, it's quite therapeutic. It's all about life, not death. And there is definitely something about trees. They seem to lift the spirits somehow.'

Wendy smiled. She ran a hand across the bark of a eucalyptus tree that swayed gracefully at the edge of the fern garden. 'Shinrin-yoku. It's a Japanese therapy we call "forest bathing." I read about it in the Daily Telegraph the other day. They reckon fifteen minutes spent among trees can lower cortisol levels, boost the immune system and reduce anxiety.'

'Good Lord! Really?'

'You seem to have tapped into it organically, Eve Anderson. We'll make a forest therapist out of you yet!'

'Very funny.' Eve looked up. 'There's a car down in the lay-by at the end of the drive.' For a second the old fear came back.

'I think I recognise it,' said Wendy warily, 'but I'm not sure who owns it.'

'Let's check it out.'

They began to walk out of the fern garden. Wendy touched Eve's arm and whispered, 'There's someone in the old graveyard.'

They threw each other puzzled looks, and hurried quietly towards the gateway.

'Morning, ladies! Hope you don't mind. I didn't think anyone would be up and out so early.'

'Leon!' Eve heaved a sigh of relief. 'Of course we don't mind. We just wondered who it was.'

'Fancy a cup of tea, Leon?' asked Wendy. 'I'm just off to put the kettle on.'

'That would be lovely. Thank you.'

Wendy left, and Eve joined Leon in the wildest area of the Monks Lantern garden. 'What brings you back here so soon?'

Leon stared around. He looked troubled. 'I don't know.'

'What's bothering you?' Eve said. 'Can I help at all?'

They walked through the dewy copse, looking at the moss-covered tombstones and chipped stone angels.

'It's these deaths. The ones your daughter is investigating.'

'The fires?'

He nodded slowly. 'I'm the only link to the three victims, Mrs Anderson, and one of my parishioners told me there was another fire last night, an old farmhouse out near Frampton.' He looked thoroughly miserable. 'And if it turns out to be Michael Porter's home, I know him too.'

'Oh dear. I see. But you have no idea why these people have been murdered?'

'I have no idea at all. I knew them all for different reasons, and to my knowledge, they were complete strangers to each other.' He stopped and stared at a cobweb strung between the branches of a birch tree. 'The thing is, when we were here yesterday something flashed through my mind. I didn't really think about it at the time, and now it's gone.'

'But you think it's important? About the fires?'

He shook his head as if to clear it. 'I don't know what it was. But I thought that if I came back here, something might jog my memory.' He sighed. 'But it hasn't.'

'It will come back. They always do, those elusive thoughts. But it doesn't help to try to force them to the surface. Come and have some tea, then maybe walk around again, calmly, and with an open mind. It's worth a try.'

Leon smiled at her. 'Absolutely. I'm probably just being an idiot, but you can see why I'm worried. I'll be suspect number one, if things go on as they are.'

'Then maybe we should try to reconstruct our meeting yesterday? Wendy will help. She has good recall. Let's have that tea, and then we'll all come back out here and try to remember where we walked and what we were talking about. What do you think?'

'Thank you, Mrs Anderson. I appreciate it. I wouldn't trouble you, but I honestly think it's important.'

* * *

Tom Black was exhausted. He had sat up half the night with his sister as she fought her way through another asthma attack. Then Giles, who had been on his way to an early meeting in Lincoln, came back in to say that the house had been daubed with slogans. Now he and Corinne were trying to clean the filthy words from the front door.

'This'll never come off, Tom.' Corinne stared at the results of ten minutes spent scrubbing at a single word.

She was right. 'I'll call a professional to come and sort it all out. If necessary, we'll just have to re-paint them. Bloody vandals!'

'I think we should call the police, but Giles said no,' Corinne grumbled.

'He's right. We don't want the police back. You know that.' He gave her a faint smile. 'Ten to one it'd be our charming, nosey, PC Collins who turns up.'

'I suppose. But does it really matter? There's nothing for her to see here, and we can't go on suffering this kind of abuse from those hateful thugs. I'm worried about what they'll do next.' Corinne threw her sponge into the bucket of water. 'And you can't tell me it doesn't bother you as well, Tom Black, because I know it does.'

His sister-in-law was right. It did. 'Then maybe it's time I found some other way to rid us of this curse. There's more than one way to skin a cat.'

Corinne made a face. 'I hate that phrase. What are you getting at anyway?'

'What's the point of being surrounded by all this power and influence if you don't take advantage of it?' he said reasonably.

'You mean use the members themselves to help deal with the thugs?' Corinne sounded dubious.

'Needs must when the Devil drives, don't you think?'

He gave a wicked smile, and for the first time that day, Corinne laughed.

* * *

Rory was back in the morgue early. He had taken a brief look at Michael Porter's body on his way out to the crime site, and he was anxious to start the post-mortem. Spike, his technician, had just arrived, and so had Ella. They were almost ready to go.

It was Rory's belief that this particular death would be the one to lead them to the killer. This silent witness would speak the loudest. He was certain of it.

'Ella! My little Ack-Ack girl! Come in and bring your trusty camera.'

Spike looked puzzled, but didn't ask. He too was used to Rory by now.

'We'll start by photographing the deceased Mr Porter as he was delivered to us. Then we'll proceed to photograph him unclothed. I particularly want pictures of any unusual features, Ms Ack-Ack, okay?'

Ella glanced across to Spike and grinned. 'The wedding? The costumes? Second World War? Get it?'

Spike raised his eyes to the ceiling. 'Thank you for that.'

'Back to work, kiddies! Mr Porter awaits. Now, this time we aren't looking for the usual things — the time, mechanism or manner of death —because we know all that, almost to the second. We are looking for more subtle clues. So, let's proceed. Have you got your initial shots, Ella? Then, Spike, measure and weigh the gentleman, please, and we can start to record our information.'

It didn't take long to conduct the initial external examination and carefully remove the clothes and prepare them for the crime lab to process.

'We need to examine the body for injuries, both old and new. The extent of burning is considerably less than the others, due to his getting into the bath and covering himself up, but he didn't escape completely unscathed. Ella? Photographs, please. Then we'll turn him, for posterior and lateral shots.'

She took several shots, and then Rory and Spike turned the body onto its front for her to take pictures of the man's back.

'Oh!' Ella exclaimed. 'I see what you mean, Prof!'

'Exactly. What do you make of that then?' Rory stood back.

'Old scar tissue,' Ella said.

Spike leaned closer. 'Scar tissue from serious burns.'

'This wasn't the first time Michael Porter was subjected to fire,' Ella murmured. 'The poor man! He'd been severely burnt before. He must have been terrified.'

Rory nodded. 'Unimaginable.' They looked at the puckered, scaly skin that stretched across the back of his left arm, along his shoulder blade, and down his ribs. 'It would appear he lifted his right arm to shield his face, then pushed through whatever was ablaze, and sustained these burns.' He paused. 'Or possibly something ignited right in front of him, like a blast from something flammable thrown onto a bonfire, and he turned and lifted that arm to protect himself.'

'That last conjecture sounds more like it, Professor,' observed Spike. 'Funny that there's evidence of skin grafts on the arms, but not the rest of him.'

'I'm told grafts can be very painful. Maybe he didn't think it was worth going through it, since they were on his shoulder and back.' Rory stared at the body on the table. 'One thing I'm certain of. These burns will help our friends in CID find the killer. This chap must have been pretty seriously injured when the accident happened, assuming it was an accident. I would think he needed specialist treatment, probably even in a burns unit.'

'And that would mean Nottingham City Hospital, I think,' said Spike, 'or maybe the Queens Medical Centre, but I know it would be Nottingham for this area.'

'And they would keep records. I'd be very interested to see what happened to this man, and how long ago. Those scars aren't recent, not by a long chalk.' Rory straightened up. 'Right. When we've finished here, I intend to find out.'

CHAPTER NINETEEN

Yvonne drove down a narrow fen lane to the farthest end of Nuthatch Lane, where it joined the road to the town. She'd been sent on door-to-door enquiries and knew the area well enough to know that there could be half a mile between each of those doors.

Her first call was to a pair of old farmworkers' cottages at the junction. They had recently been sold and knocked into one good-sized dwelling. It stood alone, commanding a view across hundreds of acres of arable fields. Yvonne reckoned that from their upstairs windows you'd see for miles in every direction. If anyone left Nuthatch Lane in a tearing hurry the night before, the home owners could well have noticed them.

The door was opened by a youngish man in stained jeans and a sweatshirt that had more plaster on it than her ceiling.

'Sorry, sir, bad time?' Yvonne said.

'No, a pretty good one actually. I'm just beginning to realise there are some things an amateur should *not* attempt.'

Yvonne smiled and showed him her warrant card. 'I won't keep you long, sir, but I was wondering if you heard or saw anyone out here last night?'

'Apart from what seemed like twenty fire trucks flying down the road?' He held the door open. 'Come in. My wife is just making tea.'

Not one to turn down a brew, Yvonne followed him in. 'That's kind of you.'

'Millie! Another mug, please. We have a visitor.' He turned to Yvonne. 'I'm Andy Brothers, and my wife Millie is on kettle duty.'

'How long have you been here, Andy?'

'About three or four months. Living like squatters, but we're getting there.' He grinned. 'Well, that's what I keep telling the wife.'

For all his joking and despite his coating of plaster, he was making a great job of the old place.

'Hello.' Millie popped her head around the kitchen door. 'Milk and sugar?'

'Just milk, please,' Yvonne replied. 'This is lovely. You're making a beautiful home out of these old cottages.'

Andy looked chuffed as little apples. 'Sit down, Officer. You want to know about the fire, I guess? Heck, you could see the flames for miles!'

Millie placed a mug of tea beside Yvonne. 'Horrible it was. I hate fire. Scares me.' She sat down in an armchair opposite and said, 'Was it deliberate? Is that why you're asking questions?'

'We believe so,' said Yvonne carefully. 'I'm very interested to know if you saw anyone around, just before the fire started?'

Husband and wife looked at each other. Andy said, 'There was a vehicle, but neither of us actually saw it.'

'We heard it though, and whoever it was, they weren't taking too much care on these fen lanes. It was going like a mad thing.'

'And the time, approximately?'

'Oh, around half eight, nine o'clock, or thereabouts. Is that right, Mil?'

'I think so, yes.'

From the timing, Yvonne was pretty sure that this had been the killer.

'I *do* know it was a van,' said Millie abruptly.

Yvonne looked up. 'Why?'

'I used to be a florist delivery driver, Officer, and vans just sound different to cars, especially the older ones. Kind of tinny.'

'Did the one you heard sound old?'

'Well, it wasn't a brand new one, I know that. As a matter of fact, I've seen a small van, a white Renault Kangoo, out here a few times in the last week. That's the sort of van we're talking about.'

Yvonne couldn't recall ever getting so much helpful information from the first door she knocked on.

'Before you ask, I didn't get the number. After all, I had no call to, did I? But it was a 2013 plate, that I did notice.' Millie wrinkled her brow in concentration. 'And it was one of those Compact vans, with lettering on the side.'

Were things finally coming together? Yvonne was getting more hopeful by the minute. 'Do you know what the writing said?'

Millie frowned. 'Can't recall the name, but it was a property care company — you know, painting and decorating.'

'I saw it too,' chimed in Andy. 'I almost stopped him and asked if he wanted a job.'

Bit of luck you didn't, thought Yvonne. He could well have been our killer on his way to nail a few windows shut.

She finished her tea. 'You've been incredibly helpful.' She looked at Millie. 'How come you're so clued up on makes of van and years of registration?'

'My dad was a used-car salesman. We lived over the garage when I was a kid.' She smiled. 'Cars and vans are part of my life, always have been.'

'Oh, I see. Well, thank you. I'm sure I don't have to tell you, but if you see it again?' She handed Millie her card.

'We'll be on the blower like greased lightning, never fear.' Millie's smile faded. 'The man who lived there died, didn't he?'

Yvonne nodded. No point in denying it.

'We didn't know him. He seemed very detached, if you know what I mean? He'd acknowledge you if you spoke to him, but it was clear he didn't want conversation.' She looked sad. 'I thought he was a very unhappy man, Officer. Or maybe just very lonely.'

Back in her vehicle, Yvonne scanned the fields and the lanes, trying to think who else she knew lived out here. One person did come to mind, although she wouldn't accept a cuppa there if offered. Meg Brownlee wasn't the most hygienic of people. Her heart was in the right place, and she adopted any orphaned animal brought to her door, but housework was not high on her list of priorities.

'Vonnie! How lovely to see you, me duck! It's been ages! Cup of tea?'

'Thanks, Meg, but I've just had one, and I'll be wanting to wee if I have another. Got a moment?'

The old lady stood on the doorstep of her ramshackle bungalow, a scraggy ginger cat under one arm and a coal shovel in her other hand. 'For you, of course.' She looked over her shoulder. 'I'd invite you in, duck, but Mr Grumpy is having one of his moods, so maybe we could just talk here?'

'Absolutely,' said Yvonne gratefully. Mr Grumpy was a ten-year-old rescue Chihuahua, and not renowned for his people skills. 'Have you seen a white van out here recently, going in the direction of Nuthatch Lane?'

'Yes, dear.' Meg tickled the cat's ears and seemed to think that was all that was expected of her.

'Well, when was that, Meg?'

'This week? Yes, that's right. I seen him twice this week. Day before yesterday around lunch time, and the same time the day before. I know, because that's the time I have to give Clucky her medicine.' She gazed toward a makeshift chicken run. 'She's had worms, you know.'

Lovely, thought Yvonne. 'Did you see what was written on the van, Meg?' She wasn't hoping for too much here, but at least she had some more times to add to her report.

'It was a decorator's van, duck. Fred someone. Didn't get the rest, but as Fred was my dear husband's name, God rest his soul, I noticed that bit.'

Better and better, thought Yvonne. 'Is your phone working, Meg?'

'I've had it cut off, duck. Pointless really.'

'But . . .' Yvonne was about to tell her how foolhardy that was when the old lady produced a smartphone from her cardigan pocket.

'Pointless now I've got this, dear. My nephew set it up and showed me how to use it. Much more fun than that stupid old landline.'

Yvonne stifled a giggle. 'Ah, good. Well, if you see that van again, ring me, okay?'

The old lady placed the cat on the floor. 'Let me just pop you in my Contacts, then I can get you if I need to.' To Yvonne's surprise, her fingers flew deftly over the tiny keyboard. 'Sorted. Now, are you sure about that tea? I'm sure Mr Grumpy will have calmed down by now.'

Yvonne declined again, turned to leave and paused. 'I suppose you didn't notice the driver of the van, did you?'

'Youngish man, Vonnie. Lovely thick brown hair and a nice smile. He waved as he went past.'

Yvonne swallowed. Cool as a cucumber, wasn't he? On his way to prepare a funeral pyre and he waves to old ladies. That told her a lot about their man. Maybe more than she wanted to know.

* * *

Niall listened to what Yvonne had to report. 'Let's take this to the DI, shall we? And, Vonnie? If they can use you, you can lend them a hand if you like. I can swing it this end.'

'Can I still keep an eye on the Black House though?' Yvonne said.

'Sure, if you think it warrants it, but this is really important stuff, so put it first.' He cuffed her arm affectionately. 'But I don't have to tell you about priorities, do I, grandmother?'

'Button it, *Sergeant* Farrow, or your grandmother might just clip your ears.'

'I miss you, Vonnie,' Niall said quietly. 'I know I had to move on. I have a wife now, and a home, oh, and a dog to consider, but I still miss you and the beat.'

'The feeling is reciprocated, young'un. It's not the same, and that's a fact. But as you said, you have responsibilities now, and you'll do fine, never fear. You're a good boy, Niall. The best.' She sniffed. 'Now let's go see the DI.'

* * *

'What?' Nikki exclaimed.

'It's as I said. Michael Porter sustained serious burns in a previous accident some time ago. It's awful that he should now die in a house fire, having survived what I suspect to have been a very nasty incident.' Rory paused. 'I've tried to trace his medical records but I've hit an impasse. Adult health records are reviewed and destroyed eight years after the patient was discharged or last seen. Or, if he was considered a child at the time of the accident, they would have been destroyed after his twenty-fifth or twenty-sixth birthday. It appears that he never attended the hospital again after his treatment was finished, hence no records.'

Nikki recalled Michael's last words, about it not being his fault, that it was just a bit of fun and that he was sorry. What had he done? Cogs were turning, and pieces were slipping into place. 'This could be the answer to why our killer uses fire, couldn't it?'

'I definitely think so.'

'A prank that went wrong on Firework Night, or the night before — Mischief Night. Rory, this *has* to be traceable. We'll get straight on to it! Thank you, my friend.'

'My absolute pleasure. Now, while I have you on the phone, I've had some more thoughts about your costume for the wedding. I was thinking along the lines of—'

'Stop right there!' Nikki said. 'Rory, *dearest*, this kind of thing doesn't come easy to a simple plod like me. I really think you have to allow me to work it out all by myself, okay? No more suggestions, right?'

'But . . .'

'Not another word.'

'I . . .'

'Rory!'

'Spoilsport. Oh well, I shall just have to wait with bated breath, won't I?'

'Got the message at last! Thank you for your info, Rory, I appreciate it. Now I'm off to chase it up.'

There was a loud theatrical sigh. Nikki hung up, smiling.

She hurried out to share Rory's news with Joseph and the others, and found them deep in conversation with Niall and Yvonne.

'We've had a sighting, boss!' Cat called out. 'Tell the DI, Vonnie.'

'He drives a small white Compact van, with a painter and decorator's name on it, Fred someone. Could be a Renault Kangoo, with a thirteen plate,' Yvonne explained. 'And he's been seen on several days prior to the fire, heading towards Rycroft Farm. I've checked with every house out on that stretch of the fen, and no one has been having work done. Then, just before the emergency services got out there last night, one of the residents heard a van being driven at breakneck speed away from the fire.'

Nikki beamed. 'Headway at last! Well done, Vonnie. I suppose no one could ID the driver, could they?'

'Youngish, and lovely brown hair is as good as it gets, I'm afraid, but it sounds like our arsonist, doesn't it?'

'No question, and I've got something that might help too.' Nikki told them about Rory's discovery of burn scars on Michael Porter's body and her suspicion that whatever had happened to Michael was the link to the killer.

'Shall I chase that up, guv?' asked Dave.

'Go for it, and if anyone else is at a loose end, you can help Dave.'

'Ma'am? If you can use Yvonne, I've squared it downstairs,' Niall offered.

'Certainly can! Vonnie, get onto finding that van. CCTV should be your first stop, and Spooky in IT will help you with that. You two know this area better than any of us.'

'Wilco, ma'am.'

Vonnie went off in search of Spooky, and for the first time since the fires started, Nikki felt as though they were finally making real progress.

The others went back to their desks, leaving Joseph apparently deep in thought. 'That man is so organised, so in control!' he said. 'I've just been calculating that he was actually sealing up Rycroft Farm on the day he torched the stolen car and killed Jez. And they say men can't multi-task!'

'John Carson was right when he said the arsonist wants this over as quickly as possible. I'm just praying that he doesn't have too many more victims on his list.' Nikki frowned. 'Because he does have a list, doesn't he?'

'Well, if we can find out who else was with Michael Porter in this prank gone wrong, we might know who they are.' Joseph looked at her. 'I'm finished with my reports. Shall I give Dave a hand?'

Nikki nodded. 'Do, and after I've updated Cam, I'll pitch in too. This could be the turning point.'

* * *

Inside the garage, he went round the van peeling off the stick-on vinyl signs and replacing them with new ones. This time the little Renault proclaimed him to be JJ's Pet Supplies. With the addition of a colourful stripe and a series of vinyl muddy dog paws, it looked completely different. He didn't want to use it too often — he knew the police would be looking for a Renault — but he would only need it for a couple of days, then the vinyl could be peeled off again and the little white van returned to where he had "borrowed" it from, hopefully without its holidaying owner ever knowing it had gone anywhere. It doesn't do to sit in pubs and tell the world you're off to Thailand. You never know who might follow you home.

He was feeling much better today. Maybe it was just a reaction to the stress. He was sure that was the reason for his dreadful headaches. Hopefully they would go when it was all over.

He finished his work and sat on a big old toolbox, trying to collect his thoughts. He had to move on to the next part of the plan. But he was tired. So tired. This project was taking its toll. He told himself he'd have plenty of time to sleep after he'd set the final fire. Until then, he must concentrate, keep calm and make them burn!

He stood up and went back into the house. He hadn't eaten today, and he couldn't afford to grow weak. A late breakfast, some vitamin pills, and back to the drawing board. This next one would not be straightforward.

CHAPTER TWENTY

Despite Wendy's near total recall of the conversations in the graveyard at Monks Lantern, nothing jogged Leon's memory. By the time he left them, he looked utterly bedevilled.

'I wonder what it was?' Eve mused.

'Whatever it is, it's going to drive him crazy until he remembers.' Wendy lowered herself into a garden chair. 'But I was interested to hear what we can and can't do with our graves.'

'I don't know about you, but I'm thinking he has a point about not digging up these poor souls. After all, they were laid to rest here for all eternity.'

Wendy looked down at the notes she made while Leon had talked. 'Well, we can level old and broken edging stones and anything already laid flat, as long as we record the exact location of the grave.' She looked up. 'He says he's put in a request for the burial and death records for this place. Apparently they're recorded in the parish registers, and they go back to the 1500s, whereas official census records don't go back further than 1837. But he isn't sure he'll be able to find them for a tiny chapel graveyard like this one.'

'And we can't touch the standing stones. Is that correct?' Eve asked.

'He's going to query that. There are conflicting views, it seems. Some other disused graveyards have been given approval to move headstones and memorials over eighty years old to the periphery of the grounds, as long as a record of names, date of death and position within the graveyard is posted clearly.' She sucked in air. 'Others have had to retain the larger standing stones and monuments and burial vaults.'

'We don't have any of those anyway. Vaults, I mean.'

'Not that I've seen, but there are a couple of areas that are pretty overgrown.' Wendy grinned. 'I wouldn't be surprised to find that some wealthy old Beech Lacey family had a vault here.'

Eve nodded. 'Mmm, could be. But whatever we decide, I suppose the first thing we have to do is have a really good tidy up. Get rid of the brambles, the nettles, the elder and all the weeds and dead branches, and then see what we have.'

'And who do we rope in to do that? The scouts? People doing Community Service? It's a big job.'

'I'm willing to pay for all the professional stuff that needs doing — tree maintenance and that sort of thing, but why don't we mobilise the village to help with the ground work? The gardening club would help, I'm sure. We could talk to Cam Walker. He and Kaye know a lot more people than we do.' Eve was starting to feel positive about their new venture, no matter how it finished up.

'Good idea,' said Wendy. 'Let's ring Cameron this evening, and then make a plan of action. Meanwhile, do you think there's anything we can do to help that young curate? I hate to see a person so troubled.'

'I was thinking the same myself.' Eve narrowed her eyes. 'We have five senses, and hearing is only one of them. Leon assumes it was something he heard, but what if it was something he saw?'

Wendy looked thoughtful. 'And what do you see in a graveyard, but memorial stones? You're thinking he noticed a specific name on a tomb, but it didn't fully register?'

'Exactly. So why don't we take a little stroll around our new project, and list all the names that are legible? We can show them to Leon. One of them might just jog his memory.'

'Good thinking! I'll get a notepad.'

* * *

Just before two o'clock, Joseph and Dave believed they'd made a breakthrough. After doing tests on the skin graft tissue, Rory had confirmed that Michael must have been in his late teens when he had his accident, so they were targeting incidents around the end of October into early November, from 2005 to 2007.

Dave had chanced on a report of a bonfire that had got out of control on a piece of waste ground. Several youngsters had received burns, two seriously.

'You say it was on 4 November, 2007?' asked Joseph, fingers hovering over his keyboard.

'That's right. It was on the outskirts of a village called Dewdyke. That's a little place near Saltern-le-Fen, I think. Some teenagers built a bonfire with old pallets and rubbish they pinched from a nearby farm, and it looks like they weren't too careful about what they chucked on the fire.'

Joseph searched a newspaper archive for the date and location. 'Ah, got it.' He squinted at the screen. 'Doesn't tell us much though, and no names.' He tried another site, but again found nothing to help them. He sat back. 'John Carson! It's just occurred to me. He said he remembers every call he ever went to. Maybe he dealt with this one, or knew someone who was there.' He picked up his phone.

'John? We need to pick your brains. It's a long shot mind you, a fire that occurred over ten years ago.'

'Tell me what you know about it,' said John.

'November 4, 2007. Bonfire out of control. Dewdyke. Several injuries.'

'Ah yes,' John said ruminatively. 'Not my case, but several youngsters were hurt, so it was investigated. I seem to

171

recall that one of the youngsters was transferred to the specialist burns centre at St Andrew's, Chelmsford.'

'Do you know any more, John? Will it still be on record with the fire and rescue service?'

'No need for us to chase up records, Joseph. The guy who dealt with it is a friend of mine. I'll give him a bell and ring you back. What are you looking for in particular?' John asked.

'Everything he has, please. Names are the most important. We'd like to know if the name Michael Porter comes up at all.'

'Oh, I see. Give me a minute or two.'

Joseph ended the call. 'This is promising.'

'Good, because I can't find anything else that fits the bill.' Dave frowned. 'I never realised how many fires are reported each month, mainly due to faulty electrical appliances.'

'I can believe that,' Joseph said.

John Carson was soon back on the phone. 'This is all I have for now, but if the need arises we can try to get into the archives for you. My old colleague remembers that the kids were celebrating Mischief Night and were pretty drunk. They took old pallets and firewood, and all manner of rubbish from the farm outbuildings, then a couple of them broke into a store and grabbed all sorts of stuff, including canisters of agro-chemicals. Their bonfire turned into a toxic inferno. Two of the kids, a boy and a girl, got in the way of a fireball. Very nasty indeed.'

'Their names? Did he remember them?' Joseph sat forward, hunched over the phone.

'Darren Smith and Sally Brooks. Sorry, Joseph. No mention of Michael Porter.'

'Damn and blast! We thought we had it there.'

'Don't forget there were others hurt too, just not as badly, and they weren't named. So he could have been involved. In fact he could have been one of the idiots who got hold of the flammable stuff in the first place.'

'That's possible. I suppose they were taken to Greenborough General, were they?'

'Most likely. Although I doubt whether they still have the records. And I'm not sure how you'd find their names in the first place. We only had the two I've given you. Oh, and the girl died a week later, by the way.'

'That's awful. Poor kid.' Joseph had seen horrendous injuries while he was serving with the special forces, men and women who'd begged him to shoot them to end their pain. He hoped the girl had at least been saved such agony.

'Sorry I can't be of more help, Joseph. Can I ask something? What's the time frame you are looking at for Michael Porter's accident?'

Joseph told him. 'You could be our main hope, John. We thought we were getting somewhere, but I'm not so sure now. And meanwhile, that madman is out there somewhere, with a fresh box of matches and itchy fingers.'

* * *

Ben and Cat were trying to get a handle on Michael Porter's past, but were faring little better than Joseph. They'd tried all the usual routes, but he'd never been in trouble, never been registered as living anywhere other than Rycroft Farm, and seemed to be a complete loner. They had his age, and a few other personal papers that had survived the fire inside a metal document box. His siblings had already been notified. They appeared to be shocked, but more concerned about losing their inheritance than losing their brother. Neither was forthcoming about Michael's earlier accident.

Ben decided to phone Michael's brother, Jared.

'Mike didn't come home for a long time after the accident,' said Jared. 'Our parents told us he was in hospital. They said he'd been mentally affected by what happened, and we weren't to talk to him about it when he came back, so we didn't.'

'But they explained about the fire, didn't they?' asked Ben.

'Not really. They just said he'd been burned. He'd been somewhere he shouldn't, and got injured.'

'And you didn't think to ask? Wasn't it in the local paper?' Ben was puzzled and more than a little angry at the brother's lack of concern.

'It didn't happen locally, and frankly, Mike was always up to something he shouldn't. Claire and I just let him get on with it.'

'He was never in trouble with the police. We checked.'

'I didn't say he was stupid, just always up to something.'

'Sir, your brother was severely injured. He had major burns on his arm, his shoulder and right across his back. He had skin grafts, which must have been agonising for him, and you tell me he suffered problems related to the trauma afterwards, but you *let him get on with it*?' Ben raised his voice. Cat flashed him a warning glance from across the desk, and pulled an imaginary zipper across her mouth. 'I'd just like to understand why,' he said.

There was a long silence, and then Jared said, 'We had a happy childhood. Our parents spoilt Mike, who was the youngest, and as he grew older, he became insufferable.' He paused. 'Sorry, Officer, bottom line, Claire and I grew up, Michael didn't. We were both at university when Mike got hurt. I didn't think it was that serious, if you must know. We thought he was milking it. He wasn't academic, and his future wasn't exactly rosy, so we thought he was trying to get on benefits, and get out of having to make a living. That's why we were less than sympathetic.'

Ben still felt they might have been at least a little curious. He was their flesh and blood, after all.

'Then, when Mum and Dad died he changed completely. He was always lazy, but after that he seemed to give up on everything. Claire and I couldn't do anything to help with the house. She lives in Ontario, and I'm based here in Riyadh. I'm an English teacher.' He sniffed. 'Look, I'm sorry this has happened, really I am, but it was probably his own fault. Left a pan on the stove or something. He was like that.'

Ben sighed. 'How much detail have you been given about your brother's death, sir?'

'That he died in a house fire, when Rycroft Farm, our home, burnt down. And someone would contact us and update us when they knew more.'

'Sir, I'm sorry to have to tell you this, but Michael was murdered. Someone locked him in the farmhouse, then set it alight.'

There was a long silence. Jared whispered, 'Oh, dear Mother of God! Poor little Mikey!'

Ben couldn't help heaving a sigh of relief. At last, some emotion. 'I'm very sorry, sir. But I'm sure you can now understand why we're having to ask so many questions. We believe his death is connected to the accident he had eleven years ago.'

'But why? I don't understand.'

'Michael is not the first victim to have been killed in this manner. We think it's connected to something called Mischief Night, and an incident that occurred years ago.'

'He always loved Mischief Night, Detective, especially when he was little.' Jared paused. 'I need to come home. I'll ask for compassionate leave. I'm not sure what use I'll be, but maybe I can recall something our parents mentioned. I'll do all I can to help, for Mikey's sake.'

Ben almost whooped aloud. 'Thank you, sir. We'll see you when you get here.'

Ben hung up.

'You enjoyed telling him that, didn't you, Ben Radley.' Cat looked at him with wide reproachful eyes.

'What is it with families? For heaven's sake, the kid gets barbecued and his brother and sister decide he's swinging the lead to get a benefit cheque! I ask you!'

Cat shrugged. 'Stranger things have happened. Anything useful come out of it in the end?'

'One thing. Michael's accident didn't happen close to home. We'll press Jared harder when we see him, but he said it wasn't in the local papers.'

Cat stood up. 'I'll go and tell the Sarge. He and Dave are checking out local fires, not ones further out of our area.'

175

'That'll please them. It makes this hunt a damn sight more difficult, too.' Ben scratched his head. 'Surely someone must know Michael Porter well enough to know what happened to him? He must have talked to *someone*.'

Cat stopped mid-stride. 'Of course! Who did the others talk to?' She beamed at him. 'Leon Martin! Bet he knows him.'

Ben slapped his temple. 'Duh! Of course!'

'So move your butt, Detective, and let's go see our curate.'

* * *

'Michael Porter should never have been left to live alone in that big old place. He wasn't capable of looking after himself, let alone the house,' Leon said.

'So how did you know him?' asked Cat.

Leon paced up and down the nave of St Saviours. 'He came to see the Reverend Taylor, but Allan was out visiting a sick parishioner, so I did what I could to help him. We got talking.' He sank into a pew. 'Well, I talked. I could see he was disturbed about something, but he didn't tell me what. He just asked about redemption. Would you still get into heaven if you'd done something terrible? Stuff like that.'

'He came back?' Ben asked.

'Often. He told me he'd been involved in something pretty horrific, and he'd survived, but whoever he was with didn't. He obviously felt guilty about it. He said it haunted him.'

'Did he ever say what that something was, Leon? You see, we believe that what happened then is connected to his death.' Ben looked hard at him. 'It's important, Leon.'

'It had something to do with drink and drugs. Not heavy drugs, some sort of psychoactive substance.'

'What we used to call legal highs,' said Ben.

Leon nodded. 'That's right. He said that way back in 2005, he and a couple of others tied up with two students who were out looking for some fun on Mischief Night. It all went wrong, apparently. People got hurt, and one of them died. He said it wasn't his fault, but he still felt responsible.' Leon hung his head. 'I cannot believe that Michael had to suffer all over again. I've prayed for him to find peace, but he was a troubled man, Detectives. Very troubled.'

'Did he say where this happened?'

'No. He told me no more than I've told you, I'm afraid.' Leon bit his lip, then looked anxious. 'I'm sure there's something about these deaths that I ought to know.'

Cat and Ben stared at him, not understanding.

'I don't know what it is, but there's a connection, and I can't make it. I've tried and tried, but it won't,' he smacked his fist into his other hand, 'it just won't come to me.'

Cat took her card from her pocket. 'If it does, ring me immediately. We really need your help.'

'Oh I will, believe me.'

Cat and Ben left him sitting in the pew and made their way down the aisle to the main doors. As they went through, two familiar figures were on their way in.

'Eve? Wendy? What are you doing here?' Cat asked.

'Oh, hello, Cat dear. And Ben too! How are you both? We're just coming to see Leon. He's kindly helping us with a problem regarding a disused graveyard.'

Cat frowned. 'Disused graveyard? No, second thoughts, I don't think I want to know right now. Gotta fly. You two take care. Oh, and try to stay out of trouble!'

Outside Cat glanced back. 'I don't trust those two one inch, do you?'

Ben grinned. 'No further than I could throw them. They're up to something alright. Did you see the look on their faces?'

'Shall we tell the boss?'

'Nah. Give them the benefit of the doubt. Maybe they just need a bit of spiritual guidance,' Cat said.

'But disused graveyards?'

'Let's not go there.'

'Good idea.'

* * *

'That's the last we see of him.' Spooky pointed to the monitor screen, where a small white van with a property maintenance logo on the side was turning off the main road into Greenborough.

'Damn. I hoped we'd track him back to his lair.' Yvonne stared at the innocuous little van. 'Perfect cover vehicle, isn't it? You see them everywhere and take no notice at all. Plus, he can use it to ferry his incendiary materials without raising the slightest suspicion. He could have parked in the industrial estate where Clary was killed, and never attracted a second glance.'

'I've enhanced the image, just to see if there are any features that would identify it further. You know, like a busted wing mirror, or bodywork damage, though of course we do have the vehicle registration number.'

'Although it's no use whatsoever,' Yvonne grumbled. The van had passed an Automatic Number Plate Recognition camera and hadn't been recognised. It did throw up an attention drawn, but the plate was false, a random number that didn't exist.

'I thought you couldn't get plates made up without proof of identity and proof of entitlement?' said Spooky.

'Not legally.' Vonnie gave her a tired smile. 'But there's a dozen ways to get around it.'

'There always is.' Spooky pushed back her chair. 'I'm sorry, Vonnie. That's all I can do. The road he's turned down has no cameras, and neither do any of the other minor roads leading off it. We're stumped, I'm afraid.'

Yvonne got out of her chair and gathered up the printed images. 'Well, we have these, and we also know the direction he was heading, unless he was throwing us off the scent. Thanks, Spooks, much appreciated. I'd better go pass this on to the boss.'

* * *

John Carson closed his old notebooks and stared at them deep in thought. The year 2005 rang a bell in the recesses of his memory, but he'd scanned every case he'd attended at the time and nothing came to mind. Joseph had told him the incident might not have happened in the Greenborough area, which did muddy the waters somewhat, but in his work as an investigator he had covered a much wider stretch than the local police divisions.

John went upstairs to the bathroom. He stood at the basin, hardly recognising the face that stared back at him from the mirror. It was haggard, deeply etched with worry lines, the eyes were sunken, red and sore. He turned on the tap and splashed himself with cold water.

He had a very good memory, he knew. So it really wasn't one of his cases. He shut his eyes tight and concentrated while the chilly water ran down his face. Gradually his thoughts cleared. What had he heard from his colleagues at the time? Did one case in particular stand out?

He wiped his face with a towel and went back downstairs, opened the conservatory doors and stepped out into his garden. Everything drooped, sad and damp, but the cool autumn air kept his mind sharp. He ran through the different kinds of fires: house fires, car fires, fires in factories, storerooms, kitchens, barns, farm buildings, outbuildings . . . Wait!

Outbuildings! Could it . . . ? John ran back indoors and logged onto his computer. He searched for ten minutes but nothing came up. With a curse he picked up the phone and called his friend again, the man who'd been his counterpart for many years. After a few minutes, John put down the receiver and picked it up again immediately.

'Cameron? It's John Carson here. Can I come and see you? It's urgent. I think I've found the case that got this whole thing going.'

"Please, come over right away,' Cam said.

'I obviously wanted to tell Nikki and Joseph, but you need to hear about it first. I'm sorry, but it's far from straightforward.'

He heard a muttered curse on the other end of the line.

'Sorry, Cam. You're not going to like what I have to tell you, but I'm certain that I'm on the right track. I'm on my way.'

He practically threw the handset back on its rest, snatched up his coat and keys, and rushed out to his car.

CHAPTER TWENTY-ONE

Eve and Wendy sat in the church vestry while Leon went through the list of names. Eve watched his finger creep lower and lower down the list, and wondered whether her bright idea was so clever after all.

'That's it!' Leon's voice echoed through the church. 'You two ladies are angels!'

Wendy smiled. 'We're in the right place at least.'

'Well, Leon? Tell us,' said Eve.

'This name here. Applegarth. They're a prominent local family, one of the oldest names in this part of the Fens. William and Edith Applegarth are long gone, but years ago I knew their great granddaughter. She disappeared.'

Eve and Wendy glanced at each other.

'Go on,' said Wendy, a little too casually.

'Well, I studied theology for three years, then I did volunteer work in the community for a while to help my interpersonal skills. That was when I met Natalie Applegarth.'

Eve heard longing in the young man's voice and wondered if he'd had feelings for the girl.

'At first I thought she was a street kid.' He gave a tight laugh. 'I couldn't have been more wrong. Her father was one of the most influential men in the county. Not that he spent much time here. He was a diplomat, posted abroad somewhere. Anyway, she used to help out with community stuff, and over time we got quite friendly.'

Eve decided she was right. There was a sad honesty in his eyes when he talked about this girl.

'What I liked about her was the way she was completely unaffected by her family's status. To Natalie, it was just irrelevant. She was her own person. She had wealthy friends, and friends who were on the streets. She could communicate with anyone — with children, the elderly, academics and idiots. She was a very special person.'

'She obviously meant a lot to you, Leon.' Wendy smiled at him.

'She helped me, Mrs Avery. I knew I had a calling to go into the church, but it's still a massive decision to make. Natalie was able to put all my doubts and concerns into perspective. She is one of the reasons I am here now.'

'What happened to her, Leon?' asked Eve gently.

'I don't know. I guess I never will. We'd arranged to help the Salvation Army at a soup kitchen they ran, but she didn't turn up. I never saw her again.'

Tears glistened in Leon's eyes. He blinked.

'You made enquiries?' Wendy asked.

'Oh yes. I even went to her home. By then, the family had moved up the county to Cassington. I was told that Natalie was needed for a family reunion in, oh, Geneva, I think it was, and that she was considering staying and finishing her studies there.'

'Was that possible?' Eve said.

'It was possible, but far from probable. Natalie never let anyone down, and she knew I was expecting her. She wouldn't have left without a word, she just wouldn't.'

'Forgive me for asking,' Eve said, 'but what does this girl's surname have to do with the recent fires and the deaths? Why were you so distraught?'

'I hadn't considered it before, but I think Ronnie knew Natalie Applegarth, and possibly Clary did too. Michael,

I don't know about. But the police are looking for a link between the victims, and Natalie could be that link.' His eyes widened. 'And another thing. When I went to the house to look for her, I was told there'd been an incident a few nights before, a fire of some kind. They said a boy had been hurt. They were saying it was lucky that Natalie had already gone away. A fire! Does that mean something?'

'Yet another fire,' whispered Wendy. 'It certainly could.'

'You need to tell this to my daughter, Leon, right now! I think it's important.' Eve glanced at her watch. 'It's four o'clock. She'll still be at the station.'

'My car's in dock until tomorrow.'

'Come on, we'll take you.'

* * *

Nikki was getting anxious.

'I saw John Carson going into Cam's office over thirty minutes ago. What the hell is going on? Why aren't they keeping us in the loop?'

Joseph gnawed on his bottom lip. 'I don't know. I'm as worried as you are.'

'Ma'am? Sorry to interrupt, but you have a visitor, well, three actually.'

Nikki noticed a slight smile playing around Niall's lips. 'Well? Who is it? A deputation from the Women's Institute? Half the flock of St Saviours collecting for a new roof?'

'Very close on both scores, actually, ma'am.' Niall grinned broadly. 'It's your mother, Mrs Avery, and Leon Martin, the curate at St Saviours.'

'What on earth . . . ?'

'Shall I arrange an interview room? Or bring them in here?'

'Bring them up here, Niall, please.' She turned to Joseph. 'I dread to think what this is about. I thought the Daredevil Sisters had given up sleuthing and taken up gardening.'

'Didn't think it would last.' Joseph chuckled. 'But it could be important, if Leon's with them.'

When she'd heard what Leon had to say, Nikki silently blessed her mother for getting involved once more. Without Eve's dogged refusal to let a thing go, they might never have been given this piece of information.

'So far, other than you, Leon, we have found no connections at all between the killer's victims. So, if they all knew this Applegarth girl, and we'll assume for now that Michael did too, she is the link.' Nikki nodded slowly.

'Which makes it quite possible that though they never knew each other, they all knew Natalie,' Joseph mused. 'We need to find Natalie, no matter where she is. We have to talk to her.'

'I don't think you'll be able to, Sergeant.' Leon sighed. 'I tried for years. I'm sure her family sent her away. I have no proof, but they certainly didn't want me looking for her.'

'We might have a little more leverage than you, Leon, no offence meant.'

'None taken, Sergeant, and good luck to you. Just don't get your hopes up too soon.' Leon stared at the floor. 'Her father is a powerful man. I sometimes wonder if he sent her away because of me.'

'Why on earth would he do that?' Eve exclaimed.

'Maybe he didn't like the idea of his only daughter becoming a curate's wife.'

'The clergy not good enough for him?' Wendy said.

'No, it's not that. He had his own beliefs, and my faith didn't exactly conform.' He stared pointedly at Nikki. 'He was very chummy with the Black family from Ferry Street.'

That explained Leon's agitation when she asked him about satanists. It wasn't just because of his religious beliefs, it was more to do with losing the love of his life.

'Thank you for telling us all this. We'll start following it up immediately. And, Leon? If we should find out what happened to Natalie, or where she is now, do you want to know?'

'More than anything, DI Galena. If she's happy, all well and good. I'll leave it there. I wouldn't do anything to spoil her life.'

Nikki nodded. 'Okay. We'll be in touch, one way or the other.' She looked at her mother and Wendy, 'And it's back to Gardener's World for you two. We appreciate your assistance, but leave it with us now, okay?'

'Delighted we could be of some help to you.' Wendy's grin said, "But *we* got there before *you*, didn't we?"

Not long after they left, she and Joseph were finally called to the superintendent's office.

'At last!' And Nikki strode out of the office.

* * *

It was getting late, but Yvonne was haunted by the image of that little white van turning off the main drag and into a side street. So she decided to drive the same route herself.

The van had taken a well-known back-way that avoided the congested A-road running through the centre of Greenborough. You could either come back out onto the A-road much closer to the edge of town, or take one of several smaller roads. One had a parade of shops that catered almost exclusively to Eastern Europeans. Another led to a rabbit warren of cul-de-sacs full of bungalows for the elderly. This last road led into a more expensive area of town, with wider, tree-lined streets and older and more expensive dwellings.

He could have taken any one of them. He could have just circled back, but then he would have hit another CCTV camera, and Spooky had been certain there were no more sightings.

Yvonne drove slowly, trying to think of where he could be heading, keeping a sharp eye open for white vans. Common sense dictated that he hadn't gone into the bungalow estate. It was almost exclusively owned by a housing association that dealt in retirement homes.

The East European part of town was not a likely destination either. Few locals still lived along that stretch of road. That left the upmarket area.

Yvonne pulled over for a moment or two to consider the layout of Towergate Lane and its side roads. There were perhaps five or six of these, pleasant avenues consisting of "desirable" residences. For some reason, Yvonne was certain that here, behind someone's "desirable" garage door, a little white van was parked.

She was just about to start her reconnoitre when she noticed a group of four or five youths huddled together on the corner of the parade of Baltic shops. Yvonne narrowed her eyes. She knew them all. They were Carborough Estate lads, and prominent among them was the leader of the gang who had threatened the Blacks and their group in Ferry Street. 'Now, what are you boys up to, I wonder?' she said to herself. Then she noticed their odd behaviour. They were usually a cocky bunch, all testosterone and attitude, but today they looked more like a gathering of people who'd just received bad news, or had witnessed a fatal accident.

Yvonne sat back in her seat and watched carefully. After a bit of desultory conversation, they drifted off, leaving their leader alone. He stood for a moment as if unsure of what to do. Then Yvonne saw that one side of his face was severely bruised.

She slammed the car door and hurried over. 'Lee? A word, please. What on earth happened to you, son?'

Lee Brown stared at the pavement, his hands shoved deep in his jeans pockets. He said nothing.

'That looks nasty. Have you had treatment for it?'

And it did look nasty. Yvonne had seen a few beatings in her time, and she knew a fractured cheekbone when she saw one. She gently said, 'You might be a right little shit at times, Lee, but whoever did that to you needs a good talking to.' She touched his arm lightly. 'I'll certainly do that if I know who to look for.'

She felt the boy flinch at her touch. His face wasn't the only part of him to take a battering. 'I think you could do with a lift, lad. Come on. I'll take you to A&E and get you checked over.'

Instead of replying, the boy suddenly jack-knifed forward and retched.

Yvonne stepped back quickly. If you valued your boot leather, you got pretty good at that after years of Friday-night patrols. Then she saw the blood. 'Okay, Lee. Sit down.' She helped him to the ground and leaned him back against a wall, then radioed for assistance. 'Ambulance, please. Corner of Sadler's Parade and South Street. Name, Lee Brown, eighteen-year-old male. Collapse, following severe beating. Conscious but vomiting blood.'

Lee was now struggling to breathe. Yvonne suspected either a pneumothorax or a haemothorax as a result of a chest injury. Probably broken ribs after a vicious kicking. She relayed that to control and spoke softly to the boy, telling him that help was on its way.

'Lee? Who did this to you? You have to tell me.' Yvonne was seriously worried that this might finish up as a murder inquiry. 'Come on, son. Who was it?'

A look of terror passed across his battered face. 'Can't.' He gagged. 'Daren't.'

Somehow she managed to keep him conscious until the paramedics arrived.

'Good job you found him, Vonnie,' said one of the technicians. 'Biddy' Baxter had been on the ambulances almost as long as Yvonne had been a policewoman. 'He's in a pretty bad way.'

'Well, he's a pretty bad boy, but he didn't deserve this.' She paused. 'Well, I hope he didn't. You can never tell with some of these tearaways.'

As the ambulance moved off, Yvonne began to think about the boys he'd been talking to. One of them was a teenager, a bit younger than the others, a boy called Tiger Boxall. She knew where he lived and had noted which way he'd gone.

Yvonne returned to her car and turned it around. Not far from the town centre she found Tiger talking to another group of teens. Again, there was no banter, no bravado, just earnest, hushed conversation. She parked the car, walked over and the little gang dematerialised like fen mist. But she only wanted Tiger, and one commanding yell, something she had perfected over the years, brought him to a sharp halt.

'You do know your mate Lee's on his way to hospital and is fighting for his life?'

Tiger suddenly found something terribly important under one of his fingernails.

'Who hurt him, Tiger?'

The finger still held his attention. Yvonne took a step closer.

The lad pulled his hoodie tighter round his face. 'Dunno, Constable Collins, honest.'

'Tell me, because I'll find out one way or another, but if it takes too long, someone else could finish up with blood pouring into their lungs and choking up on the pavement. Someone just like you, Tiger.'

His face paled, making the spots stand out. His Adam's apple rose and fell. 'I don't know! That's the truth! I promised not to say, but it was a warning, right? They threatened his family too. He said they told him to back off or, yeah, you're right, the same thing could happen to us.' He looked at her with wide eyes. 'Can I go now?'

She nodded and stared after his retreating figure. Why was she thinking about the Black House? Surely that wouldn't be their way? They said they hated violence, and neither of the Black brothers looked the type to send the boys round.

She walked back to her car, deep in thought. Whatever had happened to Lee Brown, the Black House meetings should now take place in safety. Was that just luck? Or had something more sinister happened?

Too late now to start hunting for white van man, Yvonne drove back to the station full of a nagging doubt about the peaceful followers of Lucifer, supposed bringer of light.

CHAPTER TWENTY-TWO

Nikki exploded. 'Only *we* could inherit a problem like this! For heaven's sake, what kind of police force have we become? Our hands are tied tighter than a bloody villain in cuffs!'

They allowed the rant to subside. 'No one here is disagreeing with that,' Cam said. 'We just need to work out a way to proceed that won't bring someone barging in and shutting us down.'

Nikki shuddered. That very thing had happened only too recently, right here in this station. 'Okay. John, can we run though the basics again? I need to get this straight in my head.'

John nodded. 'It starts with a 999 call on November fourth, to a fire in the grounds of a big rambling old house on the borders of the Fens and the Wolds, a village called Cassington. When the fire service get there, they find an extensive Victorian summerhouse on fire and five young people out on the lawns. One has serious burns. It's clear they were using the summerhouse to hold a clandestine party. Most of the survivors are the worse for drink, or maybe drugs. By the time the firefighters bring it under control, the owners of the house have taken the teenagers inside and are caring for them. One is taken to hospital and subsequently transferred to Nottingham.'

'And we think we're talking about Michael Porter, right?' Nikki said.

'I believe so, although there are no records of the names of those that were present. The owners didn't want to press charges and had the youngsters driven home as soon as they'd been checked over and were fit to leave. The owner was a very rich man with a lot of clout. He had three children himself and said they often allowed their friends to use the summer-house. He maintained it was his fault for not making sure that the old place was better secured.'

'So no one died in the fire?' Nikki asked.

'No. There was no evidence to suggest that,' John said.

'And none of the owner's children were actually at this party?' Joseph queried.

'All away from home that night. In fact, they were out of the country — some annual family thing in Switzerland. The parents were supposed to have flown out the following day to join them, after some important meeting that the father had to attend.'

'But we aren't allowed to know the name of the family,' Nikki growled. 'Or where exactly this took place.'

'As someone was injured, my friend from fire and res-cue was sent along as a matter of course, but found himself suddenly taken to HQ and told no further action was to be taken. Even though it appeared that the youngsters had broken in, the owner assumed responsibility. The fire was a simple accident. Case closed.' John raised his eyebrows. 'He wasn't happy. He was a good investigator and sensed that something wasn't right about the situation. A small area, a kind of anteroom with a couch and some bookshelves was relatively undamaged, and there he found several brightly coloured packets with odd names like "bath salts" on them.'

'NPS. Bloody legal highs,' Nikki said angrily.

'We think that's the reason the owners were anxious to hush it up. As I said, he was an influential man, although I don't know what in exactly.'

'A whitewash to keep his family name untainted by association with drugs,' Joseph added.

'And if we tie all this in with what we've just learned from Leon Martin, we have an even bigger mystery — and a dilemma. Because *we* know the name of the family. It's Applegarth, and Daddy Applegarth is, if Leon is correct, a diplomat.'

'But Michael Porter told the curate that a teenager had died in the accident where he was burnt. Said it wasn't his fault, but he felt guilty.' Joseph was struggling to make sense of what they knew. 'It had to be the same accident. He said drink and drugs were involved. In fact, he mentioned legal highs by name.'

'Plus he said it happened on Mischief Night, which is November fourth,' Nikki added.

'And on that night, no other serious injuries were reported across the county, no fires, no fatalities,' concluded John. 'I think you're right. It *had* to be that particular incident.'

'So who died?' asked Cam, rubbing at his temples.

'My money's on the girl Leon had fallen in love with, Natalie Applegarth.'

'But she was out of the country, according to her father,' said John.

'Diplomats have silver tongues. Maybe Natalie *was* at the party. Someone had to invite the other kids. Maybe the family covered it up rather than have their daughter labelled a drug addict.' Nikki grimaced. 'We've seen far worse things happen to protect some precious family name.'

Cam shook his head. 'How could they possibly magic her body out of a burning building, and then make it disappear before the fire service arrived? That's pushing the bounds of possibility a bit too far, don't you think?'

'Then show me Natalie,' Nikki said flatly.

'If her father finds out that we're looking into his family in an official capacity, we'll end up with no jobs.' Cam gave Nikki a long, knowing stare.

'Ah, so we look into them in an *unofficial* capacity!'

'I never heard that.'

'Good, because I never said it.' Nikki rubbed her hands together. 'Two things bother me, John. You said there were five teenagers when your colleagues got to the fire, didn't you?'

'Yes. The injured boy and four others.' He glanced down at some notes he had scribbled. 'My friend thought the fire crew said there were three boys and two girls.'

'Ronnie, Michael, Jez and Clary. Only four deaths so far, so if someone is trying to murder all the kids at the party, then there's one more to come.' She exhaled loudly. 'Probably another female.'

'And the other thing, Nikki?' asked John.

'The Applegarth children. Any idea how old they were at the time?'

'No one said. Although if they were bringing their mates around to hang out, I'd say a similar age to the kids at the party — seventeen, eighteen, nineteen?'

Nikki turned to Joseph. 'We need to see Leon again. We need every bit of info about Natalie that we can get. Then we dig deeper.' She looked at Cam and smiled sweetly. 'And do it very, very quietly.'

* * *

Nikki phoned her mother to find out if they'd dropped Leon off yet. Eve said he was still with them.

'Where are you, Mum? We have some more questions for Leon, and it's pretty urgent.'

'Café des Amis, just round the corner, Nikki. Poor chap seemed so low we thought we'd treat him to a coffee and a chocolate éclair before we took him home.'

'Stay there, Mum. We'll come and join you.'

'Any excuse for a slice of cake,' muttered Joseph.

'Actually I thought he'd be more relaxed talking away of the station. That's all.' Nikki sniffed.

'So you won't be having your usual apricot Danish while you're there?'

'I hadn't even thought about it, but now you mention it, bring some money, will you?'

'Me and my big mouth.' Joseph checked he had his wallet and followed her out. 'Your mother looks so much more relaxed, doesn't she?'

Nikki nodded. 'I just hope it was a temporary wobble, a bit of a delayed reaction to what happened to her friends.'

'It wouldn't be surprising, would it? Everything happened so quickly and Eve was heavily involved. She never had the chance to grieve at the time.'

'And neither did Wendy and the others. Maybe that's why they all feel so shaky.' Nikki paused. 'Oh, don't let me forget. Rene and Lou are going to be at Monks Lantern this weekend. If we can steal half an hour, I'd love to see them again.'

'Me too.' Joseph chuckled. 'What an amazing group of women! If it hadn't been so terrifying, it would have made a great film comedy.'

'*Ladies in Lavender* meets *The Dirty Dozen*? Something like that?'

'Or *Cocoon* — the 2018 version.'

* * *

Joseph placed their coffees on the table, and Nikki was relieved to see a Danish pastry. She smiled at Leon. 'I know it's late and I'm sorry to have to take more of your time, but there are some things we are very anxious to know.'

Leon sipped at his second coffee. 'What can I tell you?'

'I know this will be painful, but we have to learn all we can about Natalie Applegarth.'

Leon looked at them apprehensively. 'I'm not going to ask why, because I think I can guess.' He sighed. 'So, what do you need to know?'

'Well, we understand she has siblings. Would you know their names and how old they are?'

Leon frowned. 'Let's see. The oldest was Polly, her sister. She'd be around thirty-one by now. Then there was Natalie, the middle child, and then Lyndon, her brother. He was two years younger than Nat, so he'd be twenty-seven, I think, or thereabouts.'

'And were they close?' asked Joseph.

'Very close, although they were all completely different. I've told you what Nat was like. Polly was the complete opposite. She was very good with figures, down-to-earth but not a people person. Lyndon was clever with his hands. He liked the natural world and exploring. Nat used to say she could see him in one of those natural history documentaries, striding through rainforests or trudging through snow to find some rare plant or bird.'

'We need to trace them, Leon, but we have a big problem.' Nikki looked at him.

'Don't tell me — Daddy! Richard Applegarth.'

'Kind of. He's a diplomat, and they have certain privileges—'

'And they also have the ability to talk their way out of anything,' interrupted Leon, his tone bitter. 'It's what they do. They protect interests, they facilitate strategic agreements, they resolve differences. DI Galena, this man is no ordinary citizen, and he has the state behind him all the way. He's their spokesman, and a member of a very exclusive profession.'

Nikki mulled this over, chewing a mouthful of pastry. 'It's true. We've already been told not to proceed with any investigation into the Applegarth family. That's why we need your help, Leon, and why we are not climbing all over his stately home and gardens. Anything you can tell us could help. Any small thing that she mentioned to you, no matter how insignificant it seemed, could be vital.'

Joseph leaned closer, adding, 'We are sure that Natalie is the key to everything.'

'You think Natalie is the girl who died, don't you? If what Michael Porter told me was true, then she was the girl who died in the fire that injured him.' Leon's voice shook. 'You think she's dead.'

'I hate to say it,' Nikki felt a wave of sadness for Leon, 'but I'm afraid we do.'

'Leon? Would it have been unusual for the three siblings to bugger off to Geneva for some family bash?' asked Nikki.

'Not exactly. As you know, her father spent most of his time abroad, and his brother lived in Geneva. Natalie went there on several occasions in the time that I knew her.'

'But at such short notice? What did he have? A private plane?'

'Actually, yes. I don't know about now, but he used to fly out of Greenborough Airfield on a regular basis. A six-seater Beechcraft Bonanza.'

Nikki glanced at Joseph. 'So they could have gone to Switzerland.'

'But if she was as nice as Leon says, she wouldn't have gone away without telling him, would she?' Joseph said.

'You're right, she just wouldn't.' Leon looked close to tears. 'I didn't say before, but it wasn't just the Salvation Army soup kitchen that we were meeting to help with that day. She was going to answer a question I'd put to her the day before.'

'You'd asked her to marry you,' said Eve softly. She and Wendy, both signatories to the Official Secrets Act, had been listening quietly.

Leon nodded. 'It was a huge step for both of us. I mean, marriage is a big thing for anybody, but with my calling and her high-profile family . . . We were both young, and we had a lot to take into consideration. I didn't want to rush her, but I did suggest it.' He stared into his coffee. 'Now I wish I'd spoken earlier, said, "Be damned, let's just do it." *If only* are the saddest two words I know.'

'I'm sorry.' Eve placed her hand on his arm. 'It's very hard to lose the one you love.'

Nikki avoided looking at her mother, not wanting to see the hurt that Eve still felt over Nikki's father.

With his usual sensitivity, Joseph broke the silence. 'We need to know the truth. And you do too, don't you, Leon? Will you work with us?'

Leon nodded. 'Of course. And you're right. It's time for me to move forward, and that means finding the truth, for Natalie's sake as much as mine.'

'Good man.' Joseph gave him an encouraging smile. 'We'd rather not talk at the station — walls have ears even there. Would the church be a good place?'

'I can't think of anywhere better, although,' he paused, 'there are a couple of meetings going on there this evening, so maybe . . .'

'Come to Monks Lantern,' Eve said, with an enquiring look at Wendy.

'Of course,' said Wendy. 'We'll take Leon and go on ahead. See you two there.'

* * *

Eve and Wendy left them to it, and Nikki, Joseph and Leon sat in the lounge. 'How did Natalie view her father's career?' Joseph asked. 'Was she proud of him? Did she resent his living abroad for so long?'

Leon thought about this. 'She loved him very much, I know that. But, she didn't love a lot of the people he mixed with, the hangers-on, the ones who wanted to bask in his glory or take advantage of his position. And I think she did come to resent his work as she got older. She said it was great fun living in foreign countries when she was a kid, and she learned several different languages, but later she wanted to settle here.'

'So they were pretty solid as a family, even though they were privileged and very wealthy? No weak links in the chain?' Nikki asked.

'Absolutely none. I was the problem. I was not in their class, plus I was, and still am, totally dedicated to God and the Church.'

'Don't have a go at me, Leon, but I have to ask. Was Applegarth a Satanist? Or one of these Luciferians?'

'I don't honestly know, DI Galena. I assumed that he was because of his relationship with the Black family. They were very friendly. And he just didn't like the fact that I was ordained into the church. That was why I wanted Natalie to think carefully about marrying me. She loved her family, and I know she loved me, but I couldn't make her choose between us. It wouldn't have been fair.'

'Have you ever seen any of her siblings since Natalie supposedly went abroad to live?' Joseph asked.

Leon frowned. 'No, I haven't. I've seen the father and the mother, but not Polly and Lyndon.'

'You actually met them, did you?' Nikki said.

'Yes, on the one or two social occasions when her father actually tolerated my presence.'

'You liked them?'

'Lyndon, yes. I could appreciate his love for nature, and he was a likeable guy, but I found Polly a bit intimidating. She was blunt to the point of rudeness. She had a superior, "academic" air that I never managed to penetrate, even though I'd been to university myself.'

'Did they know about your plans?'

He shook his head. 'Oh no, and I'm sure Natalie wouldn't have said anything without speaking to me first.'

'I suppose you don't have the uncle's address in Geneva, do you?' Joseph chanced.

'No, sorry. But I do know he was CEO of a big fund-raising organisation. Natalie was very fond of him. I think he inspired her, and lit the fuse for her own charity work. His name is Clive Applegarth.'

'That's a start.' Nikki looked at Joseph, then nodded towards the door.

Outside in the hallway she said, 'Off the record, I'm going to ask Spooky to do a little private work for us. Strictly unofficial, from her personal computer at home.'

'Can you ask her to do that? That's a custodial offence if she gets caught hacking into diplomatic immunity.' Joseph looked mildly horrified.

'One, do you want another girl condemned to the flames?'

'Of course not, but—'

'And two, I'm not asking her to hack into anything. I want her to use perfectly legal channels, just not from the police station. I promise you I won't be asking her to infiltrate Daddy Applegarth's personal affairs. I would just like a few details on Natalie's Uncle Clive.' Nikki smiled sweetly. 'And Spooky will love it, believe me.'

Nikki walked back into the room. 'We need to get back. Thank you, Leon. I know that was hard for you. Can we run you back to town?'

'No thanks, DI Galena. Your mother and Wendy have kindly asked me to stay for supper, then she said she'd take me home. But thank you.' He stood up and offered his hand. 'This has been cathartic. I've had my head in the sand for far too long.'

As they left, Nikki wondered about Leon. He was both complicated and direct at the same time. She wondered how he would really feel if they found that Natalie Applegarth had indeed died.

* * *

Nikki and Joseph reported in to Cam, and then decided to call it a day. The others had gone home and there was little more they could do.

They drove home mostly in silence, then Joseph suddenly said, 'Do you think we're becoming a bit blasé about our relationship, now we know that Cam is so laid back about us? I'd hate to inadvertently ruin things.'

Nikki hadn't even considered that point. 'Like using the same car so much?'

'Yes, and generally being so . . .'

'Comfortable?' She smiled. 'If Cam doesn't take the job permanently, then we'll reassess, okay? But right now, we're fine, I know we are. And it makes perfect sense for neighbours to car share on occasions.'

CHAPTER TWENTY-THREE

'Sergeant Farrow? I think I've found what PC Collins was asking for yesterday.' Chris Hale, a young rookie PC, stood in front of Niall's desk. He had been given the task of sitting through hours of CCTV footage from the Greenborough streets.

'Good. I'll come and take a look,' Niall said. He walked down to where Chris had paused the recording.

'I picked up Lee Brown leaving the pool hall down Brewer Street at 10.37 p.m., Sarge. From the direction he took, I reckoned he was on his way home. Then, as he turned into Bloxham Alley, on the outskirts of the Carborough, this happens . . .'

Niall watched as two men came out of the shadows and manhandled Lee up against a wall. The area was rundown, occupied mostly by old disused stores. There were no houses.

One of the men delivered a vicious punch to Lee's gut. Niall winced. They then hauled him up straight, and brought their faces close to his. Niall could see that they were shouting at him.

Lee Brown struggled. He was no angel, Niall knew, but these two thugs outclassed him. Niall was forced to sit and watch a young man being beaten relentlessly. It wasn't a part of his job that Niall enjoyed. Violence on this level sickened him.

'This bit might be of interest, Sarge.' Chris pointed as the two attackers stood and watched their victim writhing on the pavement. One raised a hand, as if he were about to do a high five, then the other man did the same, but instead of the usual slap, they did a strange punching motion with their fists. 'Some kind of gangland thing?' Chris asked.

'Not sure, but good lad for noticing it. That could help, if we can find out who uses that sign.'

Niall had seen a lot of different gangland signature hand signs, but he didn't recognise this one. 'Print me off a couple of stills of those two guys, Chris, both their faces *and* that hand thing they did, and if you can, get them enhanced, okay?'

Chris nodded. 'I'll do it now, Sarge.'

Niall went back to his desk. He was pretty sure these two weren't local. He had spent years on the streets and still recalled most of their villains. They might not even have been British. There was something about them that just didn't fit with the Fens. And that strange gesture. He hoped Vonnie would get back soon. Without her to confer with, he felt as if his right arm was missing.

He sighed. He'd better hurry up and get used to it. Vonnie would be retiring soon. Things changed, he knew, nothing stayed the same forever. But that didn't stop him missing their time together on the streets. They were very different, but they'd made a great team, and he still felt like a shit for breaking up that partnership.

Come on, Farrow, he told himself, *get a grip,* and he pulled out his phone and rang her. 'Vonnie? Got some pictures of your villain taking a beating. Are you free to come back to base?'

* * *

When she received Nikki's call, Spooky told her techies that she'd be going out for a while, and left the station.

Five minutes later, she was sitting on a bench in a tiny garden close to the banks of the Westland River. After another few minutes, Nikki sat down beside her.

'This is unorthodox.' Spooky grinned and ran her hand through her dark, shaggy hair.

'More than you know.'

Spooky looked at Nikki's grave expression and wondered what was so terribly wrong. 'Alright, how can I help?' She listened with growing concern as Nikki explained. 'So you think another woman is in danger, but you can't use the usual channels to carry out your enquiries?'

'Exactly. I need to trace the whereabouts of three members of the Applegarth family. A woman named Polly, a man called Lyndon, and their uncle. I really need to speak to the uncle, but I don't know how to get in touch with him, not without bringing Armageddon down on my head.'

'His name?'

'Clive Applegarth. Used to live in Geneva and as far as we know, still does. Brother to diplomat Richard Applegarth, hence the problem.'

'Leave it with me,' Spooky said. 'I have a secure laptop at home, with some brilliant software. I'll do a little ferreting and report back to you.'

Nikki touched her arm. 'Nothing illegal, Spooky, and I mean that. I shouldn't even be asking you to do this. I'm sure there'll be something in the public domain that can lead us to the Applegarths. The uncle is a fundraiser, so it seems logical to start with him. We just can't do it from HQ. You don't *have* to do it either, and I mean that.'

Spooky shrugged. 'How do you think I'd feel if another woman died, and I could have helped?'

'As bad as me, I guess.' Nikki gave her arm a squeeze. 'But be careful, won't you?'

'Oh, Nikki! There's a wealth of stuff out there if you know where and *how* to look. Plus I know how to search without being spied on.' Spooky stood up. 'I'll go now. I can be home and back to the station before you've ordered your second coffee of the day, how's that?'

'If you can find anything that might help us, I'll be in your debt forever.'

Spooky had never seen Nikki look so worried.

* * *

On her way to the police station, Yvonne saw a vehicle she recognised pulling out of Ferry Street. Billie Seager. The sight of his "Graffiti Cleaning and Removal Company" van set alarm bells ringing.

She waved him down.

'Haven't been to the Black House by any chance, have you, Billie?' she said.

'Spot on, Vonnie. Little shits did a smashing job of redecorating that lovely old house.'

'When did it happen?'

'Night before last. They found it when they got up. We did a lot of work on it yesterday but there was still a bit of ghosting, so I came back this morning to sort it.' He smiled at her cheerfully.

Yvonne knew the culprit wasn't Lee, unless he'd done it before getting attacked. Possible, she supposed. 'Maybe I should pop in and see if they want to report it.'

'I told them to call you guys, but they said they didn't want any more hassle. They just wanted it gone.'

'Okay, well, thanks Billie. Give my love to the wife.'

'Will do. You take care, Vonnie.'

Yvonne watched the van drive away, turning this news over in her head. Was it coincidence that Lee'd been given a good thumping, very shortly after the Black House had been vandalised? The Blacks had both declared that they abhorred violence, but was that true? Had someone from their little coven decided to warn the louts off in language they could understand?

Yvonne was glad Niall had asked her to check that CCTV footage. She could run her concerns past him, and see what he thought. She smiled to herself, certain he would think exactly as she had . . . that there was no such thing as coincidence.

* * *

Eve and Wendy sat at the kitchen table in Monks Lantern and talked over what they'd heard the night before. 'That young man needs some definitive answers, doesn't he?' said Eve.

Wendy nodded. 'He'll never find peace if he doesn't.' She stirred her drink and stared into the cup. 'We could help, of course.'

'I'd thought of that,' Eve said, 'but . . .' She shrugged. She had promised Nikki that they'd keep to the garden.

Wendy sighed. 'I guess it comes down to a matter of conscience. If we have the capacity, which we *do*, shouldn't we use it to help? I'm wondering whether Nikki and Joseph spoke so freely in front of us because they were asking for our help.' She put down her teaspoon and looked at Eve. 'It won't be pleasant for us, just when we were feeling so much freer from past events, but,' she shrugged, 'it would only be a single phone call, and poor Leon does need answers.'

Eve wholeheartedly agreed, though she was still anxious about Nikki. She had worried her badly on the last case, and had sworn that she would never again cause her daughter such grief.

'Why don't *I* make a few enquiries, Eve?'

Eve wondered if her friend could read minds.

'I could very easily make the odd call, a casual chat with an old friend, and not even mention it to you until afterwards.'

'You could.' Eve smiled slowly.

'I think that would be agreeable to all concerned, don't you?'

'Absolutely. But there is one other thing.' Eve set down her cup. 'We are both agreed that, somehow, Natalie died on the night of the fire?'

'And because drugs and drink were involved, the family hushed it up.'

Eve drew in a breath. 'So, if we start asking questions, we could be opening up a very nasty can of worms because, if Natalie did die, what the hell happened to her body?'

Wendy puffed out her cheeks. '*But*, if someone in a position of trust and privilege chose to act dishonestly, he should be investigated, shouldn't he?'

Eve knew she was right, but she continued to hesitate. In the past, her life had been her own to do what she wished with. She had come close to death last year, and because of the close bond that she'd recently forged with her daughter, suddenly she had someone else to consider. However, right was right, and wrong was something that needed to be addressed. 'Make your call, Wendy. And even though I know nothing about it, give David my best, won't you?'

With a grin, Wendy pulled her smartphone from her pocket.

'David! How are you?' She glanced up at Eve. 'I'm sorry but we need your help again.' She paused. 'Thank you, I appreciate it.' She ended the call. 'He's ringing back from a different line.'

As they waited for the call, Eve wondered what on earth they had set in motion.

* * *

Yvonne stared at the CCTV images of the men who had attacked Lee Brown. 'I've never seen either of those men before. They're strangers to this area, no doubt about it. Vicious bastards, too.' She squinted at the peculiar handshake and shook her head. 'Not something I've come across either, but I know someone who might be able to explain it.' She looked at Niall and raised an eyebrow.

'Mickey Leonard?'

She smiled. 'I might just take a stroll down to the engineers where he works, and show him these.' She waved the printouts. 'Can I pinch them?'

'Be my guest, Vonnie. The sooner we get these guys off the streets, the happier I'll be.'

Yvonne had to hide her smile. Niall really cared, unlike some of the others that had drifted into the job in recent years. 'Niall? I need to run something past you. Do you remember Billie Seager?'

'Graffiti Bill? Of course.' Niall laughed. 'Used to spray-paint any available surface right across the town, then met a girl and settled down, only to open a graffiti removal company! Great stuff that. Why?'

'I saw him this morning. He had just finished cleaning up the Black House.'

Niall's smile vanished. 'Ah. You're thinking Lee Brown?'

'Probably. He's pretty handy with an aerosol can. Now he's in hospital.' She swore she could hear the cogs whirring in Niall's brain.

'Surely not? I thought the Blacks were pacifists or something?' His face darkened. 'Or maybe all that spiel was just for our benefit.'

'I wish I knew. That family has me well confused.'

'Not like you, Vonnie. Must be a first.'

Yvonne mumbled something unintelligible.

'Want me to swan past?' Niall looked at her hopefully. 'Tell them I'd seen the graffiti, and wondered if they'd like to make a complaint? I'd like to get my nose in there.'

'I think they're too canny for that, my friend. A sergeant, enquiring about a bit of random property defacing? With our budgets? I don't think so. You'd be hard pushed to get a PCSO to follow that up.'

'But it's not the first incident, is it? I could have read your report, then seen the graffiti, and being such a dedicated officer, decided to take action. I'd be able to give you the benefit of my valuable opinion on the Black family then.'

Yvonne shrugged. 'Okay, but I'll bet you don't get across the doorstep.'

'You're on.' He held up his hand for a high five. 'Loser buys coffee and doughnuts. Sorry I can't afford any more than that. I have a wife and dog to support.'

Yvonne slapped his hand. 'Get yer money ready.'

* * *

Spooky walked into the office, her face a tapestry of frustration and pique.

'Not good news, I'm afraid.' She plonked herself down into a chair. 'For starters, Clive Applegarth, the uncle, is dead. He died of septicaemia after some kind of lung infection. That's a matter of common knowledge and it was posted on the net by a big charity organisation. Lyndon's sister, Polly Applegarth, now Polly Favre, is still living in Geneva. She's a statistician, married with one child. She has a job as an analyst for a technology company. I found all that on LinkedIn.' She ran her hand through her hair. 'And that is that. No more. No mention anywhere of Natalie or Lyndon. It's as if they went into hiding after the fire happened.'

'That's not exactly awful, Spooks.' Nikki smiled at her. 'Polly is a good lead, and if she's putting herself out there on social media, we can probably find out more.'

Spooky glowered at her. 'Thanks for being nice to me, but we both know you need a hell of a lot more than that.' She scratched her cheek. 'There are other ways, Nikki. I could—'

'No! Definitely not. This is too sensitive. We'll find another route to get to Natalie. Don't worry, and thank you for what you *have* discovered. At least we won't be busting a gut looking for a dead man. And we know Polly is alive and settled with her own family. Maybe Lyndon did what Natalie always thought he would, and buggered off to some rainforest to chase rare bugs.'

But Spooky looked grim. 'And Natalie? Personally, I think she didn't go anywhere that night. Certainly not to

Switzerland. Young people these days live through technology. They spend their lives glued to their smartphones. Natalie and Lyndon have left no footprint anywhere, and that's strange.' Spooky gave Nikki a despairing look. 'I have a very strong feeling that something happened, not only to Natalie, but to Lyndon too. He's not even thirty yet, son of a diplomat, well-off and apparently good-looking, and he might just as well not exist.'

'The trouble is,' Nikki said, 'we can't use proper police channels, or illegal ones either. We can't even find out if they boarded a flight to Geneva that night. We're totally stuffed.'

'So, you've been banned from contacting Applegarth himself, and the only people that could have told us what really happened that night, that is, the kids at the party, are all dead.' Spooky muttered a curse.

'Bar one, and as we don't know who she is, that's about as helpful as a chocolate poker,' Nikki grumbled.

'I'm sorry, Nikki. I feel I've let you down.'

'Don't be daft. That's just how it goes with police work. You follow a lead, it dries up. You chase another one, same thing happens. But then you get a lucky break. Let's just hope this one appears before another woman dies.'

Spooky stood up. 'I won't give up. If I think of something else, I'll try again and don't worry, I'll do it from home.'

'But no hacking, understand? I don't want you losing a damned good job because of one of my investigations.'

Spooky sighed. 'Understood.'

* * *

Mickey wiped his hands on a paper towel. 'Sorry, Vonnie. I've never seen that one before, and living on the Carborough I thought I'd seen them all.'

Mickey Leonard was the adopted son of the only law-abiding member of the Leonards. Like a Mafia clan, the Leonard family had run the Carborough Estate for years. Archie, the oldest member, had been one of the last of the old-school "honourable" villains, and he and Nikki Galena had struck up an unlikely friendship. He had died not long ago, and his son Raymond had taken up the sceptre. Nikki and Joseph had saved Mickey's life back in the bad old days, and he'd remained loyal to them ever since. He acted as a willing go-between and helped them whenever he could.

Now he held his hand out for the pictures. 'Can I have those? There's a lad I know who works in the pool hall down by the docks. He sees a lot down there. Maybe he could identify that sign for you?'

Yvonne smiled at him. 'I could go find him, Mickey, if you give me his name.' But she already knew what his answer would be.

'Ah, well, no offence, Vonnie, but he'd run a mile if he saw your uniform come through the door. I'll go down there tonight when I finish work, okay? And I'll ring you. Might be late, though.'

Yvonne gave him her mobile number. 'Thanks, Mickey. No problem, I'll wait for your call.'

Yvonne walked back to the station, wondering where those two thugs could possibly have come from. And if they weren't from the area, why pick on Lee Brown? He was hardly someone who merited the attention of some powerful gang from another town. Again, her thoughts returned to the Black House. Their church, for want of a better word, apparently had a large following of powerful people, but would any of them stoop to such a brutal warning? Joseph and Ben had mentioned secret societies that were a front for all manner of illegal goings on — fraud, money-laundering, and embezzlement. She hoped she'd lose her bet with Niall. If he did manage to get in, he might see something she'd missed. It would be well worth getting him a coffee and a doughnut!

CHAPTER TWENTY-FOUR

Around lunchtime, Nikki was called to the front desk. She was seized with panic when she saw Wendy Avery waiting for her. Was something wrong with Eve?

'I wondered if I could have a few moments of your time?' Wendy said.

'Of course.' Nikki hesitated. 'There's nothing wrong, is there?'

'Oh no. It's just that I have some information for you. I know that Eve promised to keep strictly to her house and garden, so I've been a bit naughty and kept her out of it.'

Nikki led the way to her office and offered Wendy a drink that was declined. 'I won't take up too much of your time, I promise.' She lowered her voice. 'Do you remember David Danbury?'

'Your friend in GCHQ? How could I forget him? I'm not sure how things would have panned out without his help.'

'Well, as a matter of fact, I spoke to him this morning.' Wendy raised her eyebrows.

Nikki narrowed her eyes. 'Oh, really? And did he have anything interesting to say?'

'Interesting, but I'm not sure that it's terribly helpful to you.' Wendy avoided Nikki's stare. 'He was kind enough to make a few low-key enquiries for me, just a bit of background on the Applegarth family.'

'And?'

'It appears that Richard Applegarth's happy family life fell to pieces at around the time of the fire in the summer-house. David didn't mention the fire, you understand, I just calculated the dates.' Wendy took a breath. 'David said that it followed a family get-together in Geneva. You already know he shipped the whole family off to Switzerland for a reunion party, well, Natalie was apparently taken ill and never attended. Lyndon and Polly were there, but then Lyndon came down with the same thing, reportedly a stomach bug. Richard told his friends and family that Natalie was probably not really ill, but angry with him for vetoing her "inappropriate" relationship with a religious man. He thought she'd get over it if he took her away from England, but he said it must have made the situation worse, because shortly afterwards, Natalie left home.'

Nikki puffed out her cheeks. 'Convenient.'

'Absolutely. Then David told me that two years later, Lyndon upped and left to live in France, leaving only Polly in Switzerland, where she married a scientist.' Wendy shrugged. 'As I said, not much help, is it?'

'I think it is.' Nikki thought carefully. 'So, there is a very good chance she never left the Fens in the first place.'

'You need to know about that flight out of the country, and exactly who was on it,' mused Wendy. 'I could ask David to dig deeper.'

Nikki pulled a face. 'I better not, Wendy. I know we can trust David, but I don't think I want to push things any further. If I get found out, my superintendent's neck will be on the block, as well as mine, and the whole team with me. Thanks, but right now, I'll hold fire.'

'Then I have one more suggestion.' Wendy's smile was mischievous. 'As you know, I hold a pilot's licence, and I've been flying locally for years. What if I could track down the Applegarths' private pilot from the time of the fire? We are a pretty close community and I know a whole lot of flyers. It's a thought, isn't it?'

'Now that I can handle! But Wendy, be very careful who you talk to, won't you?'

Wendy sighed. 'I've been through wars, DI Galena, and worked at a very high level in the MOD. What do you think I'm going to do? Wave a banner with the Applegarth name on it?'

'Sorry,' said Nikki, chastened. 'I'm just so on edge about this case, I was forgetting your history.'

'You're forgiven.' Wendy stood up. 'I must get back.'

'How much does my mother know about this, Wendy?' Nikki asked with a smile. 'Everything?'

'Some, but it was my decision to talk to David, not hers. And, Nikki, she does respect your wishes as much as she can. It really bothers her, though I suspect that if the boot was on the other foot, you'd do exactly what you thought necessary if it meant catching a killer.'

Nikki nodded slowly. 'I know what you are saying, Wendy, but since my mother came back into my life, even I have moments when I hold back, just because of her.'

Wendy paused in the doorway. 'Maybe you should both just do what you have to, in the full knowledge that you love each other, and nothing will change that.'

The door closed, leaving Nikki alone with the echo of her words.

* * *

Unable to sit and do nothing, John Carson rang his old friend from the fire-investigation team, then jumped in his car and drove to Skegness, where Dougie spent the summer season in his holiday chalet.

'Dougie! Good to see you.' John took stock of his old friend. Retirement seemed to be suiting him. He looked relaxed and, though a little heavier, still pretty fit.

Dougie made tea, and they sat on the veranda of the wooden chalet looking out over a pond.

'Nice spot. Quiet too. Some of these complexes can be a bit busy, can't they?' John said.

'Come on, John, no need for small talk.' Dougie grinned, his smile toothy and a little crooked. 'I've known you long enough to know you're itching to ask me something.' The grin widened. 'And as the last conversation we had was about that hush-hush fire at the Applegarth place, I guess it must be that.'

John poured out his story. 'We're on borrowed time, Dougie,' he concluded. 'This killer wants his reign of terror over as much as we do, I'm certain of it. The next fire might not be tonight, but it'll be very soon. I *have* to find out all I can about that fire, and find the identity of the remaining teenager. She, or maybe *he*, is in terrible danger. We must discover who they are and get to them before the killer does.'

'A reluctant arsonist. That's pretty unusual.' Dougie pulled a face. 'But I'm not sure how I can help you. I didn't even see the kids. By the time I was called in, apart from one small area, there was just a smouldering wreck in the garden, and everyone was desperately trying to play it down. All I got was apologies for wasting our time, there'd be no charges brought, just a silly accident, blah blah blah.'

'Regarding that last comment, would you say they left it rather a long time before dialling 999?'

'So the fire boys told me. It had really taken a hold by the time they were called.'

'But one youngster had been burnt quite badly.'

'Yes, and he'd already been taken to hospital when I arrived. I was told later that he'd been transferred to Nottingham for treatment. I did find alcohol and drug residue at the site, and my friend Simon, one of the fire-fighters, saw it too. Then we were politely told to drop the investigation.'

John leaned forward. 'Do you think Simon saw the teenagers?'

'Bound to have. He was first on scene.'

'Is he still serving with fire and rescue?'

'Oh yes. At the moment he's the acting watch manager at Skegness fire station.'

'What? Right here?'

'Churchill Avenue. And he'll be on duty this afternoon because it's drill night tonight, so he'll be on the lookout for new blood to join the on-call crew here in Skeggie. Fancy a trip down memory lane?'

John was already on his feet. 'My car or yours?'

Dougie waved his car keys. 'I know this patch better than you, John, so allow me.'

* * *

Simon Briggs was a tall man, with iron-grey hair and a ruddy face. 'Lord! As I live and breathe! It's the two legends of the fenland fire-investigation unit! Both together! I'm honoured.'

'Cut the crap, Si! We want to talk to you," Dougie said.

'Then grab a seat and fire away, if you'll excuse the pun.'

'This enquiry is rather sensitive,' John said sombrely.

'Then you'd better shut the door before you sit down.'

'Cast your mind back, Simon,' said Dougie. 'Do you recall the summerhouse fire out at that big house on Elm Lane, oh, some ten years back?'

'Yeah, I do. That was the one with a load of pissed-up kids, wasn't it? And one kid got burnt trying to rescue one of the others.'

This was news to John. 'Do you know the facts, Simon?'

'Only that the boy in question made a heroic dash into the flames to get one of the girls out. He did it very well too, except he took a roasting in the process. The girl had only a couple of very minor burns, as I recall. As did the other kids.'

John frowned. 'Simon? Was there anything odd about that evening? Especially regarding the owners of the property?'

Simon exhaled. 'Well, it's a long while now, and it was pretty manic. People everywhere, trying to help the teenagers and get them to the main house, and,' he paused, 'the householder seemed to be all over us like a rash. He certainly wasn't hiding behind a cordon and quaking in his boots. He kept saying that he was so grateful his own kids were away at the time, or they could have been involved too.'

Making a point, thought John. 'I know this is a long shot, but do any names come to mind? I'm thinking about the teenagers.'

Simon closed his eyes. 'The boy who got hurt, don't hold me to this, but I think I heard him referred to as Michael.'

John smiled to himself. Nikki Galena needed to hear this. This wasn't a wild goose chase, after all. This was behind what was happening in Greenborough.

'Is there anything else? Anything at all that stood out, Simon?' Dougie added, as they prepared to leave.

'There was a bit of a fight, if that has anything to do with it. One of our lads, Brian — remember him, Doug? Brian Coots? Big lad, he was, well, he waded in and sorted it out. Three lads getting really stuck in. One got dragged off by the homeowner and taken straight into the house.'

'Any idea why?'

'Don't forget they were well hammered, so no, I've no idea what caused it, but I got the distinct feeling that, even though the man had sworn his own children weren't around, the boy who got frog-marched back to the house was his son. There was a clear family resemblance.'

'You've been a fantastic help, Simon,' John said. 'Thank you. We might well be back to pick your brains again, if that's okay?'

Simon nodded. 'If I think of anything else, I'll get in touch with Dougie straight away. Nice to see you, John. You take care.'

They drove back to Dougie's chalet, where John picked up his car. 'Thanks, mate. I owe you one. Anything else that comes your way, ring me, day or night, okay? This is vital.'

'I know.' Dougie looked at him pensively. 'I've never seen you like this, John Carson, and I can't say I like it.'

John knew he looked like some kind of tormented soul. Well, there'd be time to sort himself out after they caught the arsonist. 'I'm fine, honest. I just need to make sure we get this killer before more innocent people die.'

'Look out for yourself too, John. You'll be no good to anyone if you burn out.'

'Great choice of words, Dougie.'

'Hell, John! You know what I mean. Just get some sleep! You look like—'

'Shit. I know. I've been told already.' He clapped a hand on his friend's shoulder. 'Thanks for all your help. I'll be in touch.'

Back in his car, he called Nikki and told her what he'd discovered, 'So somehow, you have to check out the Applegarths' son, Lyndon. If he waded in and attacked the teenagers on the night of the fire, he could be the man you're looking for now. A man with a long memory and a grudge to settle. It's my very strong belief that his sister Natalie *did* die in that fire. He blamed her drunken friends, and still does!'

* * *

Nikki called Joseph into her office and told him what John had said. She felt supremely cool and calm, as if a light was emerging over the horizon and everything was becoming crystal clear.

They discussed their options for almost half an hour, and then went to find Superintendent Cameron Walker.

'We are aware that this doesn't constitute irrefutable evidence, Cam, but it leaves us believing that we could well be looking at Lyndon Applegarth as our arsonist. It all fits. Including using fire as a means of revenge.' She glanced at Joseph, and noted his tight smile and encouraging nod. 'We've talked it over, Cam. A short while back, this team was involved in a cover-up. The investigation we were conducting was closed down and taken out of our hands. That's not going to happen again.' Her expression hardened. 'We are going to pursue this lead like we would any other. We're going to use every channel available to us, and do it openly.

I don't care if this man is privileged. I don't care if he's the son of a diplomat or the crown prince of bloody Woo-Woo Land. If he's a suspect in a series of horrific murders, he's going to be hunted down, brought in and charged, like anyone else. We've locked up peers, lords and high court judges before. This case will be no different. It's about the restoration of order in our town.'

'And about truth and justice.' Joseph nodded vigorously. 'We don't want to drop you in it, Cam, but if this police force isn't allowed to do its job properly and fairly, then we don't want to be part of it. After what we've seen, it's gloves off regarding this killer. We'll do whatever it takes to find him — press, media, the whole lot, and sod red tape. Sorry, but that's the way it is.'

Cameron sat back, obviously digesting what he'd just heard. Then he said simply, 'I agree.'

Nikki felt as if a chain had been cut from her. At last she was free to move forward.

'Thank you, Cam.'

'No need. It's the simple truth. If we can't do what we signed up for, and protect life and property, then we might as well give up. But we're not going to do that.' His brow furrowed. 'If you say that this Lyndon Applegarth went to France to live, the first thing you must do is get onto all the European official bodies — border control, employment records, everything you can think of — and find out if and when he returned to England. These murders were well planned, so he clearly didn't turn up last week.' He stared at Nikki. 'But I don't have to tell you how to do your job. Do whatever it takes to find him. Just do it as quickly as possible. I'll throw a blanket over it for as long as I can, but be prepared for heavy artillery when the shit finally hits the fan.'

'Wilco, sir!' Nikki and Joseph stood up.

They hurried back to the CID room and gathered everyone together.

'We need photographs of this man, and if we can't get recent ones, find whatever you can and get IT to produce an age progression image for us. Then get out there and show the whole of Greenborough. He's been moving among us, someone must know him. Stick his picture in every single shop window if you have to.' Nikki looked at Ben. 'Get this onto the PNC, and issue an attention drawn to all forces. He's about to kill the remaining survivor of that Mischief Night fire all those years ago. We have to find him before he can complete his task. So go! Do your job! Find him!'

Nikki's phone rang in her pocket. She glanced at the display and saw Wendy's name.

'Can you talk?' she asked.

'Go ahead, Wendy.'

'A friend of mine, a chap called Dennis at the Greenborough Airfield, knew the pilot who worked for the Applegarths. His name is Nathan Lowe. Apparently Lowe came into some money and emigrated to somewhere hot and sunny around ten years ago.'

'Oh, did he?' Another underhand dealing the Applegarth family may have been involved in.

'Dennis told me Lowe was very stressed in the weeks before he left the country. One night he even had to be prevented from flying because he'd been drinking. That had never happened before. Lowe was a good, well-respected flyer, and certainly not a drinker. Dennis said he seemed to be very bothered about something, but he never told him what it was.'

'Then I'd hazard a guess that he'd either done something he wasn't comfortable with, or had witnessed something equally distressing.'

'I agree. I have one more thing for you. It may be of no consequence, but there is an unlicensed airstrip on the Applegarth property. It's just a grass runway, tricky to use but that's part of the fun of flying, and Lowe sometimes flew from there, instead of Greenborough Airfield.'

'Is that legal?' asked Nikki.

'Oh yes, it's quite common practice. You don't need planning permission as long as you don't use it more than twenty-eight days in a year.'

'Ah, well, that makes a cover-up even simpler.' Nikki sighed. 'I appreciate all that, Wendy. Now I think you can stand down. I've changed my thoughts on how this investigation should be handled. From now on we're proceeding openly.'

'Well, if I can help, you know where to find me.'

'In a disused graveyard!'

'That's the place. It's back to gardening for us. Bye for now.'

Nikki went into her office and closed the door on the bedlam in the CID room. For a moment or two she sat in silence, breathing slowly and getting her head in order. She knew there was a risk that their sudden and very visible onslaught could force their man to act sooner rather than later, but it was a chance she had to take. She also knew that the station would be inundated with calls, some valid, many hoax. But again, she had no choice. Fortunately she had Sergeant Niall Farrow to rely on, so uniform would be right behind her.

She leaned back in her chair. This was policing as it should be. No more cloak and dagger for her. If some Special Branch unit turned up to close her down, they would be no better than the people who had found it expedient to conceal a lovely girl's death, and in turn, sentence a group of decent people to die in agony. And she, Nikki Galena, would hold them to account, even if she did so as a civilian.

'Bring it on!' she growled, and strode back out to join her team.

CHAPTER TWENTY-FIVE

At four in the afternoon, Nikki had confirmation that Lyndon had come back to England the month before. Officers traced him to a small hotel on the outskirts of Greenborough, where he was positively identified by the hotel manager. He had openly registered as Lyndon Applegarth. According to the manager, he was a quiet, pleasant man. He'd left over a week ago, saying that he was going back to France, since his business here was complete.

'Why didn't he go to the family home,' asked Cat, 'if he wasn't bothered about concealing his identity?'

'We've heard that he fell out with his father, which is why he moved to France to live and work,' said Nikki. 'And possibly he couldn't face being back at the scene of his sister's death.'

'I made a few discreet enquiries with the Applegarths' neighbours,' Ben added. 'It's been closed up for over six weeks now. Richard and his wife are in residence abroad. There's a caretaker who keeps an eye on things while they're away, which can be months at a time.'

'So where did Lyndon go when he left the hotel?' mused Joseph. 'Somewhere where he could prepare to execute his plan, I guess, but where?'

'My best guess would be a rental property,' volunteered Dave. 'But would he have used his own name again?'

'I doubt it,' said Nikki. 'And there's a lot of other places he could choose, like caravan parks, holiday chalets. He could even be house-sitting.'

'Legally, or *il*legally,' added Cat.

'The most important thing is that we can place him here in Greenborough at the time the fires started. We've just had confirmation that he hasn't left the country. Lyndon Applegarth is right here, and he's preparing another fire. And we have no idea who his next victim is, or where he'll strike.' Nikki rubbed her eyes. 'It's so exasperating!'

Joseph massaged the back of his neck. 'And time is not on our side.'

'Our best chance is for someone to spot him,' said Ben hopefully. 'We've plastered the town with his likeness. Someone will recognise him before long.'

'Sorry, Ben, but I'm betting I could change my appearance enough to walk right past you in the street, and you wouldn't know me.' Cat winked. 'Not that I'd want to, you understand, but I'm just saying, disguise is easy.'

'It is if you're a chameleon, like you.' Dave smiled. 'But you do have a point. We can't just sit back and wait for a break, can we?'

'I've had a couple of pool detectives going back over the four dead victims' old friends and acquaintances,' Joseph said, 'but they haven't found anyone who was at that party on Mischief Night.'

'And I've had no joy trying to contact Polly Favre, nee Applegarth,' said Dave. 'I've been told by her place of work that she's holidaying with her husband and child on some remote Greek island. It has an intermittent ferry link, and so far we've had no luck tracing them. Apparently, when they go away they don't welcome communication.'

Nikki stood up. 'Then I think it's time to make a phone call. And someone with a little more clout than me will have to do it.' She looked rather anxiously at Joseph. 'Cam is going to have to contact Richard Applegarth, give him the chance to tell the truth about what happened and help us find his son.'

Joseph's eyes widened, and then he nodded. 'You're right. He might even know where Lyndon might hide out. We have no choice, Nikki. And if he cares about his boy, he'll have to help us.'

Nikki wasn't convinced of Richard Applegarth's fatherly affection. She could see him clamming up and then using his position to get the case closed. Well, just let him try. She gritted her teeth.

* * *

'Why are there Applegarth family members in our little cemetery when they live in a big house up on the edge of the Wolds?' Eve asked.

Wendy looked up from her gardening book and frowned. 'Leon said they were a local family, didn't he?' She put the book down and fetched her laptop. 'Time for a spot of silver surfing, I think.'

'While you do that, I'll make some tea.' Eve went to the kitchen.

She kept turning the case over in her mind, putting herself in Nikki and Joseph's place. They must be at their wits' end, knowing that some poor soul had a death sentence hanging over them, and powerless to stop it unless they found the killer before he struck again.

She went back into the sitting room. 'Any luck?'

'Local history is fascinating, isn't it?' She looked up. 'For generations the Applegarths lived right here on the outskirts of Beech Lacey. And guess what?'

Eve placed her tea on a coffee table. 'Go on . . .'

'Their home burnt down! Destroyed! It was razed to the ground. After that, the family upped sticks and moved up county to Cassington Village. Now it's that rather nice bungalow and apartment complex for senior citizens — Lyndon Court.'

'*Lyndon* Court? As in Lyndon Applegarth?'

'Named after the son. It has a community hall called Natalie House, and a studio where they can do arts and crafts or have a cup of tea and a chat, and that's called Polly's Place.'

'Well I never!' Eve sat down. 'Well, that answers that, doesn't it? Another fire! That's creepy, isn't it? Do they know how it started?'

'Ancient electrics, according to a newspaper report.'

'Was anyone injured?'

'It doesn't say. I suspect not. It did mention that the children were very young. Apparently the smell of smoke woke the father in the early hours of the morning, and he got them all to safety.' Wendy switched to another site. 'I wonder if Cameron Walker knows about this? I mean, if they were in the neighbourhood up until, well, fifteen to twenty years ago, you'd think he would have recognised the name.'

Eve sipped her tea. 'I don't think the Walkers have lived here that long, Wendy. As far as I know, they came here about ten years ago because Cam was posted here. If the Applegarth family moved away, perhaps they just faded into history. There are a lot of new faces in the fen villages these days, incomers looking for a better, cheaper life in the country, and even villages like this move on. I've not been here for long, I know, but I've never heard the name mentioned.'

'Maybe. I'll ask him, though.' Wendy closed down the laptop. 'Not that it means anything. House fires do happen, and nine times out of ten, it's faulty appliances or wiring.'

This was true, but Eve also felt that every tiny piece of information about the Applegarth family could be important. 'You're right, of course. But I think we'll tell Nikki when we speak next.'

'Absolutely.' Wendy picked up her book. 'Now, back to my autumn pruning.'

* * *

He sat still, regulating his breathing and meticulously going over his next move in his head.

Earlier that afternoon he had stripped the van of its phoney logos, and had driven it back to its rightful owner, parking it with the spare key taped back behind the visor, just as it had been. He wouldn't need it to get to the last venue. He was certain he had not been seen, but just in case, he'd worn a stretchy fleece beanie hat pulled down around his face and covering his hair. He was also wearing a walker's anorak and weatherproof trousers and had carried a small backpack. Just a rambler, nothing more sinister than that.

He'd been particularly careful on this occasion. His picture was all over the town, but so far no one had identified him. They would, he knew, and he couldn't afford to fall at the final hurdle.

He made sure that he had the new throwaway phone to hand. It was a vital part of the plan. For the tenth time he checked the three numbers stored in the contacts list, and then shut it off. He verified the time. That was crucial, but he'd managed it before, especially with the car fire that had ended Jeremy Bedford's life. He could do this, he would. For Natalie.

* * *

Cameron Walker sat alone in his office and stared at the display on his smartphone, waiting for his wife to answer. She did, and he told her he loved her. 'I hope you'll forgive me, Kaye, but I think I've just signed my death warrant with the force.'

A heartbeat, and then Kaye said that she loved him too. 'But did you feel good about what you just did? Honestly?'

'Without a doubt.'

'That's fine then. Will you be home for dinner tonight?'

Cam wondered what on earth he had done to deserve such an amazing partner. He was filled with love for her. 'Probably not, darling. But I'll keep you updated.'

'Then take care of yourself. There are some bad people out there.'

'Aren't there just! I'll do my best to steer clear of them. Love you. Speak later.'

Cam ended the call and went to find Nikki.

Inside her office, he heaved a big breath and flopped into a chair beside Joseph. 'Bottom line, someone "in authority" is going to speak to him immediately. I'm not sure if that means some Special Branch unit, or Interpol, since it concerns international police cooperation. But at least I wasn't dismissed out of hand. The chief super listened to every word I said, and by the time I left, he looked as worried as me.'

'Well, you can't do any more, can you?' Joseph gave him an encouraging smile. 'That took guts, after the warning they gave you!'

Cam ran his fingers through his hair and shook his head. 'I surprised myself, I must say, though who knows how it'll pan out. I could still be down the job centre tomorrow!'

'In the queue behind us,' added Nikki grimly. 'If it all goes tits up, it was because of me.'

'We didn't have to agree with you though, did we?' Joseph said. 'We went along with you because we believe it's the right thing to do.'

'I guess you're right, but I still feel responsible.' Nikki sighed. 'I wonder how long it'll take before we hear back?'

Cam glanced at the clock. 'Two hours, I reckon. I really made a big deal about the imminence of this next fire. I even said he'd have the death of an innocent person on his conscience if he didn't pull his finger out.'

'Bet he liked that,' Joseph said. 'Let's just pray that Richard Applegarth has a conscience too, and realises that it's finally time to 'fess up about what happened to his daughter.'

There was a soft tap on the door. 'Come in,' Nikki called.

Laura Archer entered the room, her beautiful face almost gaunt with anxiety. 'Cat has just been bringing me up to speed on what's happened.'

'Do you have any idea how this arsonist's mind might be working right now?' asked Nikki hopefully.

Laura raised an eyebrow. 'Fetch me a crystal ball, someone!' She gave a tight laugh. 'If what you believe is correct, and this is his last kill, he'll be fighting to hold it together. He's not a thrill killer, who'd grow more and more excited by every new kill. This is a strategically planned operation, something *you* would understand, Joseph.' He nodded. She knew his background. 'He's completed four stages, and now he's facing the final one, and in his eyes it's the most vital. He *has* to get it right.'

'It's the culmination of the whole campaign,' Joseph said softly. 'You're right, Laura, it will be essential that it goes to plan.'

The four of them sat in silence. After a while, Nikki said, 'Can I ask you something, Laura? I keep thinking about the victims, and somehow my picture of them as young people, teenagers, doesn't gel with what I know of them as adults.' She frowned. 'Each victim, although very different in character, was basically a good, caring person. Jeremy Bedford was a positively *inspirational* charity worker. And Clary . . .' Nikki thought of that beautiful, diaphanous painting that she'd admired so much. 'Clary was almost saintly in her generosity with her art work. Could these people really have been an unruly gaggle of drunken, drug-taking kids?'

Laura grinned. 'Were you ever a teenager? And are you the same person now? I doubt it very much. I know I'm not.'

'Me neither,' muttered Cam, sounding heartfelt. 'I was an appalling teenager!'

'I guess you're right,' Nikki said.

'And to be honest, it was only hearsay that the legal highs belonged to them. The drugs could have been stashed there by one of the Applegarth kids. They might not have ingested them at all. Drink, sure. After all, they *were* students, and teenagers, and it *was* Mischief Night.' Joseph sat back in his chair and stretched out his legs, 'Which one of us has never, ever, taken an exploratory drag on a spliff?'

Nikki looked around, and realised that she was the only one with a hand raised. 'Bugger! That will do my reputation as a tough nut the world of good!'

'Just proving a point.' Joseph smiled affectionately at her. The sound of her phone made them all start.

'DI Nikki Galena.'

Niall's voice filled her head. 'You have a visitor, ma'am. It's Michael Porter's brother, arrived from Riyadh. He's come directly here from the airport.'

'Could you arrange one of the interview rooms, please? Get him a drink, and I'll be right down.'

'Wilco, ma'am.'

She looked at her colleagues. 'Michael's brother. Let's hope he's remembered something on his long flight home.' She looked at Joseph. 'You stay here. I'll take Ben, as he was the one who spoke to him initially.' She stood up. 'I'm not expecting too much from this, but you never know.'

* * *

Yvonne's phone rang. It was Mickey, the last person she'd been expecting.

'Vonnie? Your weird hand gesture in the picture had me thinking, so I went straight to my mate Dan's home and spoke to him before he went to work. He'd never seen it before around here, but he had seen something similar when he was in London. He's going to try to make a few enquiries for me.' Mickey drew a breath. 'But that's not exactly why I phoned. He told me to be careful on the streets over the next couple of nights.'

Yvonne's hackles rose. This was not something she wanted to hear. 'Did he say why, Mickey?'

'There's an ugly feeling out there. We noticed it on the Carborough too, though not like Dan described. He thinks it's to do with Lee Brown getting done over. It all started with people feeling threatened and pretty scared. Now they're angry.'

Yvonne groaned inwardly. They'd seen this kind of thing before in the town, and it always ended in violence. Just what they didn't need when they were chasing a killer. 'Mickey? Are these angry people directing their anger anywhere specific?'

'Rumour has it they have some religious group fingered for the attack on Lee. I don't know any more than that, but if I hear anything, I'll pass it on.'

'Thank you, Mickey. You're a star.'

'It's been said before, Vonnie. I'm beginning to believe it! Ciao.' He ended the call. Yvonne was left with a sinking feeling in the pit of her stomach. Time to talk to Niall again.

* * *

Nikki was pretty sure that Jared Porter hadn't flown first class. The man looked ragged.

'All the way back, I've been thinking about just how wrong I got my brother. I can't believe that we didn't ask more questions at the time.' He looked at Ben. 'And you really put me straight on that one, DS Radley. Don't think I'm complaining, mind. I deserved a damned good talking to. What a fool I've been! Poor Michael, how he must have suffered. I think I'm going to have nightmares about that. Trapped in a burning building twice in your life! It's inconceivable.'

Nikki smiled at him. 'I'm thinking that your parents played down his original accident far too much. Only to protect him, I expect, but it didn't have a good outcome. You probably believed what you were told and took it no further. Everyone gets things wrong sometimes, Jared. You can only work with the information you're given.'

'We were too involved in our own lives, DI Galena. After my sister and I went abroad, we never gave Michael a second thought. An occasional phone call, a birthday card, and that was it really. Then we got mad with him because he let the house get run down. How self-centred can you be? Now he's gone, and I can't even say sorry to him.'

Nikki felt for him, but couldn't afford the time to listen to this flood of self-recrimination. She couldn't spend too long here if Jared had nothing for her. 'Jared, is there anything you've remembered? Maybe from when your parents talked about his accident. The smallest thing — a simple name of a friend. Anything?'

'I've been thinking of nothing else, Inspector, and only one name surfaced.'

'Which was?'

'Natalie. No surname. But I definitely remember Michael speaking about a girl called Natalie. I think he had a crush on her. I came home from university one weekend, and although my dad had insisted we didn't mention his accident, we did chat a bit more than usual. I told him about a girl I'd met that I was thinking of asking out, and he said to go for it. He'd really liked a girl called Natalie, but he left it too late, and now she was gone.'

'Did he say what he meant by "gone?"' asked Ben.

'No. That was all he said, but I could tell he was pretty upset even thinking about her.' He pulled a face. 'Not much, is it?'

'On the contrary, sir. It's another link, and one we needed. Now we can connect your brother to the person at the very heart of this case. Thank you.'

'Where are you staying?' asked Ben. 'Can we contact you if we need to?'

'I'm in a small hotel, just off Victoria Avenue called the Salthouse. Sorry, I don't have their card. I booked it from Riyadh. I haven't even seen it yet.'

'We'll get the number, don't worry, sir,' Ben said.

They stood up, and Nikki thanked him for coming in. 'Jared? It might help you to know that although we are a long way from understanding what happened, we do believe that your brother sustained his original injuries in the course of saving a girl's life. We don't know her name, but someone who attended the fire said that Michael risked his life in that burning building to help someone else.'

Tears welled up in Jared's eyes. 'Thank you, Inspector.' He swallowed noisily. 'Right now, I feel even worse, but I know it'll be a big help when I finally get my head around it all.'

Nikki watched him go. Funny how life had a habit of making saying sorry out of the question.

CHAPTER TWENTY-SIX

'You're thinking it's this religious group, these satanists, or whatever they call themselves?' Niall asked, looking dubious.

'Luciferians. Well, what do you think? Lee made it his business to confront and assault the Blacks and their followers, and was most likely responsible for the graffiti on their home, then he gets beaten up. Bit of a no-brainer, wouldn't you think?'

'Talk about bad timing! Just when we're stretched to capacity hunting for this Lyndon Applegarth, we might have a riot to contend with.' He groaned. 'And I don't have enough officers to put any sort of watch on the Black House, and certainly not on the strength of a rumour about an *ugly feeling*.'

'But at least we have a heads-up, don't we? It won't hit us like a freight train out of the blue, if something does kick off.'

'Vonnie. Always the optimist.' Niall smiled wryly. 'But you're right. I'll log it, and the late shift will do what they can to keep a lid on any trouble that might be brewing.'

Yvonne smiled to herself. She knew Niall. He was not the kind of man to walk out on a situation, despite his talk of handing it over to the night shift. 'If you need me, I'll be upstairs. My neighbour Ray will look after Hobo till I get home. I have a feeling the guv'nor is edging closer to this damned fire-killer. And if she is, she'll need all the help she can get.'

Niall nodded. He'd soon be ringing Tamsin to ask her to hold dinner tonight.

* * *

An hour later, Cameron Walker's commanding officer, Chief Superintendent Owen Sims, walked through his door, along with two men Cam didn't recognise. His heart sank. This was it.

Cam stood to attention. 'Sir? Gentlemen? Can I help you?'

No one answered until the door clicked shut behind them.

'Sit down, Cameron,' said the chief super. 'This is Warren Bell and Marcus Lander from the UK SIRENE Bureau.'

Cam held his breath. SIRENE was the network that supported cooperation between law enforcement agencies in the EU member states, and was part of the National Crime Agency. But why were they here? They normally dealt with terrorism, people trafficking, money-laundering and other serious crimes.

The three men pulled up chairs and sat facing him.

'We are here, sir, to tell you that your concerns were acted upon. Richard Applegarth has volunteered to give us his full cooperation regarding the hunt for his son, Lyndon. And to facilitate this, he is returning to England tonight, where he will be met and escorted to his home in Cassington Village.'

Relief washed over him. At least Applegarth hadn't pulled strings and brought the investigation to a grinding halt. 'And has he offered to help us with regard to his daughter Natalie?'

'He claimed to be unaware of any problems, sir. He said he and his daughter were estranged, and he hadn't seen or heard from her in years. He said this was a matter of deep sadness for both him and his wife.'

I'll bet it is, thought Cam.

Lander leaned forward. 'I'm sure we don't have to tell you to be cautious, Superintendent. If a crime has been committed, then of course it must be pursued, but we cannot afford to make mistakes. Applegarth is a powerful man. It could be costly. Very costly.'

Cam gritted his teeth. 'I shall be the soul of discretion, but if I think he's covering up a death, then he and I won't be politely drinking tea in his country retreat, we'll be sitting in an interview room right here in Greenborough police station.'

'He's agreed to help with our enquiries,' Warren Bell said crisply. 'You may accept that assistance. But be very wary of making any accusations unless you have hard evidence.'

Which I don't, thought Cam, *Not yet. But give me a little time and we'll see about that.*

'Just tread warily, Cameron,' said Chief Superintendent Sims. 'We don't want you making too many waves, but probably not for the reason you are thinking.' He glanced across to Lander.

Lander was impassive. 'We are on your side, Superintendent. The thing is, we can find no trace of Natalie Applegarth. Naturally, our investigation has only just begun, but we do liaise closely with mainland Europe, and the young lady in question hasn't shown up in any border control records, neither has she legally worked anywhere. There has been no driving licence issued or any other recorded transaction — and her passport has not been used, which is of grave concern.'

'We consider your suggestion that she never left this country to be valid,' continued Bell. 'But,' he looked straight into Cam's eyes, 'we have to have cast-iron proof. And while we search for it, you will direct all your efforts toward finding the son. You must make Richard Applegarth believe that that is all we are interested in. Can you do that?'

Cam was dumbfounded. He had expected these men to obstruct or delay, but they seemed to want to help. 'Yes, yes, of course I can.'

'We have your report,' Lander said, 'and we have to say that your DI Galena and her team have made pretty remarkable headway in a very short space of time. We are now taking some of the intelligence they gathered a step further. The pilot, for instance. We know where he relocated to in Portugal, and,' he glanced at his watch, 'I should think someone is having a chat with him as we speak. He could be the key witness, *if* Natalie was indeed spirited away that night.'

'*If* he talks,' added Bell.

'We have more than one lead to follow. For instance, we know exactly where Polly and her family take their holidays. But right now, the biggest concern of all of us is this sadly unidentified target of Lyndon Applegarth. And the ball for that, Superintendent, is firmly in your court.' Lander looked intently at Cam. 'Applegarth will be home within the hour. I hate to tell you how to do your job, but you should get up to Cassington without delay, and strike while the iron is hot. The flight was short, so he hasn't had much time to formulate what he's going to say, so get in there quickly.'

Cameron stood up. 'Is that all, gentlemen? If so, consider me *en route*.'

On their way out of the office, the chief super lightly touched Cam's arm. 'Kid gloves?'

'Yes, sir. I'm fully in the picture now. I know how to handle it.'

The big man nodded. 'Good, good. I know you're the right man for the job, Cameron, but take care. And for heaven's sake, find that arsonist!'

* * *

Joseph paced his tiny office like a beast in a cage. No one knew how to proceed, and it was getting to them all. And to make matters worse, there was unrest on the streets of Greenborough. He'd experienced that before, and it wasn't pleasant. He sank onto his chair. There seemed to be no way to track the fifth partygoer. Why did none of those teenagers ever talk about what happened on Mischief Night? Why didn't they keep in touch? They had shared a terrible experience, after all. All the evidence indicated that they never even knew each other in their adult lives. What were the chances of that?

'Can I join you?' Dave looked as fraught as Joseph felt.

'By all means. Come in and share the agony,' Joseph said grimly.

'I've been thinking about those kids,' Dave said.

'Me too. That's exactly what my little grey cells are working on right now.'

Dave went and found an office chair, and jammed it up against Joseph's desk. 'I've been going over what the fire investigator told John Carson.' He exhaled. 'The sequence of events doesn't fit the usual pattern. For a start, there was a delay in raising the alarm. Then the kids were taken into the main house, where they stayed for quite some time before the paramedics attended to them. Okay, the one we think was Michael Porter was hospitalised, but the others were all taken home by people attached to the Applegarth family. Isn't that odd, Sarge? Wouldn't you call their families and get them to come out and pick up their kids?'

'Absolutely, unless there was no family or close relative. Where's this going, Dave?'

'I think intense pressure was put on those teenagers when they were taken into the Applegarth house. I think they were got at, either through intimidation or bribery, and whatever they were threatened with lasted a lifetime.'

Joseph had been thinking along similar lines, but it was good to hear it from someone else. 'It would've had to be something pretty terrifying to shut them up for ten whole years.' He thought for a while. Was it possible? They were intelligent, educated kids. Could someone intimidate them badly enough that the fear would stain the rest of their lives? Joseph knew it was more than possible. He'd seen people before who had been terrorised into silence, spending their whole lives pretending something never happened, denying a horrible truth. 'Let's say that they all knew Natalie had died in the fire. Could the family have threatened them with a murder or manslaughter charge? Could they possibly have been wicked enough to tell those teenagers that if they kept their mouths shut, the body would disappear?'

'There was something in the papers around that time, a rumour that Applegarth was due for some award or other, and a possible step up the diplomatic service ladder. If this drink/drug-taking party threatened all that, I'd say yes, they could have been.' Dave nodded slowly.

'And five kids lived with the guilt for the rest of their days.'

'Made new lives far apart from each other,' said Dave pensively, 'and all tried to make up for what they'd brought to pass on Mischief Night. They turned into do-gooders, to make amends for what happened.'

'A guilty conscience could do that I suppose, although I've often seen it go the other way, and the accused person turns into a right little shit.' Joseph smiled faintly.

'They weren't bad kids, I don't think. I reckon they just got drunk and acted stupidly,' Dave said.

'And paid with their lives,' Joseph concluded. 'I think we should see what the boss thinks of this, don't you?'

Dave nodded. 'Yes, I do. It makes complete sense, though proving it, now that they're all dead, won't be easy.'

'You can say that again, but we still need to find the arsonist, and stop him before he can get to the last target.'

Dave carried his chair back outside. 'We have every available officer out there, and his picture's plastered all over town. I'm not sure what else we *can* do.'

'Nikki has even given a statement to the press and the media. It was short and very succinct — no mention of the fires, of course. She simply urged the public to look out for Lyndon Applegarth, because we need to speak to him in connection with four unexplained deaths. The phones'll be ringing all night, I should think.'

'Then wherever he is, he must be feeling like a hunted animal by now.' Dave grimaced. 'And you know what wild beasts do when they are cornered?'

Joseph knew only too well. 'They attack.'

* * *

Giles Black straightened his tie and examined his reflection in the mirror. The meeting he was due to attend this evening was being held at the house of one of the other members. It was an opportunity for him to introduce a new acolyte to the group. The woman was a powerful presence in the food industry, and he had been patiently grooming her for some time now.

He was hoping that tonight she would commit to joining them, so he was being careful about every detail. He was even going alone. His wife's presence, and even his brother's charm, could be a distraction from the job he needed to do. This woman could prove to be a very influential player in their game, if he made all the right noises. Their group was expanding, and he was on his way to becoming a very wealthy man, but it was essential to bring in new blood.

'Looking good, brother.' Tom walked into his room and flopped down on the bed. 'Think she's in the bag?'

'Pretty sure, but you never can tell with a woman like that. She's understandably cautious, and she's no fool.'

'Play it cool, Giles. No pressure. Just reel her in gently.'

'That's the plan, bro. I shan't ask you to wish me luck, because this is entirely about skill.' He put on his gold cufflinks, engraved with a small fireball emblem, and shook his arm, admiring them.

'Well, I'm glad to see you're confident but not too cocky, for once.'

'Fuck off, Tom!' Giles grinned at his brother. 'I can do without being badgered by you right now. So, what are you doing tonight?'

'Nothing. I thought Ollie and I could play chess for a bit, then maybe watch some TV together. Your lovely wife is leaving us too, going to a baby shower or so she says — whatever that is.'

'Some heathen thing. It's her friend Pattie's. You shower a new or expected baby with expensive gifts and try to outdo all the other fawning mothers.'

'Sounds wonderful.' Tom pulled a face. 'You aren't telling me Corinne's getting broody, are you?'

'Hardly.' He snorted. 'My wife is far too self-centred to want a baby stealing the limelight, or taking up all her precious time.' Her attitude had been a disappointment to him, so he changed the subject quickly. 'How is Olivia today? I've barely seen her.'

'Not bad. She went out for a while today, just a trip to Café des Amis with an old friend of hers. It did her good, I think. She spends far too much time incarcerated here.' Tom stood up and stretched. 'I'm going to order a pizza tonight. Ollie said she fancied one, so as you guys are partying elsewhere, we are going to pig out and to hell with the calories.'

'I'm *working*, Neanderthal, not partying,' Giles said haughtily.

'Yeah, sure. There won't be any wine, I guess, or champagne or delicious food? No music? No beautiful women?'

'And I'll be working my butt off, trying to acquire a very special commodity for our group, as you well know, Thomas Black.'

'Then happy shopping, Giles. Bring back a nice juicy bargain.'

Giles flung a pillow at Tom's retreating back. *That's just what I intend to do, brother, and I'm about to land a very big fish indeed.*

CHAPTER TWENTY-SEVEN

Cameron saw at once that Richard Applegarth was in the right job. He was quietly spoken, with an air of confidence and integrity. He came over as honest, intelligent and believable. But in his time, Cameron had met many suave con men, people who, in his mother's words, could charm the birds out of the trees.

'Thank you for seeing me at such short notice, sir,' Cameron said.

'It's the least I can do. This is a terrible business, terrible. But I still find it hard to believe that my son has anything to do with such a heinous crime,' Appegarth said.

Applegarth was tall and lean, with a full head of silver-grey hair cut in a neat, wavy style. He had a pale complexion, and his blue eyes matched his soft blue shirt and tie. He was every inch the elegant gentleman. He looked a bit like George Clooney.

'We don't know this for sure, sir, not yet. But your son can be placed in the area, and has been described in detail by several witnesses to these fires. We need to talk to him, at the very least to eliminate him from our enquiries.'

'How can I help you, Superintendent?'

'Tell me about Lyndon. What kind of man is he?'

Applegarth lowered his eyes. 'I can tell you what he *was* like, but I'm ashamed to say I haven't seen Lyndon in several years. He went to live in France, and has had nothing to do with his family since. We had no idea he'd returned to England.' He sighed. 'My wife's heart is broken.'

The name Natalie rose to Cameron's lips. He bit it back. 'A family row?'

'More than that. After his sister ran away ten years ago, we were a family in crisis.'

It would be only natural to follow this up, wouldn't it? 'That's awful, sir. So you have two estranged children?'

Richard Applegarth nodded sadly. 'Natalie. I forbade her to marry a priest. She was only nineteen, and I was certain she hadn't thought about the long-term consequences. I thought it would stunt her life. If I'd known what would happen, I would have given my blessing immediately.'

Nice words, thought Cameron, beautifully put. 'And she ran away? That's quite extreme, isn't it?'

'Natalie dreamt of improving people's lives. She wanted to make things better for everyone, and she was passionate about causes. I think she saw my rejection of her young man as a rejection of her ideals.'

'And Lyndon?'

'He adored Natalie. He loved Polly too, but not like Natalie. He stayed with the family for some time after she left, but eventually made the break. He said he blamed me for causing her to leave.'

True, thought Cameron. If Lyndon was the arsonist, he probably did blame his father, not for her absconding, but for all the subterfuge and underhand dealings surrounding her death. You can only live with lies for so long.

'Lyndon was a gentle boy, good at crafts and he had an all-encompassing love for animals, trees, birds — all natural life.' Applegarth seemed to drift into a trance as he spoke of his young son. Then he shook his head. 'How can such a happy family, filled with love and respect, suddenly sour to a point of disintegration?'

Keep it simple, thought Cam. 'So, after Lyndon grew up, what did he do for a living, sir?'

'He never really settled down to a proper job. One month he'd be volunteering at an elephant orphanage, and the next he'd be helping to clean beaches or dredge waterways. We never knew what he'd be doing next.'

'And he never trained for anything in particular?'

'He loved working with wood, so he did a stint as a trainee carpenter. Then he tried his hand at metalwork. He enjoyed that too, but it lasted as long as the carpentry. I'm ashamed to say that he became a drifter.'

'But he worked in France, didn't he?'

'If he did, I don't know what his job was. He had his allowance, so I knew he wouldn't starve, but I know nothing about what he did or where he lived.'

Cameron frowned. 'But he kept in touch with his other sister, didn't he?'

'Infrequently, but he told her very little — in case she passed anything on to me, I suppose.' Applegarth shrugged. 'At least Polly and I still have a good relationship, thank the Lord.'

Was that the dark lord? Cameron pushed the notion away. He needed to find where Lyndon might be staying now. 'Sir? We know Lyndon hasn't been here. The place was shut up and your lodge-keeper told us as much, but is there anywhere else he would go? Some other small property, maybe? Near, or in Greenborough?'

'I never owned any other house. After we were forced to leave the family home in Beech Lacey, this became our only property.'

'Nothing at all?'

'No. We kept the plane at Greenborough Airfield, but we had no *pied-à-terre* there. And I hate water, so we never owned a boat or a boathouse.' Applegarth wrinkled his brow. 'Sorry, but I can't think of anywhere he might go.'

'No place he loved to hang out in as a kid?' Cameron was getting desperate.

There was a long silence. Applegarth sighed again. 'Sorry, but nothing comes to mind.'

'If I could ask you to reflect on that, sir, and phone me if you do think of anything.' Cameron handed him his card. 'Sir, we *have* to find him.'

Applegarth rubbed his chin. 'Well, he had a friend, a boy called, um, Arthur, I think. They used to go birdwatching together, down on the marshes. He was an odd kid, but Lyndon liked him. If Lyndon needed help, I think he'd go to Arthur.'

'Do you know any more about this Arthur?'

'His surname was Kent, I do know that, and he lived in one of the poorer areas of Greenborough. Rough family, as I recall. But that's it, I'm afraid, Superintendent. And I'm very tired. Could we continue this at a later date?'

Cam narrowed his eyes. 'I do apologise, sir, but you can see the urgency of our situation, can't you? Our probable killer — Lyndon, or someone else — has another victim in his sights, and we have no idea who it is. But we do know it all stems from the fire that took place ten years ago, on this very property, in the summerhouse. All the victims were kids who were present at the fire, Mr Applegarth. You saw those kids, those teenagers, and now they are all dead, bar one. And right now that one is a sitting target firmly in the killer's cross-hairs. Doomed to die by fire. How sick is that?'

Applegarth's voice shook. 'I have no idea who they were! I never even knew their names, except for the boy who was burnt — Michael it was — and I did follow his progress. I even offered his parents some financial assistance, but they turned it down. As for the others, as soon as we saw they were unharmed, I gave them a dressing down for being so foolish, then my chauffeur and my caretaker ferried them home.' He paused. 'You really think she's in mortal danger? Possibly from my son?'

'We do. We're sure of it.'

Richard Applegarth visibly deflated. 'I need to rest, Superintendent. You have my word that I'll ring you if I think of anything else.'

* * *

Ten minutes later, Cameron sat in his car staring blankly out of the windscreen. 'He knows,' he whispered. Applegarth had given himself away with a single word: *she*. "You really think *she* is in mortal danger?" Cameron had said four out of the five were dead. He hadn't specified how many were men and how many women. And even if Applegarth had looked up the deaths on the Internet, which Cameron didn't think he had, the way he said *she* sounded as if he had a particular person in mind.

'He knows who the next victim is,' Cam muttered to himself, 'and he had the chance to tell me, but he didn't. This man is up to his neck in lies, and if he can't give me a simple name, then he's covering up something far more sinister.'

He pulled his phone from his pocket and rang Chief Superintendent Sims.

* * *

'Is Yvonne in?' Nikki called out.

'Here, ma'am!' Yvonne hurried across to the office. 'Can I help?'

'I've just had a call from the super. Do you know a family called Kent? An Arthur Kent in particular. Lived here in Greenborough around ten years back.'

Yvonne closed her eyes for a moment. 'Let me see . . . Yes, Bob and Sharon Kent. They had just the one son, Arthur. The lad was lacking something, if you know what I mean. Learning difficulties. Nothing too bad, but it made him a bit strange.' She looked at the ceiling. 'Eleven, Kings Court, just outside the Carborough, and they still live there, though I think Arthur moved out some years ago.'

Nikki never ceased to be amazed by Vonnie's almost total recall of the Greenborough residents. 'Any convictions?'

'No. Poor family, but decent. Arthur had his collar felt a few times, but nothing serious.'

'Yvonne? Go and see them, will you? Find out where Arthur is. Cameron Walker thinks that Lyndon was pretty friendly with him, way back. Maybe he's gone to ground with an old friend.' She paused. 'And if you do find Arthur, don't go in alone, okay? Lyndon could just be with him.'

'Wilco, ma'am. Show me attending.' Yvonne hurried off.

Nikki watched her go. She had the feeling that something was about to happen. She just hoped it wasn't another deadly inferno. Nikki felt as helpless as she ever had, except for that terrible time when she couldn't help her own daughter. It didn't get any worse than that.

'Guv?' Cat said.

Cat Cullen broke into her dark thoughts. 'I've been thinking. After you told us about what the super said, you know, about those kids being driven home after the fire? Have we tried to talk to his old chauffeur, or the caretaker? If they drove them home, they might remember their addresses. And even if they'd moved, someone would probably know who'd lived there before.'

Nikki thought for a moment. 'Ah, I get it. We knock Michael off the list. He went to hospital. The drivers took the kids to four separate addresses, so we eliminate those of Clary, Jeremy and Ronnie, and we should be left with our anonymous partygoer.'

'And bingo!' Cat grinned. 'Okay, I know it's a long shot. We might not locate the drivers, they could be dead for all we know. But is it worth a try, guv?'

'It certainly is. I'll ask Cameron if he can trace who was in Applegarth's employ at that time. He's got some rather useful buddies working with him at present. Then you and Ben can go jog their collective memories.'

'Let's hope they have good ones. It is ten years, after all.'

'Sure, but some things stick, and it would have been a pretty memorable evening, with fire tenders and ambulances and heaven knows what all going on. I'd remember, wouldn't you?'

'Well, yes, I would. Fingers crossed for a bit of luck, huh?'

'Right. Oh, and well done to think of that, Cat. It could just lead us to our final victim.'

Cat walked away, her grin broadening. Nikki smiled too. Even after all the years they'd worked together, Cat was still hugely proud when her boss praised her.

Nikki's phone rang. 'Leon? How can I help?'

'I'm sorry, DI Galena. I know I shouldn't bother you when you're so busy, but is there any news? I'm worried sick about this murderer, and desperate to know about my Natalie. I've done nothing but think about all the things that could have happened to her. It's torture.'

Nikki took a breath. 'We are getting closer to finding out what happened, but this is no easy case, Leon. I promise to let you know as soon as we have any positive news.' A thought struck her. 'Leon? Did Natalie drink? Or take recreational drugs?'

'Natalie? No way! She rarely drank anything, and was dead set against any kind of drug. I actually saw her confiscate cannabis from a friend's bag and hide it until she could destroy it. It was her bête noir.'

'Thank you, Leon, and please, try not to worry too much. I *will* find you the truth.'

Nikki ended the call, frowning. 'Joseph, we need to brainstorm!'

Joseph looked up from a conversation with Ben. He loped over. 'You have a conundrum, I can tell by your expression.'

'You're so right.'

She opened a file and laid out several sheets of paper across her desk. 'John Carson's written report on everything his friend, the other fire investigator, told him about the summerhouse fire. With,' she passed him another sheet of paper, 'a diagram of the summerhouse prior to being incinerated.' She took a deep breath. 'Five teenagers, seemingly let into the summerhouse by Natalie. Two were students. Clary was studying art, and Jez, we are told, was doing a degree in social work. Ronnie was just a farm worker. Then there's our mystery person, who we know nothing about. Michael was a layabout and was said to be out of work at the time. And then we have Natalie.'

Joseph looked up. 'You say that as if she's different to the others.'

'She is. She didn't drink and she hated drugs.'

'Oh.'

'Yes. Oh.' She stared at the diagram. 'Bottles and cans were found strewn around this area, the main body of the summerhouse. But here,' she jabbed a finger at a smaller space at the far end of the long building, 'is where they found packets of legal highs.'

'What is that room?'

'I think the Applegarth kids used it to chill out and listen to music. It had a sofa, a divan kind of thing, and some bookshelves. It was a sort of den, I guess, somewhere to hide if you wanted some peace.'

Joseph frowned. 'I'm not quite sure where that mind of yours is taking us, Nikki.'

'Nor am I. Yet. But think about it. Five kids are getting slowly rat-arsed. One has bought some NPS. It's Mischief Night and they're looking for kicks. We can only guess they meet Natalie, and we have it on record from Jared Porter, Michael's brother, that Michael fancied a girl called Natalie. So . . .'

'Natalie hates drugs in any form, so she . . .' Joseph thought for a moment, 'so she decides to get them off the streets, to somewhere they can have a drink and party a bit but away from the bars and clubs? Something like that?'

'Something like that, yes. We may never know for sure, but as all the drugs were in the little den, I'm thinking she spirited them away and hid them. Leon told me she had history of doing just that.'

Joseph picked up the report. 'I wonder . . .' He flipped through the pages, then shook his head. 'Nothing here.'

'What?' asked Nikki.

'I was wondering if the packets they found were empty or full.'

Nikki phoned John and asked him.

'I'll speak to my friend. I'll get back to you.' John rang off.

A few moments later, he called back. 'Andy said they were unopened. Does that help in some way?'

'Just another tiny piece in a bloody great jigsaw, John, but thank you.' She hung up. 'She hid them. Natalie took them from the others and hid them.'

'And that suggests a chilling hypothesis, doesn't it?' said Joseph grimly.

'That none of this need have happened. Natalie was never taking drugs in the first place, and she was trying to prevent the others from using them. Someone, an Applegarth family member, made a serious error of judgement about that young woman.'

Joseph leaned back in his chair. 'Problem is, this is all guesswork. Not a shred of real evidence.'

'True, but it is helping *us* to see more clearly,' Nikki said. 'And when this case is over, a certain gent in high office is going to have some very tricky questions to answer.'

The phone rang again. 'Ma'am? Cross Arthur off your list. He's up county working with a cousin. He's been there for months apparently.'

'Okay, Vonnie, come back to base. And thanks for clearing that up.'

'No problem. By the way, Mickey Leonard's warning about the ugly feeling on the streets is quite true.'

Nikki nibbled on her bottom lip. 'How so?'

'There's a distinct chill in the air, and it has nothing to do with the weather. There's little gangs of youths gathering in alleyways all over town. It just feels ominous, and frankly, I fear for the Black House.'

'Then maybe we should get uniform to direct a little attention there as night falls. They are a complete enigma, that group. I still have no idea what the hell is going on in that place, but we don't want a war in Ferry Street. I know our boys and girls are stretched, but I'll talk to them.'

'Thank you, ma'am. I'm on my way back now.'

Nikki hung up. 'Arthur was a wild bloody goose chase, courtesy of Richard Applegarth. And Vonnie says she has serious concerns about marauding youths and the Black House. I need to make sure that uniform have logged her concerns.'

Nikki called Niall. As she put the phone down, there was a sharp rap at the door, and Cameron Walker hurried in. 'Got what you asked for, Nikki. Two names. Employees at the Applegarth house at the time of the fire.' He thrust a memo at her. 'Baker was the driver, and Glass was the general help and dogsbody. Both live on the outskirts of Greenborough. And one very interesting fact. Both were "retired" the day after the fire, with a very handsome golden handshake. New staff were recruited immediately. So think on that, if you will! But right now it's time to get your team on the road to talk to them.'

'Brilliant! Thanks, Cam.' Nikki looked at Joseph, her eyes alight. 'A break, at last.' She ran out into the CID room. 'Cat! Ben! You have a house call to make, and Dave, there's one for you too. One in Frampton, and one just north of Greenborough, in Beltoft End, okay? Just come back with a name. This is our best chance yet. So go to it!'

* * *

Cameron stared across the desk to the chief superintendent. 'He has to tell us, sir! He knows who this last victim is, I'd stake everything I own on the fact.'

Owen Sims rubbed a beefy hand across his chin. 'I have to agree, it's looking more and more as if he has something to hide. Sacking his staff immediately after the incident! That reeks of a cover-up. And extensive searches for Natalie have proved negative.' He drew in a long breath. 'Okay, Cameron, I'll take this upstairs, and notify Lander and Bell. It's time there was a proper, official interview, with the appropriate people. Leave this with me.'

'Sir, can you emphasise the urgency? It's *critical* that it's done immediately. The fire investigator, and all the rest of us too, believe this unknown target is really on borrowed time. The murderer could strike tonight. In fact, it's more than likely he will. He's being hunted, and his face is everywhere. He can't afford to wait.'

'Understood.'

Cameron left, relieved that the chief was on his side, but terrified that the wheels of justice might turn too slowly for the next victim.

CHAPTER TWENTY-EIGHT

The police officers who were still out following up possible sightings of Lyndon Applegarth found themselves dispersing gatherings of angry youths. By around eight o'clock, there had been several scuffles and a couple of arrests.

In the CID room, Nikki was agitated. Neither of the men employed by Applegarth was at home. Dave had no luck at all trying to track Glass, and Cat and Ben, having been told that Baker would probably be in the pub, were trawling round all the local public houses within a three-mile radius of his village.

No one had gone home. There was an atmosphere of nervous anticipation throughout the station. Joseph was munching his way through a bag of crisps, something he *never* did, and Nikki was on her second Mars bar when a white-faced Cameron walked into the room like someone in a dream.

'Cam?' Nikki jumped up. 'What's the matter?'

'He's dead. Applegarth is dead. Lander and Bell went to talk to him, and found him in his study, a twelve-bore shot-gun beside him. Not pretty, but apparently very effective.'

Nikki let out a groan. 'Now he'll never tell us who the next victim is.' She jerked upright. 'Was there a note?'

Cam shook his head slowly. 'Nothing. He took the phone call from Lander, then as far as we can tell, it was bang! Game over.'

'Wicked sod! He could have told us and saved a life! Now we're left, still scratching around looking for a missing, probably pissed, ex-chauffeur! Just wonderful!' Nikki put her head in her hands.

'I'm sorry, Nikki. I should have pushed him harder when I spoke to him, and damn the warnings to tread carefully.'

'It's not your fault, Cam,' said Joseph. 'Nothing you could have said would have made a blind bit of difference.'

'I agree,' added Nikki. 'So don't beat yourself up over it. We need all the help you can give us now to find Lyndon.'

Cameron straightened up. 'You're right. So, as soon as Cat and Ben get back, I think we should have an impromptu campfire, don't you? Throw everything we have into the pot and see if something of value comes out.'

'Okay, I'll call you when they get back.'

Nikki returned to her office. It was a horrible thing to happen, but she didn't feel sorry for the diplomat. 'Okay, top yourself if you must,' she muttered, 'but do the right thing first, and let us know who that last girl is.' Their only hope was the chauffeur, and it appeared he used a multitude of different watering holes and could be in any one of them. She felt as if a giant hourglass was poised above her head, the sands trickling through it.

'I've just heard from downstairs.' Joseph stood in the doorway, his expression grave. 'Niall and a couple of crews have broken up a gathering in the road next to Ferry Street. He said they were heading for the Black House.'

'Damn and bugger! Have they contained it?'

'Yes, this time, but he reckons the word has spread, and any thug who fancies a bit of aggro is joining in, no matter what the original cause was.'

Nikki gazed at him wearily. 'It's going to be one pig of a night!'

* * *

Tom sat with his feet up on the sofa and passed his sister the box of Celebrations. 'How many times have we watched this, Ollie?' He unpeeled a chocolate and popped it into his mouth.

Olivia smiled and shrugged. 'Ten?'

'And we still laugh at the bit when the baby says "arsehole!"'

Olivia chuckled. 'It's just so funny. Phone's ringing, Tom.'

Tom got up and padded across the room to the walnut sideboard that held the telephone. 'Tom Black.'

He listened, and then yelled, 'Where? For heaven's sake, tell me where!'

Very slowly, he set down the receiver. He didn't want to scare Olivia, but she had to be told.

'Ollie, that was the police. Giles has had an accident. A mob of youths attacked him as he was getting into his car. I have to go. Will you be okay?'

Olivia nodded. 'Of course, just go! Did they say if he's badly hurt?'

'There's an ambulance in attendance, but they didn't tell me any more than that.' Tom was hopping around on one leg trying to get his shoes on. 'It's way over on the other side of town.'

'Drive carefully, Tom. I don't want two brothers injured.'

Tom ran over and planted a kiss on his sister's forehead. 'Love you, Ollie. I'll ring you as soon as I know more. Maybe you should try to get hold of Corinne, although she does turn her phone off. I'll leave that with you.' Then he was off, out into the darkness.

* * *

The call came through a few moments after Cat and Ben had reluctantly returned empty-handed.

'Thank heavens you put a note through his letterbox! It's Baker, the chauffeur. He's on his way in. Ten minutes, tops.' Dave put down the phone. 'This could be it.'

It was the longest ten minutes of Nikki's life. After an eternity of sitting and drumming her fingers, the desk sergeant informed her that her visitor was in the foyer. She and Joseph glanced at each other, and hurried from the CID room.

By the time they got downstairs, Reg Baker had already been escorted to an interview room.

'Thank you for coming in, Mr Baker. I'm DI Nikki Galena, and this is DS Joseph Easter.'

'What's this all about?'

'Sir, we think you may be able to assist us with some information that could help apprehend a murderer.' She spoke slowly and clearly, although in her heart she just wanted to drag the name out of him and send him on his way.

'We understand you were employed by the late Richard Applegarth, some ten years ago,' Joseph said.

'Late?'

'He died today, sir.'

'Did he?' Baker looked confused. 'And what's this about a murderer?'

Nikki leaned forward. 'We want you to cast your mind back to the fire in the summerhouse.'

Baker's expression darkened. 'What do you want to know?'

'You and a man named Glass drove some of the teenagers home afterwards. Is that correct?'

Baker stared at the table. He seemed to be struggling in the horns of a dilemma.

'Did you drive anyone home, Mr Baker?' Joseph kept his tone reasonable, but there was an edge to it. 'This is very important.'

Baker raised his head. 'You say he's dead? Applegarth is dead?'

'Yes, sir, irrefutably dead.' Nikki spoke through gritted teeth.

'When we were asked to leave, we were told never to talk about the fire. Or anything connected to it.' Baker looked thoroughly miserable. 'He paid for our silence. But if he's dead, does that apply?'

251

'All bets are off, sir. You are free to talk. In fact, you *have* to talk. A woman's life may depend on it.' Nikki fixed him with a stare. 'Who did you take home and where did you take them?'

'I remember that night like it was yesterday. I took a lad to his mum and dad's place, in Rain Bridge Lane. I remember it clearly, because my sister lived down there for a while.'

Nikki wrote down the name *Jez Bedford* on a sheet of paper.

'And then I took a lass with lovely long auburn-ginger hair somewhere, let me think . . . oh yes, it was to her sister, they lived in London Road.'

Clary, wrote Nikki. 'Did you take anyone else, and have you any idea who Mr Glass took?'

'Ernie only took one kid home. A rather rough-looking lad, but it was quite a way out, on some farm I think. I don't know where, I'm afraid.'

'Ronnie,' said Joseph. Nikki wrote this down. 'So, with Michael taken to hospital, that leaves only one.'

Together they stared at Reg Baker, willing him to speak. 'The last teenager? Where did you take her?'

'Oh, that one was easy. She was the last one I dropped off before the trip back home. It was to a lovely old house in Ferry Street. I remember it perfectly. It was called the Black House.'

Nikki's mouth dropped open. 'Are you sure?'

'Oh yes. She said it had been their family home for generations.'

'Corinne? Or Olivia?' Nikki whispered. Her head spun.

'They called her Ollie, if that helps. The other kids, they called her Ollie.'

* * *

The sound of sirens tore the evening apart, and the streets were lit up by blue lights that flashed like lightning. Two cars sped towards the Black House. Nikki and Joseph, along with

Yvonne were in one, and Cat, Ben and Dave followed closely behind them. Behind them were more marked police cars, pulled away from keeping the peace on the streets.

With a screech of brakes, Nikki pulled up in front of the Black House. She flung herself out of the car, and caught the smell of smoke in the air. 'He's already torched it! Get fire and rescue!'

'Already done!' said a voice. 'They're on their way!'

Nikki looked down a wide alleyway running along the side of the property, and saw that the back of the old house was on fire.

Despite the noise surrounding her, Nikki's world was silent. Things moved in slow motion.

Some fifty yards away, silhouetted against the flames, Nikki saw a man hurrying away from the scene. He gave a quick glance back. Nikki was sure it was Lyndon Applegarth.

'Cat! Ben! He's there! Get him!' Nikki shouted.

They sped off in pursuit, and Yvonne grabbed her arm. 'Ma'am! The last time I was in that house there were oxygen cylinders! I think the girl, Olivia, has severe asthma!'

'Oh hell!' Nikki had read enough about fire by now to know that oxygen wasn't combustible, but it was an accelerant. If one of those containers were to rupture, the ensuing blast would be deadly.

They ran to the front of the property, just in time to see Niall grab a heavy enforcer from one of his colleagues and swing it at the front door. It took three strikes for the lock and hinges to shatter. Niall threw down the enforcer and with a glance at Joseph, plunged forward.

'Niall! No! Think of Tamsin!' Joseph grabbed his arm. 'Think of my daughter, son, please! Don't go in there.'

Joseph whispered something inaudible, and to Nikki's utter horror, pushed Niall aside and ran into the house himself.

'Joseph!' Nikki screamed. 'Joseph!'

For a moment she stood rooted to the spot. Then she moved toward the door.

'Nikki! No! You can't! He doesn't want you following him.' Niall took hold of her, and gripped her tightly. 'He said to trust him. He knows what to do.'

'Oh my God!' she whispered. 'My Joseph!'

CHAPTER TWENTY-NINE

Joseph moved quickly and carefully through the ground floor rooms. In the kitchen he grabbed a towel, soaked it under the cold tap and wrapped the wet material around his face. The big conservatory was ablaze, but he could see that it was empty, so he hurried on. He came upon an oxygen cylinder on a trolley close to a window in the hall. He thrust the window open and hauled the cylinder into the garden, as far as the heavy weight would allow. At least now it wouldn't add to the blaze.

If the girl was ill, she was probably in a bedroom, but he had to check downstairs first. And where was the rest of the family? Giles, Corinne and Tom? And why hadn't they dialled 999? He shook his head and hurried on, no time for questions now.

He made his way back into the hall as the smoke built up. Suddenly he wasn't alone. John Carson stood on one side of him, with Yvonne on the other.

There was no point in telling them to get out. He had seen the determined look in their eyes, and there was no time to argue.

'Upstairs!' he shouted.

'Keep as low down as possible!' John called out. 'Be aware of what is going on behind you too. Don't get trapped, okay? The fire crews will be here in a minute, but let's try to find the girl.'

The three of them fought their way upstairs, trying to keep together, but they were fighting a losing battle with the smoke and the growing heat.

One big bedroom was already a conflagration. Burning drapes writhed and fell like living things. Furniture crackled and burnt fiercely, and flames rolled over the ceiling.

John leapt forward and closed the door. He coughed, and choked out an instruction to close all doors if there was no one in the room.

Joseph's eyes stung and his chest felt as if it was clamped in a vice. He pushed a door back and found a small shower room. 'Grab this, Vonnie!' He threw a soaked towel at her, then plunged another into water for John to wrap around his mouth and nose.

In the fourth bedroom, they found Olivia lying on the floor.

Vonnie dashed forward, ripped off her towel, and wrapped it round Olivia's face.

Olivia's hands and feet were tied, and her chest was heaving. She was struggling to breathe. Joseph knew there was no time to try to free her. He had to get her out, at once. 'John! Try to clear me a way out of here! Vonnie, get downstairs and tell the others we have her, and we're bringing her down. But we need help! They'll need breathing apparatus. John? Where the fuck are those fire engines?'

He wasn't sure he could do this, but he had to try.

Yvonne hurled herself out of the room. Joseph bent down, gathered up Olivia and put her over his shoulder. She wasn't too heavy, but he had a staircase to descend. 'I've got you,' he whispered, and immediately broke into a fit of coughing.

He stepped out into the hallway, to be confronted by a wall of fire stretched across the landing.

John appeared from the flames, and threw a soaking wet curtain over them. 'Run! It's just a few steps, and you'll be through it! The stairs are still passable. Run, Joseph!'

With dry, cracked lips, Joseph uttered a prayer and ran.

Somehow he got through, but knew that without the wet curtain protecting them, they would have suffered serious burns. Tiny fires were springing up everywhere, and now hungry tongues of flame were even licking the banister rails.

With legs shaking under Olivia's weight, Joseph plunged forward, determined not to let this mad arsonist claim his final victim. He lurched forward down the stairs, and as he reached the last step, the firefighters stormed in. 'John's still in there!' he choked.

And then he was outside, into the autumn night and merciful fresh air.

He thought the cheer was just the roar of the fire, then Olivia was snatched from him and rushed into the back of a waiting ambulance. He was pulled away from danger, and a blanket thrown around his shoulders. He slipped to the ground. Then a paramedic was giving him oxygen, and suddenly, bursting through the crowd of helpers and onlookers, was Nikki.

She dropped down on her knees beside him and clasped his hand. 'Joseph? Oh, dear God! I thought . . . are you all right?'

He nodded and pulled the oxygen mask from his face. 'Okay,' he rasped. 'I'm okay. Where's Vonnie?'

'She's with another paramedic. She's pretty shaken. Shock, I think.'

'She was amazing.'

'Put that back on. You need to get your oxygen levels back up.' The paramedic placed the mask over his mouth and nose. 'This is serious, you know. There'll be time to chat later.'

Nikki looked almost hollow with worry.

'I'm sorry,' he murmured through the mask.

'You will be, Easter, believe me! If you *ever* pull a stunt like that again . . .' And Nikki began to cry.

'And I love you too,' he whispered, and sank back and closed his eyes, concentrating on trying to breathe.

Suddenly the questions came pouring in. He pulled off his mask. 'John? Is John okay? And Lyndon? Did they catch him?' He gripped Nikki's hand tighter. 'And Olivia! She has asthma, doesn't she? Did she make it?'

'Slow down! Cat and Ben caught Lyndon. Rugby-tackled him, apparently, and that was Cat, not Ben! He's on his way to the custody suite.'

'And John?' Joseph asked.

'I'll go and find out, shall I?'

'Please. If it hadn't been for him, I'm sure we wouldn't have made it across that burning landing.'

'He's a good man, and I'm glad he was there for you.' She smiled at him. 'Olivia is on her way to A&E. They have everything ready and waiting for her, okay? She's in the best hands possible. Now I'll go check on John.'

He watched Nikki talk to the fire crew with a bad feeling in the pit of his stomach. He stared at the burning building. Would this fire be the one that finally claimed him?

He half-sat and looked around. Yvonne was sitting on a wall, a paramedic at her side, and Dave standing with his arm around her. She had been incredibly brave. Now the reality of what had happened was evidently hitting home.

He lifted an arm and waved to her. His arm felt like a ton weight.

She acknowledged him with a nod and a pained smile. We did it, she seemed to say. He gave her a thumbs up. *Yeah, Vonnie we did it.*

Nikki returned, and Joseph knew the tears in her eyes weren't due to the smoke.

'Tell me,' he said.

'He didn't make it, Joseph.'

He hung his head. 'If only he'd followed us out. He'd be alive now.'

'He finished checking all the rooms, and reported to the fire crew, and then one of those cylinders blew in a room below. The floor collapsed beneath him.'

Nikki slid down and sat next to him on the pavement, and with their arms wrapped around each other, they wept for the firefighter.

CHAPTER THIRTY

Nikki saw Joseph and Yvonne off to hospital, and then with a heavy heart pulled her inspector's hat firmly back on and returned to the station.

Now, she and Superintendent Cameron Walker were sitting side by side, looking across the table to Lyndon Applegarth.

No one spoke.

Then Nikki switched on the tape and got the formalities out of the way. It was hard to imagine that the man in front of her had deliberately and brutally murdered four of his contemporaries, and attempted to kill a fifth. Lyndon gave the appearance of being a gentleman, handsome in a boyish way, softly spoken and polite. He waved to old ladies because he'd been brought up to be nice to people. What had happened?

'Lyndon, you have admitted to killing four people and attempting to kill Olivia Black. Can you tell us why?' asked Cameron.

Lyndon looked straight at them and said, 'Of course. They killed my sister.'

Nikki's stomach jolted. They were finally going to learn the truth. 'How did they do that, Lyndon?'

'They were in the summerhouse on Mischief Night. They were drinking and taking drugs. I don't know what started the fire, but it was an old building. I saw it from my bedroom window, but by the time I got there, it was ablaze.' Lyndon closed his eyes for a moment. 'And they'd already got out, all those drunken kids. They saved their own skins, Officers! And one, Michael Porter, he even risked his life to go back inside to fetch out that stupid asthmatic kid, Olivia! And they *all*, every one of them, left my sister, my lovely Natalie, to die!' Now there were tears coursing down his face. 'They got out and did nothing to save her! They deserved to die as she did, terrified, fighting for breath, and in pain.'

Nikki stared at him. 'What happened to Natalie, Lyndon? There was no trace of her after the fire, was there?'

'I found her.' He wiped his nose on the back of his hand, and Nikki found herself handing him a tissue.

'Thank you,' he said, almost shyly. He blew his nose and went on. 'I knew her favourite place was the snug, a little room at the end of the summerhouse. It had a narrow French window leading out to the side of the old place. I got in and found her there, lying on the couch, dead. The fire was licking all around her, but it hadn't taken hold. It was the smoke that had killed her.'

'You got her out?' asked Cam.

He nodded, and then gingerly rolled up his sleeves. His forearms were badly scarred.

'No one saw me. They were so wrapped up in getting Olivia to safety, they never even thought about Natalie.'

'What did you do with her body?' asked Nikki gently.

'I took her into the house and told my father what had happened.'

'And you told him about the drink and the drugs?'

'Yes, of course.'

Nikki heaved a sigh. 'You thought she'd taken drugs, and they'd show up in her system, didn't you?'

'She was surrounded by packets of them! I collected what I could, but I needed to get her out of there. I couldn't bear the thought of her burning. I loved her. I didn't want her name dishonoured, or my family's.'

'Where is Natalie now, Lyndon?'

He looked at her, his eyes huge and dark. 'I don't know. After all I'd done to protect her, he wouldn't tell me. My father wouldn't tell me.' His head fell forward and he began to sob as if his heart would break.

'Interview terminated at . . .' Cameron glanced at the clock and brought the harrowing session to a close.

Outside, Nikki leaned against the wall of the corridor and let out a long, slow breath. 'And now that his father is dead, we may never know what happened to Natalie.'

'He had that plane, didn't he?' said Cameron. 'He could have flown her anywhere. We know the pilot was a gibbering wreck after that fire, so perhaps we'll find out something from him.'

'I do hope so. I hate loose ends. And that girl deserves a proper resting place.' She looked up at Cam. 'I didn't have the heart to tell him that we believe Natalie was only trying to hide the drugs from the other kids.'

'He'll find out in court. Every detail will come out. Even things like those unopened packets of legal highs.'

Nikki yawned. 'I stink of smoke! I feel like Smokey Joe!'

'Get home, Nikki, and get a shower and a change of clothes.'

She stretched. 'I'll grab a shower here, and I've always got spare clothes in the office. Just in case.'

'And then?'

'To the hospital. I've got two officers and a very sick young woman to check up on.'

'Okay, go freshen up, and I'll come with you.'

'Are you sure? What about Kaye? Won't she worry?'

'Kaye is a good police wife, Nikki. She expects me only when she sees me walking through the door.'

'Ah, well trained.'

'No, just pragmatic and long-suffering. We've been doing this for a long time now. It's how we roll, as they say.' He gave her a friendly push. 'Go get sorted, Galena. Joseph will be pining for you.'

'Right. Well he won't be pining for the ear-bashing he's going to get for dashing into that burning building like some kind of superhero!'

They both fell silent. Thoughts of John Carson filled their minds.

'I'm so sorry, Cam. John was your friend, and here's me joking about going into burning buildings.'

'Fire was that man's life. Don't think I'm sick or anything, but I honestly believe he'd prefer a death like that to dwindling slowly away, eaten up by cancer or something else. I think he'd see it as a kind of karma. He'd fought fire and won for so many years. Now fire was just redressing the balance.'

Nikki touched Cam's arm. 'We have a lot to thank him for, don't we?'

'We do, and one thing is for sure, we'll never forget him. Now, go shower, Smokey Joe! Your prince awaits with bated breath.'

'Up yours, *acting* Superintendent.'

* * *

'Observation for thirty-six hours,' Joseph grumbled.

He was sitting up in bed. He looked pale and shaken, and it was now obvious that he had suffered an assortment of minor burns. 'And everything hurts!' he added ruefully.

'Hardly surprising, is it, if you *will* play Action Man!' Nikki squeezed his hand. 'And Action Woman Yvonne doesn't look much better! Cam's with her now. He says they're talking about commendations. Personally, I'd stick you back on traffic for your reckless behaviour, but who am I to judge?'

He squeezed her hand in return. 'I'm sorry I scared you.'

'Scared!' She lowered her voice. 'Joseph, I went to hell and back while you were in that building. I couldn't even begin to explain the thoughts that went through my head.'

'I was just trying to stop that killer claiming his last victim. I've been in a fire-fight before, and I knew I could deal with it. I was so focussed on getting us out alive—'

'Exactly. You were *doing* something. Me, I was just standing there, helpless and living a nightmare. You wouldn't have had time to even think about me.' Nikki looked down at their joined hands. 'I'm *so* angry with you, Joseph, but so proud of you, it bloody hurts!'

'It's the price we pay for caring so much, isn't it?'

'And what a price.' She exhaled. 'I need to go and see Olivia. But I'll be back, okay?'

Joseph nodded. 'I just hope we did enough. She was a sick woman to begin with.'

Nikki stood up, leaned forward and planted a kiss on his forehead. 'Love you.'

'Love you too.'

'Get some sleep, okay?'

Joseph nodded, smiled and obediently closed his eyes. 'I think it might be in my best interests to toe the line for a while, don't you?'

'And how, sunshine!'

* * *

Tom and Giles Black sat on by their sister's bed and spoke in hushed voices.

They marvelled at her self-control and how lucky she was to be alive. Olivia hadn't panicked. Knowing that her asthma, combined with smoke inhalation, could kill her, she had managed to roll off the bed where Lyndon had left her, and onto the floor. She got herself to the lowest point possible, and then endeavoured to keep her lung functions to a minimum, all the time praying for rescue. And when it came, her removal from the scene had been swift, giving her the best possible chance. The ambulance crew had been made aware of the situation and had delivered humidified, high-flow oxygen and rushed her to the A&E department on blue lights.

She had sustained no burns, so the job of the intensive care team was a little easier. Now, after a period on nebulisers and an assortment of intravenous drugs, she was sleeping, and the brothers relaxed a little. It was just sad that when she recovered enough to leave hospital, there would be no home to go back to. The Black House was beyond saving.

Tom looked up and saw DI Nikki Galena looking through the glass in the ward room door. He stood up and went out to speak to her.

'My brother and I have a lot to thank your officers for, Inspector.' He held out his hand. 'We can't thank you enough. They saved Olivia's life.'

'It's what we do, sir. Protect life. I'm just so pleased that she has pulled through. By the look on your face, I assume the prognosis is good?'

'They need to be watchful for some while yet — Bronchospasm is still a possibility, but yes, she's getting there.'

'I just wanted to tell you that the call you received was the arsonist, luring you away from the house. Olivia was his target, no one else.' She frowned. 'Strangely, the fact that someone else died in the blaze seems to have upset him more than anything else.'

Tom looked back into the room where his brother kept watch over his sleeping sister. 'Shall we go to the visitor's room?'

Once they'd sat down in the empty room, the detective asked, 'Did you know about what happened to Olivia on Mischief Night, ten years ago?'

He shook his head. 'No, DI Galena. All we knew was that there'd been a fire. But something, or somebody, terrified her that night. She never talked about it, and we were so worried that we made all sorts of enquiries,' he shrugged, 'but nothing.' He paused, looking almost embarrassed. 'Giles was afraid she'd been raped, that's how seriously she was affected.' He slumped back in his seat. 'She has told us a little about it, just now, when she was first able to speak, but it's hard to understand. She says he accused her of allowing someone to die? Is that right?'

'It's a very complicated situation, sir. We know some of it, but not everything. Your sister is the only one left alive now who can tell us what really happened. As soon as she's well enough, we'll have to interview her.'

'I understand. Of course you must. And now that whatever threat to her has gone, I'm sure she'll do all she can to help. Olivia is a good person, Detective. A very good person.'

'So were all the others, the ones who died.'

'Others?'

'There were a group of them involved, Mr Black. Olivia is the only survivor.'

Tom was aghast. He hadn't known it was as bad as all that. 'You're completely sure there's no danger to her now?'

'Absolutely. The killer has been apprehended, and the man who orchestrated the whole deception has killed himself. The danger is over.'

Tom heaved a sigh of relief.

'You've lost everything, sir? All your possessions? And you used the Black House as a venue for your, er, your . . .'

'Luciferian gatherings, yes, we did.' He managed a weak smile. 'Don't worry about us, Inspector. We have a lot of friends. We have insurance, and we are not without money. We'll rise again from the ashes. I have no doubt of that.'

'One last thing, and please don't think me impertinent. PC Collins mentioned a tattoo you and your brother have. A fireball?'

Tom rather liked this woman. 'Ironic, isn't it?' He pushed up his shirt sleeve. 'We all have one. Olivia had only one burn on her after that mysterious event on Mischief Night, a small flame-like scar just above her wrist. It bothered her terribly. It probably served as a reminder of what happened. So Corinne designed this, and we all have them — the family, and our whole branch of Luciferians. It's a sign that life goes on, and even though we never knew what happened to her, we respected her courage in surviving it.'

He noticed the detective looking at him intently. Then she said, 'So you really are Luciferians, not some secret society under the guise of a religious group?'

'We really are, Detective. As I told your lovely PC Collins at the time, we were brought up with parents who followed the Church of Satan, but that wasn't for us. However, there were aspects of it that we rather liked — shall we say the rather more hedonistic ones? So we formed our own group of Luciferians. We have a strong code of ethics, but we do believe in freedom, individuality and enjoyment, especially enjoyment. The group has grown over the years, and we network and share business opportunities. It's very lucrative indeed. We have some quite high-profile members.' He grinned. 'Not unlike yourself, in fact.' He gave her an enquiring glance. 'You'd be very welcome.'

'Thanks, but I don't think so!' The look on her face spoke volumes.

'Our loss.'

'I doubt that, Mr Black. I'm strictly police force, and for me, that's a twenty-four hour a day commitment.'

'Then I'd advise taking time out for yourself every once in a while. Life is short, DI Galena, as my sister nearly found out. Enjoy yourself while you are on this earth.'

She gave him that odd look again, then nodded. 'Thank you for your time, sir. We'll be in to see Olivia as soon as she's well enough to talk to us. We all wish her well.'

Tom watched her leave. She was an interesting woman. He suspected she'd make an excellent Luciferian.

* * *

Nikki had been sitting with Joseph for two hours when she heard a soft tap on the door. She looked up and saw Giles Black. For a moment she feared something was wrong, then she saw a weak smile on his tired face.

'We hoped you'd still be here, Detective Inspector. Olivia is awake and she wants to talk to you.'

'Is she up to it?' Nikki asked.

'She says she needs you to know certain things.'

Nikki stood up. 'Of course.'

She followed him back down the corridor to Olivia's room.

Inside, Olivia eased herself up in her bed. 'Tom tells me I'm the only survivor.'

Her voice was very soft and her breathing was still ragged. Nikki worried that she really wasn't up to this right now, but Olivia seemed determined to get it over with.

'It was one of those stupid things that happens, and afterwards you wonder how it all came about.' She took several shallow breaths. 'We didn't even know each other. Well, I'd met Jez Bedford before, but not the others. There was supposed to be a bonfire party, but it was cancelled. The rest of our friends jumped in cars and went off somewhere else, and we were stranded. We hung around for while in the town square — we'd all had a bit to drink — then this one guy, his name was Michael, said he'd pinched a whole handful of highs from a mate of his. He reckoned he'd never taken anything like that before and wanted to give it a try.'

Nikki noticed that her breathing was changing. 'Take a break, Olivia. There's no hurry. I've got all night if need be.'

'No, I'm okay.' She breathed steadily again. 'Then this really nice girl arrived — a friend of Michael's I think — and she said we shouldn't be drinking in the street, even if it was Mischief Night. She seemed really worried about us. She said that if we wanted to hang out, we could use a summerhouse in her dad's garden.'

'That would have been Natalie, I guess. But how did you get there? It was quite a way away, and you said you were all drinking.' Nikki decided that if she asked questions, it would give the girl a break from talking every so often.

'Natalie had a little van, so we all piled in the back. She drove. She said she didn't drink.' Olivia shifted in the bed. 'It was fun at first. It was a very big summerhouse, and there was a radio, so we found a music station, and a guy called Ronnie had brought some cans. We lit candles and just hung out together talking and laughing. Then Ronnie asked Michael about trying the drugs. Michael said it was probably a bad idea, but he tipped them into a bowl on the table and left them there. Ronnie was the only one still interested. He said it would be like an experiment. Natalie was very against it. She said if we promised not to take them, she knew where her brother had hidden one of her father's bottles of wine, and we could have that instead. We chose the wine, and a bit later I noticed the drugs had disappeared.'

'Natalie took them and hid them, to stop anyone doing something they'd regret.'

Olivia rested for a while. She took some oxygen, and lay back on the pillows. This was taking its toll, and Nikki could see from the brothers' faces that they were worried too.

After a while, Olivia said, 'I don't know if it was the drink, the candles, or dust, or grass, but I had an asthma attack. Not a bad one, but it scared the others. Then there was a crackling sound, and a flash, and suddenly the whole place was on fire. Everyone panicked. The drink didn't help, I guess, but it was bedlam. The others got out, but I collapsed. I couldn't breathe, and I thought I was going to die. I could see that the whole of the old timber frame was blazing. Then Michael burst through, wrapped me in a blanket, and carried me out.' She wiped a tear from her eye. 'I was unhurt, apart from one tiny burn, but poor Michael's arms and shoulders, oh, they were raw. It was horrible.'

'And Natalie?'

'We thought she'd gone to the house for the wine! We didn't know about that little room at the end of the building. I swear we never knew she was there. The brother went mad at us. He said we'd only thought of ourselves, and we'd left her to die.'

'I think that's enough for tonight, Olivia.' Nikki brought a halt to the story. 'You've answered a lot of questions. Tomorrow will do for the next part.'

'What next part?' asked Tom anxiously.

'It's my belief that Natalie's father blackmailed you and the other teenagers into keeping silent. He scared them almost to death, saying they'd be accused of manslaughter or worse, just to keep his powerful job and his family's good name. Is that right, Olivia? Did he threaten you?'

Olivia nodded. 'And he was a powerful man. We knew that if we were accused of something, he would be believed, not us. I've spent all my life in fear, waiting for his threats to materialise.' Tears filled her eyes. 'And I didn't dare speak, not even to my brothers.'

Nikki stood up. 'Please rest, and sleep. We need to tie up a lot of loose ends, but the threat has gone now. It's time for a new start.'

'From the ashes', murmured Tom, clasping his sister's hand. 'You will rise from the ashes.'

Nikki went back and found Joseph sleeping. She shut the door, slipped off her shoes, and lay down beside him. She closed her eyes and held him tightly, thinking about the case. The pieces of the puzzle were all falling into place, apart from one.

Where was Natalie Applegarth's body?

EPILOGUE

Rory got his wish.

With the formal ceremony at the Registry Office over, it was time for everyone to get into their costumes, get out to the airfield, and party like 1944! With the exception of Nikki Galena, every one of his guests had thrown themselves wholeheartedly into dressing up for the World War II wedding reception.

'This is just the best thing ever! Even if I did have to lose five pounds to get into this outfit!' Ella Jarvis, dressed in her grandmother's Ack-Ack girl uniform, drank champagne with Dave, looking every inch the air-raid warden, right down to a tin hat with ARP stencilled on it.

'Have you noticed that everyone's watching the door?' Dave grinned mischievously.

'Ah. The missing guest. Will she? Won't she?'

Dave pursed his lips. 'Mmm. My guess, knowing how much she thinks of Rory and David, is yes, she will.' He looked across the big NAAFI canteen that was the venue, and saw Cat approaching. 'Oh my! Look at you!'

Cat was dressed as a 1940s swing singer. In a scarlet off-the-shoulder dress with a figure-hugging pencil slim skirt, high heels and scarlet lipstick she looked for all the world as if she was about to break into *Boogie Woogie Bugle Boy of Company B* .

'And where's the rest of the Andrews Sisters?' asked Dave.

'Who?'

He laughed and shook his head. 'You're not old enough to know, but oh, Catkin, you *so* look the part.'

'Talking of looking the part,' Cat pointed, 'have you seen the happy couple?'

'Priceless,' said Ella. 'It's on my smartphone. I'm never going to let him forget this.'

Rory and David were both dressed in US Navy uniforms. David's was navy blue and white, and Rory's was the typical all white, tropical uniform.

Cat giggled. 'They give a whole new meaning to "hallo, sailor!" don't they? High camp or what? I keep thinking I've wandered onto the set of South Pacific!'

Ben — or was it Tommy — joined them in full British khaki battledress, complete with gas mask and dummy rifle. 'Hell, this thing doesn't half chafe the neck!' he said, tugging at the collar.

'Don't whine. My grandad went through a whole war wearing that! You only have to wear it for a couple of hours.' Cat smiled at him.

'Is she here yet?' Ben looked around.

'No, but hang on! There's the Sarge!' Dave waved to Joseph.

'That's really cool, Sarge!' Cat cooed. 'Very nice!'

Joseph saluted. He'd chosen to be an RAF fighter pilot, and was wearing a dress uniform with a peaked cap, wings, and highly polished shoes.

'Now I know why the girls all loved the fly boys!' said Ella admiringly.

'Okay, Joseph,' Dave passed him a drink, 'where is she?'

'I have *absolutely* no idea.'

They all looked at him. 'What?' Dave puffed out his cheeks. 'She is coming, isn't she?'

Joseph frowned. 'She took off immediately after the ceremony, and I haven't heard a word from her. I had to come on my own.' He looked around. 'Eve's over there. I'll go and see if she has any idea.'

'I'll come with you.' Dave followed Joseph across the dance floor. He still couldn't see Nikki letting Rory down, but she'd been very much against the idea of dressing up. Sometimes you just couldn't tell with the boss. If something really went against the grain, there was no turning her.

Eve smiled and waved. 'Gentlemen! My goodness, don't you look good!'

'And you too, Eve. Love the outfit.' Dave grinned. 'I have pictures of my mother dressed exactly like that.' Eve wore a simple 1940s dress and jacket with a matching hat, but the style was pure vintage, and it suited her. Eve was still a very handsome woman.

'Have you seen Nikki, Eve? I'm really starting to worry,' Joseph blurted out.

Eve raised an eyebrow. 'I haven't seen her, no. But,' she reached out and squeezed Joseph's arm, 'don't be mad at her. You know yourself that this is *really* not her kind of thing.'

Before Joseph could answer, the Master of Ceremonies could be heard, loudly welcoming everyone to the East Enderby airfield.

'As I'm sure you know, later this afternoon our beautiful Lancaster bomber will do a taxi run down the runway, so you can feel for yourselves the power of those amazing planes that defended the realm so valiantly. And Rory and David have kindly arranged that those of you who wish can ride with us.' He paused. 'But no fighting for the seat in the cockpit, now, or for who gets to be rear gunner!'

There was a ripple of laughter. Dave felt sad that the boss was missing this, especially as her father had been a decorated RAF pilot.

'Now, if you would like to just step outside for a moment, you can see another reason why we won the war.'

Eve looked at Joseph and offered her arm. 'Escort me, please, Captain?'

'My pleasure, ma'am.'

They all filed out of the building and stood outside.

In less than a minute, they heard a loud rumbling noise. It increased in volume, and then a two-seater Spitfire could be seen approaching the airfield at speed. The guests watched as it climbed, dived, then levelled out and flew low over their heads.

Everyone gasped, and then cheered as it banked away again.

After a few more hair-raising acrobatics, the plane slowed and landed, taxiing to a halt close to where they all waited.

Dave cheered and clapped madly along with the rest of them, as the pilot and co-pilot pushed back their cockpit covers and climbed out. It was a sight he'd seen a hundred times in newsreels and old films. The two fighter pilots descended to the runway, then, in full flight gear, walked side by side back towards their base. Home safe! Mission accomplished.

He swallowed hard. It was a strangely emotional sight, and, with all his colleagues around him dressed as they would have been when those planes came back for real, it brought a lump to his throat.

Then, just twenty metres away, the flyers pulled off their leather flying helmets. He immediately recognised the pilot as Wendy Avery. He glanced toward the co-pilot — and saw the boss grinning at him!

The whole party erupted into laughter and cheers as Nikki stripped off her parachute belts and shook her head disbelievingly. 'Oh my! Did we just do that?'

Rory and David rushed forward and hugged her.

'Excuse me! Upstaged, or what!' Rory's eyes were wide. 'It is *our* wedding, Nikki Galena!'

'Sorry. I just thought if I really had to take part in this silly pantomime, I'd do it properly!' She looked across to Wendy. 'And all thanks to this amazing woman! Is there anything you can't fly?'

Wendy grinned. 'Not much. But I'm pretty small fry compared to the woman I've come dressed as — Mary Ellis, of the air transport auxiliary.'

'Thanks for getting me back in one piece, Wendy! But I've never been so scared — or exhilarated — in all my life! And all for you, Wilkinson! You bloody owe me one!'

Joseph approached Nikki, saluted smartly, and escorted her inside.

Dave followed them in. It was going to be a very good wedding reception, now that *all* of them were there.

* * *

After the meal, the 1940s swing band began to play. Even Nikki found herself tapping her foot.

'Ladies and Gentlemen!' the MC announced. 'Can I invite David and Rory to take the floor for the first dance?'

Nikki felt a stab of sadness. Here they were, her dearest friends all gathered to share this moment of happiness. It was something that could never happen for her, unless she was prepared to leave behind the job that she loved. She looked across to Joseph, and knew that he was thinking the same thing. Maybe this was a dilemma that would always haunt them. They were torn, and always would be.

Soon the whole floor was alive with dancers, bopping, swinging and jiving.

Nikki leaned toward Joseph. 'I'm still bowled over by the present you gave me.'

'I thought it should be yours, and the Devlins were happy to let me buy it.'

Nikki had gone home a few days before to find a large, flat package covered in brown paper in her lounge. It was the painting by Clary Sage that had made such an impact on her.

'I hoped it wouldn't evoke memories of a bad case, but I got the feeling that you liked it on a far deeper level than that.'

'I absolutely adore it, Joseph. She captured all the things I love about the Fens. And at least Olivia Black is doing well now. Her brothers took Yvonne the biggest bunch of flowers I have ever seen.'

'I was relieved to hear that they had nothing to do with that vicious attack on Lee Brown. Dave followed it up after Mickey identified that strange hand sign in the CCTV. It was the signature of a Russian gang of drug dealers, wasn't it?'

'Yes, there was more to that little scrote Lee than we realised, and one hell of a warning to stay off their turf! It just coincided rather badly with his run-in with the Luciferians.' Nikki sipped her drink. 'And Tom Black admits that a couple of their members did call on the Brown family, but only with the intention of paying them to back off. By then, the Russians had dealt with Lee anyway, so no more was done about it.'

'And Olivia is recovering, that's really good news.' Joseph lightly touched an area on the side of his face that was still tender from the minor burns. 'I'd hate to have gone through all that for nothing.'

'Yvonne said Tom and Giles are more concerned about her mental state. It was the way Lyndon managed to find out about the house that scared her more than anything.'

'Oh yeah, that was sneaky. He sucked up to Yvonne's little mate, Billie Seager, for a bit of part-time work with his graffiti removal company. He vandalised the Black House, then helped Graffiti Bill to clean it up! He was there all day, used the toilet several times, had tea in the kitchen and everything.'

'He admitted that he chose that night specifically, after glancing at the open appointments diary in the kitchen. He knew Giles and Corinne would be out, so only had Tom to lure away. Easy-peasy!'

'Is this a private party? Or can we join you fellow RAF officers?' Eve sat down, shortly to be followed by Wendy.

'We have some news.' Wendy sounded both excited and anxious.

'This might be nothing, but then again it could be vital,' Eve said.

'Then get on with it, Mother!'

The two women looked at each other, and then Wendy began. 'We've started on our project at Monks Lantern. We're not going to disturb anything in our graveyard after all, just do as Leon suggested, tidy it, clear it and plant it.'

'Then add seats and pathways, and anyone can use it who wants some peace and quiet,' added Eve.

'And?' Nikki knew there was more to this.

'There is an overgrown patch that some of the gardening club are helping to clear. It has some very old memorials, and a couple of small vaults.' Wendy lowered her voice. 'One, we believe, has been vandalised. Not recently, but it has been tampered with at some point.'

It took a moment for Nikki to understand what they were telling her. She looked at Joseph.

He returned her look. 'As Eve said, it *could* be nothing, just vandals, or . . .'

'Or it could be the last piece in the Applegarth puzzle.'

It fitted. Beech Lacey was where the family originally came from. Maybe they took their dead daughter home to rest. Nikki lifted her glass and took a long drink. 'Mum? Wendy? Are you prepared for a little extra intervention in your "peaceful place?" It might include an exhumation.'

'If it gives Leon an answer and allows him to move on with his life, it's a small price to pay, don't you think?' said Wendy.

Eve nodded vigorously. 'I've always wanted to see an exhumation! How exciting!'

'I wonder about you sometimes, Eve Anderson!' Nikki shook her head.

'You can talk!' exclaimed Eve. 'Who arrived at a wedding reception in a bloody Spitfire?'

'Like mother, like daughter,' muttered Joseph. He threw a helpless look at Wendy. 'God help us!'

THE END

THE JOFFE BOOKS STORY

We began in 2014 when Jasper agreed to publish his mum's much-rejected romance novel and it became a bestseller.

Since then we've grown into the largest independent publisher in the UK. We're extremely proud to publish some of the very best writers in the world, including Joy Ellis, Faith Martin, Caro Ramsay, Helen Forrester, Simon Brett and Robert Goddard. Everyone at Joffe Books loves reading and we never forget that it all begins with the magic of an author telling a story.

We are proud to publish talented first-time authors, as well as established writers whose books we love introducing to a new generation of readers.

We won Trade Publisher of the Year at the Independent Publishing Awards in 2023. We have been shortlisted for Independent Publisher of the Year at the British Book Awards for the last four years, and were shortlisted for the Diversity and Inclusivity Award at the 2022 Independent Publishing Awards. In 2023 we were shortlisted for Publisher of the Year at the RNA Industry Awards.

We built this company with your help, and we love to hear from you, so please email us about absolutely anything bookish at feedback@joffebooks.com

If you want to receive free books every Friday and hear about all our new releases, join our mailing list: www.joffebooks.com/contact

And when you tell your friends about us, just remember: it's pronounced Joffe as in coffee or toffee!

Milton Keynes UK
Ingram Content Group UK Ltd.
UKHW012332100724
445430UK00011B/166

9 781835 266106